American Stories

MODERN ASIAN LITERATURE

A PACIFIC BASIN INSTITUTE BOOK

American Stories is the eighth volume to be published in The Library of Japan series, a selected cross-section of modern Japanese fiction and nonfiction in translation for presentation to American readers. Produced by the Pacific Basin Institute at Pomona College, as part of a plan evolved under the aegis of the Japan–United States Conference on Cultural and Educational Exchange (CULCON), this series is designed to make Americans aware of the social and cultural underpinnings of modern Japan, offering works either unavailable in English translation or difficult for most general readers to obtain.

Volumes previously published include *Silk and Insight*, by Mishima Yukio; *The Autobiography of Fukuzawa Yukichi*; *Labyrinth*, by Arishima Takeo; *Konoe Fumimaro, A Political Biography*, by Oka Yoshitake; *Kokoro and Selected Essays*, by Natsume Sōseki; *The Spirit of Japanese Capitalism*, by Yamamoto Shichihei; and Ōoka Shōhei's *Taken Captive: A Prisoner of War's Diary*. Frank Gibney and J. Thomas Rimer are the editors of the series. The editors and the publisher would like to thank the Japan Foundation for its generous support in making this publication possible.

American Stories

Nagai Kafū

translated and with an introduction by Mitsuko Iriye

COLUMBIA UNIVERSITY PRESS   NEW YORK

Columbia University Press wishes to express its appreciation for funds given by The Japan Foundation toward the cost of publishing this volume.

Photograph of Nagai Kafū reproduced from *Kafū ẓenshu*
(Collected works of Kafū), vol. 18 (Tokyo: Iwanami, 1964).
Nagai Kafū's personal seal reproduced from *Kafū ẓenshu*, vol. 4
(Tokyo: Iwanami, 1992). Used by permission of the Estate of Nagai Kafū.

Columbia University Press
Publishers Since 1893
New York   Chichester, West Sussex
Translation copyright © 2000 Columbia University Press
Library of Congress Cataloging-in-Publication Data
Nagai, Kafū, 1879–1959.
[Amerika monogatari. English]
American stories / by Nagai Kafū ;
translated and with an introduction by Mitsuko Iriye.
p.   cm. — (Modern Asian literature)
ISBN 0-231-11790-6 (cloth)
I. Iriye, Mitsuko. II. Title. III. Series.
PL812.A4A8413   2000
895.6'342—DC21   99-33508

Casebound editions of Columbia University Press books are
printed on permanent and durable acid-free paper.
Printed in the United States of America
c 10 9 8 7 6 5 4 3 2 1

Contents

CONTENTS

Translator's Introduction

Nagai Kafū (1879–1959), whose real first name was Sōkichi, was one of the major writers of modern Japan. On September 24, 1903, at the age of twenty-three, he left for the United States, and he did not return home till July 1908. He spent his last year abroad in France, mainly in Lyon, but it would not be an exaggeration to say that it was his stay in America that made a major impact on Kafū's formative years as a writer. Yet the scarcity of his written work during this period makes it difficult to assess precisely what happened to him abroad and how his writings were intertwined with his experiences there.

As the eldest son of a high-ranking bureaucrat turned business-man, Kafū had been expected to follow in his father's footsteps. Nagai Kyūichirō had married the daughter of his teacher, a famous Sinologist, and was himself well known for his poems written in the Chinese style. At age ten, Kafū was taught classical Chinese, but he was particularly influenced by his mother, an avid reader of popular literature and Kabuki theatergoer who collected colored woodblock prints depicting actors. She was also good at *nagauta* (long epic songs) and *koto* (Japanese harp). Through her, Kafū was drawn to the world of literature and arts of the Edo period.

He belonged to the second generation of Japanese in the modern era, who began their careers after their country had gone through the initial and generally successful process of "modernization" following its encounter with the West. Japan had established a constitutional form of government, carried out administrative and fiscal centralization, adopted the gold standard, universalized military training, induced the Western powers to revise the "unequal treaties," and launched ambitious programs of industrialization and mass education. In the name of "enriching the nation and strengthening the army," Japan built up a formidable military force and fought successfully against China and, later, Russia, in the process acquiring overseas colonies as well as the coveted status of a great power. In less than half a century after the arrival of Commodore Matthew Perry in 1853–54, the country had emerged as the first "modern" nation of Asia.

Japan's political and economic transformation had been achieved through contact with and learning from Europe and North America, but the modern transformation had not necessarily meant the Westernization of Japanese culture, such as literature, music, and fine art. Nevertheless, there was no doubt that the country's values, mental habits, and tastes were subtly changing as more and more Japanese came into contact with Westerners and their ideas and arts. It was natural, then, that the intellectuals of Kafū's generation should have become fascinated by the implications of modernization for Japan's cultural life and for the mental and psychological identity of the individual. Underneath the surface glamour of treaty revision and military victories, Japanese writers, artists, and musicians were beginning their long and serious quest for meaning. Each sought to find his or her own point of connection between Japan and the West. The sum total of these quests made up Japanese consciousness at the turn of the twentieth century. Among those who grappled with the problem of Japanese-Western relations in the field of literature, Nagai Kafū is significant not only because many of his writings reflect his self-conscious encounter with Western (in particular, French) literature but, more fundamentally, because his experiences and perspectives were among the most unique and sophisticated of that time.

Kafū's interest in literature intensified during his years at a middle school. At this time, he even began visiting the pleasure quarters of Tokyo. The school, whose principal was the founder of the *jūdō* hall, Kōdōkan, was known for its stress on martial values, something Kafū did not appreciate. Upon graduation from the school at age eighteen, he tried, and failed, the entrance examination for the prestigious First Higher School, known as a preparatory academy for future bureaucrats, lawyers, and businessmen as well as scholars. He then spent three months in Shanghai with his father, who was sent there as branch manager of the Japan Steamship Company. At the end of 1897 Kafū returned to Japan and enrolled in the Chinese language department of the Tokyo Foreign Language School. However, he hardly attended his classes and instead immersed himself in the lifestyle of a typical late Edo dilettante: writing short stories; frequenting the pleasure quarters, *yose* (variety halls), and the Kabuki theater; and taking *shakuhachi* (bamboo flute) and *samisen* lessons. He also had an equally brief stint as an apprentice Kabuki playwright.

In September 1898 Kafū showed a short story he had written to Hirotsu Ryūrō (1861–1928), a popular writer at that time who belonged to Ken'yūsha, the first modern literary society in Japan (founded in 1895). But unlike the mainstream of this group led by its founder, Ozaki Kōyō, Ryūrō had started writing so-called "serious novels" dealing with the darker and pathetic aspects of life, particularly the demimonde. For this reason, and also because his style stressed dialogue rather than the mixed *gazokubun* (colloquial-literary style) of Kōyō and others, Kafū decided to become Ryūrō's literary disciple.

It was also around this time that Kafū began his long association with Western literature, both in Japanese translation (frequently not straightforward translations but adaptations of foreign works) and in English. Upon reading Ueda Bin's account of French literature in a book entitled *Nineteenth-Century Literature and Art* (1900), Kafū felt a strong affinity with the French literary world and began to study the language. He attended French language classes in the evening division of Gyōsei High School while simultaneously reading French works in English, such as Ernest Vizetelli's fine translations of Emile Zola's novels from the *Rougon-Macquart* series. As a result, Kafū became a leading advocate of Zola and his naturalism, and continued to be profoundly influenced by the French writer's descriptive skills even after he came to claim that his "Zolaesque" phase had been but a youthful aberration.

By the time Kafū was twenty-three (1903), then, he was already known as a promising writer with several fairly well-received novels of middle length in addition to a series of trial pieces he had written as a self-appointed apprentice to Ryūrō. At a time when writers were generally held in low esteem, however, young Kafū's literary achievements did not impress his father, who had wanted to see his son become a bureaucrat. He settled for what many well-to-do fathers did at that time: sending his son to the United States in order to acquire enough prestige as a *kichōsha* (a person who has returned from abroad, more specifically from the West) so that he could eventually become a respectable businessman. It was in such circumstances that Kafū left Japan. He was a dropout from an elitist course, now being sent on a face-saving journey to a faraway land, with quite an uncertain future ahead of him.

TRAVELS ABROAD

Kafū's first year in the United States was spent primarily in Tacoma, Washington, with occasional visits to Seattle. For a brief period of time he attended classes at a local high school to improve his English; however, being a boarder at the home of the branch manager of a firm founded by a successful Japanese businessman (who was an acquaintance of Kafū's father) in a predominantly Japanese neighborhood did not help in this regard. He had hoped to live with an American family but could not, due to racial discrimination against Chinese and Japanese. Attending classes from time to time was not a pleasant experience, since he felt more than a little discomfort at having to study with American schoolchildren who were considerably younger. Confused and unable to adjust to the new life, he gave up the idea of writing novels of any length and instead concentrated on reading books and magazines sent to him from Japan. He also read some American and French works, but he was far more interested in the latter. Edgar Allan Poe was an exception, partly because Kafū's favorite French poet, Baudelaire, was fascinated by this American poet. But otherwise Kafū formed a low opinion of the American authors he read.

His sweeping castigation of contemporary American literature may have been a result of his acquaintance with only a few novels published in the United States at that time. Of one of them, John Fox, Jr.'s *The Little Shepherd of Kingdom Come* (1903), a hodgepodge of bits from *Oliver Twist*, *The Little Princess*, and the Bible, Kafū had this to say:

> American novels are too naive and optimistic, nothing even remotely like French or Russian writings. *The Little Shepherd of Kingdom Come*, which has been a best-seller, was heralded by critics as a pure American novel. It is a success story that deals with a young boy from the mountains who makes it big after a great deal of hardship. Indeed, a typically "pure American novel." The American people who shun profound thought and set their souls and hearts in quest of worldly success are quite well described in this novel. The United States is extremely inconvenient and unsuitable for a person like myself who wants to study literature.[1]

Part of the concluding passage of the novel went:

> Once again he was starting his life over afresh, with his old
> capital, a strong body and a stout heart. In his breast still
> burned the spirit that had led his race to the land, had
> wrenched it from savage and from king, had made it the high
> temple of Liberty for the worship of free men—the King-
> dom Come for the oppressed of the earth—and, himself the
> unconscious Shepherd of that Spirit, he was going to help
> carry its ideals across a continent Westward to another sea
> and on—who knows—to the gates of the rising sun.[2]

This passage conveys the novel's general tone, and it is easy to understand why Kafū would have recoiled from such a display of the ever
healthy and optimistic, even naive, American attitude—including the
urge to cross the Pacific and lead Japan to a life of spirituality.

In October 1904 Kafū visited the World's Fair at St. Louis, then
proceeded to Kalamazoo, Michigan, in mid-November to enroll in
Kalamazoo College as an "unclassified student" (auditor) in order
to study English literature and the French language. (His original
intention had been to go to New Orleans to meet French people
and practice his French, but he had been dissuaded by the climate.)
Kalamazoo is a peaceful, quiet town even today, and it is almost inconceivable that an overly urbanized young man from Tokyo should have
chosen to stay in such a place. Kalamazoo College, a Baptist institu-
tion, exuded a religious atmosphere, and even the biweekly meetings
of one of its literary circles that Kafū joined, the Century Forum,
opened with devotional exercises. The chaplain of this group was
Katō Katsuji, a very serious and hard-working student of religion who
was the only other male student from Japan at that time. Kafū, whose
maternal grandmother and mother had both been baptized, had been
accustomed to foreign missionaries visiting his family home. But the

infatuation (which proved to be rather temporary) of several young Japanese writers with Christianity had struck him as rather superficial, and the "holier-than-thou" attitude of some famous Japanese Christians had annoyed him to such an extent that he had satirized this phenomenon in one of his mid-length novels, *Flowers of Hell*, published just before he went to the United States.

For a time, Kafū settled down in Kalamazoo and attended classes in elementary French and English literature. He started writing again, something he had almost abandoned while on the West Coast. At the same time, he extensively read Flaubert, Baudelaire, Maupassant, Daudet, and other French authors and felt all the more drawn toward France and its culture. Desperately wanting to go to France, in the summer of 1905 he worked as a messenger boy at the Japanese legation in Washington to earn some money. The job was offered to him through Nagai Shōzō, a cousin who was a diplomat stationed in New York. As Japanese diplomatic affairs expanded during the war with Russia, Kafū was able to hold his job till early October, but then he returned to Kalamazoo, having failed to obtain another job for the rest of the year. Within a few weeks, however, he received a letter from his father informing him that a position as a bank clerk at the New York office of the Yokohama Specie Bank had been secured for him. Kafū worked at the bank till July 1907, all the while trying to persuade his father to let him travel to France. Finally, the bank manager told Kafū that he had been appointed to a position at the Lyon branch of the bank. Kafū's father had, once again, been instrumental in arranging his transfer. Yet Kafū's stay in France was to be rather short. After only eight months in Lyon, he could no longer bear to work at such a job and decided to resign his position. He moved to Paris, spent two months there, and returned to Japan in July 1908, never to go abroad again.

American Stories was published within a few months, and it was followed by a succession of mid-length novels, short stories, and essays. Among the best known of Kafū's novels are *Sumidagawa* [The river Sumida, 1909], *Reishō* [Sneers, 1909], *Udekurabe* [Rivalry, 1918], *Okamezasa* [Dwarf bamboo, 1920], *Ameshōshō* [Quiet rain, 1921], and *Bokutō kidan* [A strange tale in the east of the river Sumida, 1937]. Kafū also wrote a number of pieces of literary criticism and translated French poems; some of the translations were included in a book published in 1913, *Sangoshū* [Coral anthology].

During the war years (1937–45), Kafū continued to write, but without any prospect of getting his work published. He lost his home and all his library to the great fire caused by the U.S. incendiary bombing of Tokyo in March 1945. He was forced to lead a nomadic life till 1948, staying with his friends and relatives. But after the war and till his death in April 1959 at the age of seventy-nine, he was very popular and prolific. Among his postwar publications were his diaries, which he started keeping in 1917. These are considered among the most important literary works of modern Japan, as well as one of the main sources for the study of this period.

AMERICAN STORIES

During his four years in the United States, Kafū wrote very little: twenty-odd short stories and essays, about seventy letters, and an intermittent and laconic diary, *Saiyū nisshi shō* [Excerpts from the journal of a leisurely trip to the West]. This last was a somewhat fictional account, however, as a comparison with some of his notes makes clear. Among the short stories and essays he wrote while in America, fourteen appeared in various publications in Japan even before he returned home. And a month after he reached Japan, in August 1908, twenty-one of them appeared in a single volume entitled *Amerika monogatari* [American stories]. Subsequent editions of this volume, edited by Kafū himself, were to contain one additional story. After his death, however, publishers added another piece written while he was still in the United States, so that today twenty-three pieces are generally included in what is referred to as Kafū's *American Stories*.[3]

The original publication of *Amerika monogatari* created a sensation. It was a welcome diversion in the literary scene in Japan, which was still dominated by the Japanese adaptation of the naturalist school, usually associated with the work of Emile Zola. When the French writer was first introduced to Japan, the chief function of so-called "Zolaism" was to initiate "efforts to throw off the didacticism, the eroticism, and the excessive decoration of late Tokugawa fiction," as Edward Seidensticker summarizes in *Kafū the Scribbler* (1965).[4] It must be remembered, however, that in Japan what Zola had primarily meant by "naturalism" rapidly lost its distinctive character. In a country where no single religion had held sway over the intellectual life of the people, where the supernatural meant but little besides wandering ghosts, science as an antithesis to the long domination of religion, especially Catholicism, had little significance.

Literary banners and their actual products, of course, have more often than not little to do with actuality. Zola is a good example of this fact. In the case of modern Japanese literature, where divergent literary theories were introduced at random, frequently in the wrong historical order and in an incredibly short span of time, it would have been a miracle if naturalism had meant what it did in Europe. Scientifically proven truths, therefore, had different connotations in Japan. They had an intellectual appeal, but truths were equated with tangible phenomena, revealed in specific human instances. Thus an author's life became the most reliable, often the only reliable, source of information about reality. Scientific truths that in the West had the same universalistic connotation as God became in Japan much more specific and personalized. It may be said that the autobiographical tradition of Japanese literature was now reinforced and reconfirmed by Western naturalism and gave Japanese naturalism a distinctively autobiographical character. Thus the Japanese reader was expected to judge and appreciate novels according to their authenticity and even the amount of biographical details they contained.

Of course, there is nothing inherently wrong about a rapprochement between life and literature. What bothered most critics of Japanese *shishōsetsu* (personal novels), among them Kafū, was their monotony. As the majority of the self-appointed propagators of naturalism came from the countryside to the city of Tokyo, they had a difficult time earning their living—a reward in itself since hardship provided ample material for their work. Yet since most of them relied on true, subjective experiences and tended not to express them in literary language or to generalize about them—in other words, overestimating their own sincerity in writing down the most trivial, meanest, or most shameful details of their lives—they often produced insipid "true stories."

This was the background against which Kafū's *Amerika monogatari* and other works were greeted with such enthusiasm. Readers had grown tired of drab autobiographical novels. For this very reason, however, Kafū came under frequent criticism because he hardly dealt with so-called "real life" situations, above all the hardships of everyday life. He was even stigmatized as a writer who was not serious or sincere enough because he had an independent income. Kafū, on his part, was disconcerted by the tendency among the naturalist writers to define real life in terms of the struggle to earn a living. Had not many a French author he and his critics equally admired been independently wealthy? Flaubert had not only enjoyed such income but also led a retired life, and he was still a great writer. And if Kafū goes a bit too far when he says, "the value of art is not determined by its content but by the way the thoughts in the content are conveyed," he is also properly criticizing the shortcomings of the overall literary trends of his time.[5]

It must also be noted that the great appeal of *Amerika monogatari* lay in the sheer volume of information and observations it contained about life in the United States. No such work had ever been published in Japan, where the people's ideas about that country had been mostly formed by school textbooks and newspaper accounts. Here, for the first time, were twenty-odd vignettes from American life which, because of their intimate character and authenticity, offered readers a window to the country they had heard so much about. For a young man not yet thirty, to have collected such information from various parts of the United States was no mean achievement. Even today, these stories are striking in their freshness and intimacy.

MAJOR THEMES

The stories are fairly straightforward and need no elaborate explication here. But it would help to say a little about some themes they depict. First of all, there is much description of Japanese immigrants in these American stories. This is because Kafū's life in the United States started when, on the West Coast, he came face to face with the ugly and miserable conditions of Chinese and Japanese laborers. In a letter to a literary society to which he had belonged in Japan, Kafū wrote, "The way Japanese people are ostracized in this place is almost unbelievable. It will be enough to tell you that no decent house or apartment will rent to Japanese or Chinese."[6] But Kafū did not join other Japanese in denouncing American discrimination against their countrymen. Instead, his interest was more focused on what he saw as the law of the jungle among the Japanese immigrants themselves. "The Path in the Meadow," "Atop the Hill" (its original title was "The Strong and the Weak"), and "Daybreak" are examples. In those short stories, the reader can sense something close to impatience toward the poor and their ugliness due to poverty, along with the author's pity toward them, but at the same time Kafū is not easily carried away by patriotism or racial identity. He has been criticized for "going through the United States like a tourist, picking up knickknacks to be had more cheaply in Japan," keeping a distance between himself and the other Japanese students or businessmen in America as well as ordinary immigrants, and ending up just an onlooker, but such a view seems to be wide of the mark.[7]

In understanding his perspective on his fellow countrymen in the United States, "Night Fog" is revealing. This piece was published while he was still in America, and was not included in the editions of *Amerika monogatari* while he was alive. Its importance lies in part in the fact that among the short stories and essays he wrote while in the United States, it is the only piece written in literary Japanese. All the rest are written in colloquial style, except for "Night Stroll," which is in epistolary style. As a result, the dialogue carried on in "Night Fog" between Kafū and a poor drunk Japanese laborer is positioned on the same level, unlike in a work in the colloquial style, which would have differentiated the two individuals' languages according to their divergent social status—for, after all, there was no difference between the two as far as American onlookers, "with the disdainful look they show whenever they look at Japanese people," were concerned. The literary style not only blunts the coarse language of the laborer but also blurs the starkness of the scene, in which the author himself is obviously an equal target of scorn. Yet the language as well as the dense fog in the story enhances its nightmarish quality, and it is likely that Kafū, who was an exceptionally sensitive and proud person, did not want to advertise his deeply wounded feelings. Thus he decided to bury the only piece that revealed them in print and could damage his persona as a young artist leisurely observing the American landscape, society, and culture while nurturing his dream of going to France.

He must have felt much more comfortable once he moved to Kalamazoo, Michigan, where, of course, there was no concentration of

Japanese immigrants. A postcard written in English and sent to a friend in Tokyo described Kafū's feelings: "I am very happy now in Michigan because I am treated no more as a '*Jap*' as in Tacoma."[8] (These were his exact words.) Indeed, he was treated like a guest at Kalamazoo College, when the Century Forum, its literary society, discussed the Portsmouth peace treaty ending the Russo-Japanese War in 1905, and the members concluded, "Japan did herself an injustice in accepting the peace terms."[9] Despite such evidence of Kalamazoo College's pro-Japanese atmosphere, Kafū did not once mention it in his writings, and unlike so many of his fellow countrymen abroad at that time, all he wrote about the Russo-Japanese war in his published diary was just these words: "It was reported that Port Arthur fell."[10] It may well be that, while he was deeply hurt on the West Coast, he did not take the experience as a personal, let alone a national, insult, and that by the same token he was not going to feel elated just because his country had won a war, and a dubious victory at that. Likewise, during the Second World War, he was one of the very few Japanese writers who did not join the propaganda campaign to denigrate the United States.

Second, the *American Stories* are full of Western art and music, something rather novel in the Japanese literary scene. The World's Fair at St. Louis that Kafū visited on his way to Kalamazoo not only impressed him with its grand scale but also gave him a welcome chance to appreciate Western paintings. Included in the French section was Renoir's *Odalisque*, which may have inspired the painting mentioned in "The Inebriated Beauty," as did, undoubtedly, Maupassant's "Les Soeurs Rondoli." The only nude painting in the American exhibition was by Julian L. Stewart, an American artist in Paris.[11] Kafū had taken Japanese painting lessons as a child and developed a keen eye for the visual arts, and there are many scenes among the stories in *Amerika monogatari* that seem to be almost straight out of paintings, for instance, the window scene in "Atop the Hill," the sunset in "In the Woods," and the views of Staten Island in "A June Night's Dream."

Though Kafū was so visually oriented, the world of music was equally important to him. He was familiar with traditional Japanese music, and before going to the United States he had also attended some performances of Western music. But it was in New York City that he discovered the "hidden world of fine music."[12] He had shared the common prejudice among Japanese writers that a noisy commercial metropolis in the New World could not possibly be a home for music, but he soon realized, once he went to New York, that the city was like a World's Fair whose wealth attracted great musicians, including singers, from all over the world. Indeed, his stay in the city coincided with the golden age of the opera in America when Caruso, Scotti, Sembrich, Melba, and others came to stay for a whole season and sing in various productions. Furthermore, the operagoer in New York had the advantage of being able to listen to any piece sung in its original tongue—in contrast to Paris, where mostly French works were performed and where non-French operas were sung in French translation. Kafū became an avid concert- and operagoer and frequented the Metropolitan Opera as well as Carnegie and Mendelssohn Halls. "Old Regrets" in *Amerika monogatari* is a piece directly based on an opera, but Kafū published several other pieces, such as detailed accounts of Gounod's *Faust* and Berlioz's *La damnation de Faust*. (These accounts were included in *Furansu monogatari* [French stories], which was scheduled for publication in 1909. But its publication was banned, ostensibly because of its "offense against public morals," but more likely because some of the pieces included critical comments about the Japanese government. The volume was not published in more or less its original form till 1948, although a greatly truncated version was issued in 1915.) Even though his detailed description of Gounod's music and the production of the opera was largely based on Esther Singleton's *A Guide to the Opera* (1899), the appreciation and enthusiasm of the Japanese author who was able to attend the performances are vividly expressed and must have deeply impressed his readers in Japan.[13]

Third, the stories included in *American Stories* are heavily influenced by French literature, but it should be noted that Kafū did not merely graft his favorite French authors' or poets' works onto his own. This can be seen in the contrast between the *American Stories*, full of the youthful ecstasy of an author who has found ample raw material for his creative effort, and the *French Stories*, where the overwhelming tone is that of dejection and disillusionment. In part this is due to the inevitable sense of letdown Kafū felt when his dream, going to France, was finally fulfilled. But in the *French Stories* the melancholy tone seems to have been largely deliberate. Kafū had read Gustave Flaubert's *L'éducation sentimentale* while in the United States. Its central theme is the negative character of human desire, the fulfillment of which kills the desire itself. With Flaubert this was an expression of the psychology of a transitional generation, a *génération manquée* that had experienced in its youth the failure of both the Revolution and the Commune. Kafū too can be said to have belonged to such a generation. For the generation that preceded his in Japan, to go abroad, especially to the West, had almost automatically meant bringing back to the homeland something substantial, be it knowledge of Western technology, scholarship, or literature. But with Kafū's generation, the horizon had been narrowed; French specialists in Japan often considered his own efforts to introduce French literature to Japan dilettantish and unscholarly. However, for him the disappointment was more complex. In "Fallen Leaves," he dramatizes his own wish as an author to communicate "in elegant English" with Americans, especially American women. But in France, even such a daydream was impossible. As he was unable to communicate in French, his love for France and its culture was entirely unrequited, and he remained a complete outsider during the ten months he lived there.

Finally, it is worth considering the relationship between Kafū's American experiences and his famous fascination with the pleasure quarters. He is best known for his writings on the fast-vanishing world of Edo that still existed in Tokyo at the turn of the century, above all the demimonde and the women who inhabited it. The geisha and, later, vaudeville-house dancers, barmaids, and street girls who came to dominate Tokyo's night life were to serve as heroines in his novels. "Serious" authors and critics, for whom modern literature meant nothing more than drab descriptions of artists' financial or marital problems, often labeled Kafū a frivolous writer. Even today, he is frequently criticized for having been unable to describe "nonprofessional" women (as opposed to "professional" ones such as geisha and barmaids), for treating women, both in real life and in his novels, in a pitying or patronizing way at best and in a trifling, satirical, even sarcastic manner at worst. It is true that he had little patience with and felt sorry for the typical middle-class women of his time. He considered the traditional self-effacing, modest, and docile young woman or housewife exasperating rather than exemplary, as is clear in "Atop the Hill," "January First," and "Spring and Autumn." On the other hand, the modern, educated woman, frequently the product of a missionary school, was to him "frightfully moralistic, a self-righteous prude."[14] For this reason, many readers and critics consider Kafū a male chauvinist who looked down on women, particularly those he considered prudish, snobbish, or pedantic.

Yet he clearly had his own image of the ideal woman, who would be his social and intellectual equal and still retain her femininity; in other words, somebody like Rosalyn in "A June Night's Dream." The fact that he developed this image while in the United States cannot be overemphasized. This may explain his decision, upon returning to Japan, to write almost exclusively about the women of Tokyo's demimonde. As one of the characters in his mid-length novel, *Reishō* [Sneers, 1909–1910], puts it, "[Japanese] society is still far from requiring a woman to be other than the good-wife-and-wise-mother type . . . to discuss women in these terms is a totally utilitarian attitude."[15] He must have felt it was quite unrealistic for a Japanese novelist to introduce well-rounded and interesting female characters into his work. The typical middle-class family in Japan was simply the wrong milieu, especially for a writer like Kafū who enjoyed French works in which adultery was a prominent theme and flirtation was elevated to an art form. In contrast, the pleasure quarters at its peak during the Edo period had been a place of taste and refinement where geisha—highly skilled musicians and dancers—were frequently better versed in literature than their "nonprofessional" counterparts. It was also a place where the discerning connoisseur (with whom Kafū identified) was preferred to the socially prominent, where men and women could exchange witty comments on literature, the Kabuki theater, or music and thus embellish the crude realities of the place.

It is true that the pleasure quarters of Kafū's time no longer fit the descriptions in the late Edo popular literature he admired. Yet that world is distantly recalled in the family gathering in "Two Days in Chicago," where music is so much a part of life. In *Sneers*, the only protagonist who seems to share his wife's interests and taste is the Kabuki playwright, Nakatani. His wife, Okimi, comes from a pleasure quarters teahouse and has been brought up like a geisha. She is proud of the fact that her husband's charm enables him to exploit women rather than being exploited by them. Okimi is also proud that her young daughter is taking dancing lessons with some apprentice geisha. While watching the little girl, Ochō, another protagonist, who is a writer, cannot help feeling

that nothing could move one deeper than a house with music in it. After his return to Japan, it was only at the home of this Kabuki playwright, infected to its root by the moribund Edo and corrupt pleasure quarters, that he was able to find a single example where music took place. . . . From a strict, moralistic point of view, this home would be considered dirty to its core. But in the society of his native country, he was able to find the beautiful life of happiness and harmony, comparable to that he had witnessed in the healthy family life in the West only in this morally corrupt family.[16]

When young Kafū started frequenting the pleasure quarters in his teens, he was not completely out of step with the Japanese males of his time. It was still more or less acceptable for a married man to have a mistress or a de facto second wife (frequently a geisha or a former geisha), and the pleasure quarters were a prominent milieu for socializing among men. Yet Kafū's father was different: he kept away from the demimonde and remained faithful to his wife. As a result, his son felt defensive and at times defiant about his nocturnal activities. After spending four years in the United States, where he was able to observe first hand that a more colorful and exciting life was possible even within the confines of a healthy home, returning to the pleasure quarters was no longer a mere act of frivolity and debauchery. Nor was it just an escape into the past or an avoidance of reality, themes most students of Kafū stress. Rather, it provided him with a medium that was lacking in the middle-class Japan of his time for reconciling, however precariously, the world of the late Edo period and the French salon as he understood it.

Kafū's writing is appealing because of his evocative yet simple prose style and his sense of humor, but it is also a product of the culture shock he experienced while in the United States and the way he coped with it. Although he was not a particularly rational or profound thinker, he was gifted with an unusual sensitivity that he cultivated and relied upon while living in the West and reading French literature. Primarily nonreligious, Kafū believed in being true to his sensitivity. At a time when the encounter with a vastly different civilization was making an incredible and frequently chaotic impact on Japan, Kafū managed to develop his art, writing what truthfully represented his feelings and observations as well as his appreciation of Western literature and culture. He neither resented the West nor applauded Japan's modernization. Kafū's observations of the natural surroundings and the people of the United States at the turn of the century are vivid and informative. Even a piece like "Ladies of the Night," which seems to have been inspired in part by Maupassant's "La Maison Tellier," describes the variety of people in America that so few Japanese visitors to this country seemed to grasp.

All in all, then, *Amerika monogatari*, described by Donald Keene as "Kafū's first masterpiece," is worth reading both as one Japanese writer's attempt to come to grips with Western literature, art, and music at the turn of the twentieth century and as a unique observation of American life in various parts of the country.[17] Few Japanese, or for that matter writers from any country, have produced more intimate, sensitive depictions of America. The *American Stories* are therefore of interest not just to students of modern Japanese literature but also to historians of American culture and society.

ABOUT THIS TRANSLATION

This book is a translation of *Amerika monogatari*'s first edition (1908), containing twenty-one stories, and of the two pieces subsequently added to the collection, as explained above. I have used the texts of these twenty-three pieces contained in volume 4 of *Kafū zenshū* [Collected works of Kafū], published by Iwanami Shoten in 1992, which reprints the stories exactly as they first appeared. My footnotes indicate significant changes made by Kafū in subsequent versions.

Kafū's writing includes extremely long sentences, and he regularly mixes tenses, a practice that was not uncommon at that time. While I have tried to remain as faithful to the original version as possible in rendering his Japanese into English, I have made a small number of changes in punctuation and tense where I have felt the author's meaning would otherwise be obscure. Even so, Kafū's sentences may impress the modern reader as rather clumsy and sometimes stilted. But we should remember that the stories in *Amerika monogatari* were among his early works, published before he acquired a reputation for his mastery of the modern Japanese writing style.

Where Kafū uses Japanese terms (for food, for instance) that are not familiar to non-Japanese readers, or where his expressions are not entirely clear, I have inserted brief explanations within square brackets. Parentheses, on the other hand, are his own.

Finally, these stories contain several quotes from French poems. In all such instances, Kafū provides his own Japanese translation. I have rendered his translations verbatim into English even where he makes obvious mistakes.

Mitsuko Iriye

———

NOTES

1. Kafū's postcard to a literary friend, Ikuta Kizan, dated February 27, 1904, in *Kafū zenshū* [Collected works of Kafū, hereafter cited as *KZ*], 30 vols. (Tokyo: Iwanami Shoten, 1992–1995), vol. 27, p. 7.

2. John Fox, Jr., *The Little Shepherd of Kingdom Come* (New York: Scribner's, 1912), p. 332.

3. The first edition of *Amerika monogatari* included three pieces about France, but these were deleted from later editions and instead added to the collection *Furansu monogatari* [French stories].

4. Edward Seidensticker, *Kafū the Scribbler: The Life and Writings of Nagai Kafū, 1879–1959* (Stanford: Stanford University Press, 1965), p. 13.

5. Kafū's letter to Nishimura Keijirō, postmarked February 20, 1908, *KZ*, vol. 27, p. 23.

6. Kafū's letter to Mokuyōkai (Thursday Club), 1907, in *KZ*, vol. 27, p. 19.

7. Seidensticker, p. 25.

8. Kafū's postcard to Nishimura, postmarked December 27, 1904, *KZ*, vol. 27, p. 25.

9. Kalamazoo College, "The College Index," vol. 27, no. 2 (November 1905), p. 50.

10. *KZ*, vol. 4, p. 305.

11. The name of Julius L. Stewart, Paris, appears in *Official Catalogue of Exhibits, Department of Art*, revised edition (St. Louis, 1904), p. 37. One of his oil paintings was entitled *Grand Matin (nude figure)*.

12. *KZ*, vol. 5, p. 357.

13. Mitsuko Iriye, "'Amerika monogatari' no yohaku ni miru Kafū [Kafū as seen in the margins of *American Stories*], *Bungaku* [Literature], July 1992, p. 12.

14. *KZ*, vol. 6, p. 266.

15. Ibid., vol. 7, p. 189.

16. Ibid., vol. 7, p. 74.

17. Donald Keene, *Modern Japanese Diaries: The Japanese at Home and Abroad as Revealed Through Their Diaries* (New York: Columbia University Press, 1998), p. 492. I offer a detailed analysis of Kafū's early writings in "Quest for Literary Resonance: Young Kafū and French Literature" (Ph.D. diss., Harvard University, 1969). See also my "'Amerika monogatari'" cited above.

Acknowledgments

I am grateful to Frank Gibney and Thomas Rimer, who first suggested that I undertake a translation of Kafū's *Amerika monogatari*. It was many years ago, and they waited patiently while I worked on the project little by little. Without their encouragement and gentle prodding, it might have taken even longer to complete.

The translation has gone through several stages, as I have checked it against Kafū's original on numerous occasions. At every stage, I have had the benefit of a careful reading and editing by my daughter Masumi, who, together with her husband, David O'Brien, has given me much-needed moral support over the years. My husband has helped me as unpaid editor, typist, secretary, and agent. I am greatly indebted to our friends and neighbors of over thirty years in Chicago, Bob and Barb Thompson, who have been unfailing sources of information, geographical and otherwise. Lastly, Leslie Kriesel, of Columbia University Press, has been an ideal editor in every respect: efficient, resourceful, and truly conscientious.

I dedicate this modest volume to the memory of my parents, Yōichi and Yū Maeda, who, throughout the very difficult years during the war in Europe and the United States and after the war in Japan, instilled in me love of learning and especially of literature.

Mitsuko Iriye

American Stories

From around October in the fall of 1903, I spent leisurely time in the United States and left New York for France last summer, July 1907; on that occasion I collected the various pieces I had written during my journey, which I have now entitled *American Stories* and respectfully present to my revered teacher and friend, Mr. Iwaya Sazanami.

Nagai Kafū

Mais les vrais voyageurs sont ceux-là seuls qui partent
Pour partir; coeurs légers, semblables aux ballons,
De leur fatalité jamais ils ne sécartent,
Et, sans savoir pourquoi, disent toujours: Allons!

(*Le Voyage*—Ch. Baudelaire)

The true travelers are those who leave for the sole purpose
Of leaving. With hearts as light as balloons, unable to flee
From ill fate, they just call out all the time, Let's go
Let's go, without knowing why.

(*Le Voyage*—Ch. Baudelaire)[*]

---

[*]Literal rendition into English of Kafū's translation from the original. Kafū makes a mistake in thinking that the word *seuls* (only) modifies the verb *partent* (leave), instead of *ceux-là* (those).

Night Talk in a Cabin

Crossing the seas with no land in sight anywhere is almost unbearably tedious, and the voyage between Yokohama and the port of the newly developed city of Seattle is no exception.

Once the passengers have parted with the mountains of their homeland on the day of sailing, they cannot expect to see a single island, a single mountain, for more than half a month, until the day when they reach the continent on the other side of the ocean. It was all ocean yesterday, and so it is again today—one gets a view of the never-changing Pacific Ocean as simply vast, where all one can see are gray albatrosses with long wings and crooked beaks, flying about among giant, undulating waves. To make matters worse, pleasant, clear days become rarer and rarer as the ship steadily advances northward, and practically every day, not only is the sky completely covered by gloomy gray clouds, but it is even likely that rain or fog will come.

I have unexpectedly been a wayfarer in this desolate ocean now for ten days. During the day it is possible somehow to kill time playing ring toss on the deck or playing cards in the smoking room, but once dinner is over at night, there is hardly anything left to do. Furthermore, it seems that the weather has turned considerably colder today. Thinking that it would be impossible to walk across the deck to the smoking room without an overcoat, I shut myself up in my cabin. I was just wondering if perhaps I should lie down on the sofa and read some of the magazines I brought from Japan, when someone softly knocked on the door with a fingertip.

"Come in," I called out, sitting up.

The door opened. "What's the matter? It is swaying again a little, don't you think? Do you feel weak?"

"Oh, no," I replied. "I decided to withdraw to my room since it was a bit cold. Do sit down."

"Yes, it is really cold. They say we are about to pass the Gulf of Alaska," said Yanagida, sitting down at the end of the sofa, a smile on his lips, adorned with a rather thin moustache. He is a gentleman with whom I have become acquainted on this voyage.

Of middle height and build, he seemed to be over thirty by at least one or two years. He was wearing a brown overcoat over a striped suit and displayed a colorful necktie from a high collar. Resting one leg over his knee in a rather affected manner and knocking off cigar ashes with the tip of his ringed small finger, he said, "It will be beautiful weather in Japan now."

"Yes, indeed."

"Are you trying to remember something?"

"Ha ha. That's something you should say to the fellow next door."

"Maybe. Speaking of the fellow next door, how is he doing? He must be holed up in his cabin as usual. Why don't we invite him over?"

"Good," I said and knocked on the wall two or three times. There was no answer for a while, but presently Kishimoto, who occupied the cabin next door, appeared at my cabin door and said in his usual weak voice, "What is it?"

"Hello, come in!" the chic Yanagida called out immediately in an affected pronunciation.

"Thank you, but I am dressed like this, so . . ." answered Kishimoto, still standing.

"My dear fellow, don't stand on silly ceremony. This is my room. It doesn't matter if you are undressed or whatever. So do come in." I stood up from the sofa and opened up the folding chair that had been propped up against the wall.

Kishimoto was also about thirty years old and of rather short stature, and was wearing a *haori* [half-coat] made of Ōshima pongee over a lined pongee kimono and an unlined flannel garment.

"All right, thanks." He sat down, after a small bow, and said, "It is too cold in Western clothes, and so I was about to change into my night clothes and go to bed."

Yanagida responded in a most puzzled tone, looking at Kishimoto, "Do you mean Western clothes don't keep you warm? In my case, it is exactly the opposite. On a voyage like this, especially, if I put on Japanese clothes, I'll feel too chilly around the neck and will catch a cold right away."

"Is that so? Maybe this means that I have not quite gotten used to Western clothes."

"Not really. When it's cold, it doesn't matter what you wear," I said, just smiling and looking at both of them. "By the way, Yanagida, I know you are a drinker. Shall I order something for you?"

"Well, I don't particularly feel like it tonight. I just came over for a chat, as I was getting bored."

Pressing the bell, I said, "But it isn't much fun talking without holding glasses. So shall we hear your story again, Kishimoto?"

But Kishimoto did not respond and, looking up, said, "The ship seems to be swaying a great deal again."

"Well, after all, this is the Pacific Ocean," Yanagida put in, twisting his thin moustache once again.

I was just responding, "If this were the second or third day of our voyage, we would suffer more, but we seem to have gotten used to it and don't feel anything, do we?" when a cabin boy opened the door.

"Yanagida, do you want whisky as usual?"

The cabin boy, after hearing his "Of course," gently closed the door and went away, but at that very moment, we heard the deep roaring sound of the foghorn, followed by a sound of waves washing the decks.

"It does rock a little, doesn't it? Well, that's all right. Let's have a nice little chat this evening," said Yanagida, stretching his legs comfortably. Glancing around the ceiling of the cabin, brightly lit with electric lights, the kimono-clad Kishimoto said, "What is wrong? They are blowing the foghorn a great deal, aren't they?"

"Maybe the fog has thickened." Yanagida started to explain but was interrupted by the cabin boy, who promptly brought the ordered drinks on a tray and, after placing them on a small table by the bed, filled the glasses. As soon as he left again, first Yanagida raised his cup and offered his "Good luck!" followed by our repeated, laughing "Good luck!"s.

Time passed. In the far distance the forlorn sound of a bell tolling the time could be heard. Just then, the waves seemed to swell higher and higher until we heard them hitting the round porthole above the bed with a crushing sound and dashing against the deck area, while the wind sweeping by the tall masts sounded just like the dry winds of February in Tokyo. The grating sound of something creaking somewhere began. But this was a large ship of considerable tonnage, so the rolling and pushing were rather gentle, and, as we had become used to the voyage, we didn't worry about getting seasick at all. As we drew the curtains over the porthole and door so that the tiny cabin would be warmed by steam and reclined on armchairs, listening to the storm outside, all this somehow recalled the comfort of a fireside on a winter night. Yanagida seemed to feel the same way, as he said, putting down his whisky glass, "Don't you think that once you believe in your own safety, even raging storms outside somehow sound attractive?"

"Quite. I guess this is what is meant by 'feeling secure like being

NIGHT TALK IN A CABIN

on a big boat.' But suppose this were a sailboat, then I am sure it's quite possible that we might be shipwrecked," said Kishimoto in a serious tone.

"It's the same with everything. Whenever some are having fun, others may have to suffer. Like a fire—it is a disaster to those who lose their home, but a great spectacle for the rest." I intoned some such silly argument, having perhaps drunk too much whisky.

"It's true, it is quite true," Yanagida responded, as if deeply moved by something. "To continue your metaphor, I am one of those who have lost their homes. I lost my home in a fire and am fleeing all the way to America. Actually, it was only last year that I returned to Japan, and I am amazed at myself for having started my overseas trip again even before I had time to unpack all my trunks."

Both Kishimoto and I eagerly asked Yanagida to tell us about his aspirations behind this trip to America, assuming that he must have entertained grand thoughts; he was the kind of person who could not talk of little things without discussing such items as the civilization of a continent or the pettiness of an island country.

"Ha, ha, ha, ha. I really don't have anything like a grand idea. However . . ." Yanagida twisted his thin moustache and began telling us his story.

It went back to the time when he graduated from a certain school. Immediately, he was employed by a firm and proceeded to Australia with great eagerness. After a considerable amount of time, he returned to his native Japan with a sense of triumph immeasurably greater than when he had initially left the country. He preached and praised the civilization of the continent and the commerce of the world everywhere to whomever he met, including his old friends who gave him welcome parties. And he never doubted that the minuscule island country would surely offer him an important position. But instead, he was assigned a job as a translator at the head office, with a monthly wage of only forty Japanese (devalued silver) yen. He did not protest and accepted the job, after carefully considering conditions in Japan. But he could not help constantly feeling dissatisfied, and, in order to relieve himself of that feeling, decided to look for a wife, preferably a beautiful daughter of an aristocratic family, and started to campaign actively in that direction. He was secretly confident that being someone who had returned from abroad would recommend him to such young women or their mothers, but in reality nothing of the sort happened. The daughter of a certain viscount whom he pursued ended up marrying a university graduate of the island country, the type of person he scorned the most. Not only had his self-confidence been shattered twice, he now had to suffer from a broken heart.

But Yanagida never completely gave up hope. As a reaction against his pain, he began denouncing everything about the island country even more strongly than before and decided to undertake another joyful trip abroad.

"As long as you are in Japan, it is simply impossible to shout with delight from the bottom of your heart. Luckily, it so happened that a raw-silk merchant in Yokohama wanted me to study conditions in the United States, and I gladly accepted. When it comes to business, you must really go abroad at all costs. I am very happy to see that you gentlemen, my compatriots, are also going to the United States." Yanagida picked up his glass, took a sip, and turned his body around, saying, "Kishimoto, didn't you tell me that you wanted to go to school in the United States?"

"Yes," Kishimoto answered, pulling the neckbands of his kimono closer together.

"Are you planning to enter some university?"

"Well, I'd like to, but right now I don't have the language and don't quite understand how things work. . . ."

"Do you see, Yanagida? Kishimoto has left Japan in order to pursue his studies, even at the expense of leaving his wife and child behind." As I said this, Yanagida leaned forward and asked, "Kishimoto, do you already have a child?"

"Yes," was all Kishimoto said, blushing a little.

"Then you must really have made a great commitment."

"Well, I would like to think I made a big effort when I left the country. There were some relatives and others who were violently opposed to my plans." This time it was Kishimoto's turn to tell his story.

He had also worked for a company in Tokyo; however, not only did he have little prospect for career advancement, he was constantly being pushed down by others, the reason presumably being, he thought, that he had not graduated from any school and therefore had no degree. While he was pondering these facts, his company undertook a reorganization, and he was going to be dismissed. Luckily for him, since his wife had inherited a considerable fortune, he was spared the plight of an ordinary person under the same circumstances. On the contrary, his wife actually seemed happy and thought that this was a good turn of events, telling him that they should leave the noise of Tokyo behind with their sweet little child and move to some quiet countryside and live in peace and comfort, making use of her money.

But Kishimoto was not about to yield to his wife's gentle words. Instead, he told her that, if possible, he would like to make use of the property she had inherited from her late father and study in the United States for a couple of years. She, however, was firmly opposed, not because she begrudged him the money but because she simply did not want to part from the husband she loved dearly. She told him that she didn't want him to strain himself to succeed for her sake, that he should not feel embarrassed that he was being passed over by former houseboys with bachelor's degrees, and besides, wasn't it enough for everyone to act according to his ability and live a peaceful life every day? Yet, faced with her husband's resolute entreaties, in the end she yielded and tearfully saw Kishimoto go off to a faraway land.

"So, I am hoping to shorten my stay as much as possible and go home with whatever degree I may obtain from a school. A diploma will be the best present to show my wife."

Having said this much, Kishimoto gulped down a mouthful of whisky while making a face, as if to cheer himself up.

"Yes, I really feel for you. At the same time, though, I congratulate you on your daring decision with all my heart." Yanagida raised his glass after him, then changed his tone. "But you must be reminded of your wife all the time, even though I myself don't know yet what it's like to have a wife."

"Ha, ha, ha, ha. I can't be so spineless now that I have come this far . . . ha, ha, ha, ha." Kishimoto forced a laugh but looked quite distressed.

Just then, the clanging of the bell could be heard once again. The waves and the winds were still raging outside the porthole, barely kept out by a single pane, but inside the closed cabin it was already too warm, with the aroma of alcohol and cigarette smoke. We had grown a little weary of talking and, as if for the first time, looked at the electric lights that were brightening up every corner of the cabin. Before long Yanagida pulled out his watch, as though he suddenly remembered something, and said, "It's already eleven o'clock."

"Is that right? Forgive me for having stayed for such a long time. I shall be going now." Kishimoto stood up first.

"Oh, please stay."

"Thank you. I have really enjoyed myself tonight, thanks to you. It will be nice to spend tomorrow like this again. I must be going."

Opening the door, Yanagida said "Good night" in English, and while he mumbled some unintelligible English poem, his footsteps soon faded away in the direction of his cabin. In the cabin next door, in the meantime, I could hear the faint sound of the bed curtain being drawn. Kishimoto, who had also left my cabin, must already be lying down in his lonely bed.

(November 1903)

NIGHT TALK IN A CABIN

A Return Through the Meadow

If I remember correctly, it was already the last Saturday of October in Tacoma, where I was staying at that time.

Fall was coming to an end, and just about all the leaves—from those on the rows of maple trees planted on both sides of the streets to those on the trees that had provided cool shade in the parks and people's gardens during the summer—had fallen after the previous night's dense fog. Not just here in Tacoma but along the Pacific Coast of the United States, it would be the sad month of November in less than a week. From then till next May it would be rainy and foggy practically every day, and it would be next to impossible to see clear skies. People said the day's cloudless weather might give us the last chance this year to look at a blue sky. So, on the advice of a friend who knew the local conditions very well, I decided to spend the day bicycling in late autumn's prairies with him.

Leaving the house, we ride toward the east along a straight road uptown called Tacoma Avenue. The city of Tacoma faces Puget Sound, an inland sea with very heavy traffic, and is built on a sharp incline, so that, as we turn around, we can see the whole city in one glance—countless roofs and chimneys, vast landfills, docks, several ships at anchor, trains belonging to the Northern Pacific Railway. And atop the mountain range beyond the bay, the snow-clad Mount Rainier, called "Tacoma Fuji" by the Japanese, rises majestically, now with one side dyed deep red by the late-rising sun of the north country.

In no time we crossed a couple of bridges built over a large ravine at the edge of the city, and we cycled on for about four miles along a wide, specially built bicycle path; we passed a small village called South Tacoma, then came at once upon a vast field that we biked through, going uphill or downhill as the road went, feeling as if we were small ships being rocked by waves, until we finally reached the end and entered an oak woods. The road became somewhat steeper, and the straight pine trees that form dark and dense forests everywhere in this region, particularly in Washington State, in no time blocked our way, just as the oak woods had. We managed to find a moss-covered trail and, following its lead, took a short rest by a lake in the forest called the American Lake. Then we again changed course and finally arrived at a solitary village on a promontory called Stillcome.

My companion then said, "I'll take you to the lunatic asylum on top of this hill on our way back. It's the state asylum of Washington, so it's pretty well known around here."

So I followed him and climbed up the hill; we could readily identify the tall and wide brick building as the asylum, against the background of cheerful meadows far away and solid forest in the foreground.

The spacious compound was enclosed by a low white picket fence and completely covered by a bright green lawn, except for a footpath that displayed a dazzlingly fresh color against the trees with delicate branches and the various flowers planted on it. At the rear of the building, the glass roof of a huge greenhouse could be seen, and there were benches here and there along the path, while in the shade of the trees in the open space there were swing seats. But silence reigned all around, and not a single person could be seen.

We pedaled at a leisurely pace along the dirt road in front of the iron gate and started going downhill toward the meadow from which we had come. On our way back, my friend explained various things to me and mentioned casually, "There are two or three Japanese confined in this asylum."

For some reason this seemed like a rather serious matter. Then my friend added immediately, "They are all immigrant workers."

I cannot help but be agitated anew by the words, "immigrant workers." It is all too easy to recall how I felt looking at these workers from the upper deck while taking a walk, on my voyage last year from my native land to this country.

They are being treated less as humans than as cargo and are loaded to capacity in a small, dirty, and smelly hole; when they notice good weather, they come up to the deck from the bottom of the ship, like so much rising smoke, and stare at the boundless sky and ocean. But unlike the rest of us, oversensitive souls, they do not seem particularly struck by any feeling; they gather in groups of three or four, five or six, and after talking loudly for a while about something, they smoke tobacco with *kiseru* [long-stemmed straight pipes] they have brought from Japan and scatter ashes on the deck till reprimanded by one of the crew who happens to go by. Or, later, on moonlit nights, they begin singing some provincial popular songs that reveal their native places. I can never forget one of them, a white-haired old man who appeared proud of his voice.

Sustained by the vision alone, that three years of hard work abroad sow the seeds of ten years' wealth and happiness after they go back home, they leave behind the farmland where their ancestors were born and died, bidding farewell to the eastern skies more beautiful than those in Italy, remain patient all through humiliations such as immigration regulations and health examinations, and arrive in this new continent.

But no matter where one goes in this world, drudgery is everywhere. How many of these people will ever be able to attain their wishes? Such sad thoughts occurred to me as I looked at the meadows, which until now had appeared to epitomize peace and comfort but which all of a sudden impressed me with their loneliness. And the dark and deep pine forests seemed like hiding places of terror and secrecy.

I took the opportunity presented by my friend, who had pulled up his bicycle to the shade of a tree, and approached him asking, "But why did they lose their sanity, do you know?"

"Oh . . . you mean the laborers?" My friend replied after a while, as if understanding my question for the first time, "In most instances, loss of hope is the reason, but in the case of one of them, there were other causes as well. . . . A really sad case. But such cases are not unusual in America."

"Do explain what you mean."

"I heard about him from someone else . . . even in the pretty lawless Japanese society, this was extreme. He told me that it happened already six or seven years ago," my friend began, taking a tobacco pouch from his inside pocket and skillfully rolling his cigarette with his fingertips.

At that time, Japanese had just begun arriving in large numbers in Seattle and Tacoma; things were not as settled as today, and many crimes were pretty openly committed. Old-timers from Japan, such as ruffians wandering up from California or sailors of dubious origin who had crossed some ocean and then turned labor bosses, vied with each other for the lifeblood of the uninformed newcomers. To such a dangerous, hellish place he—that is, one of the inmates at the asylum—had come from Japan with his wife to earn a living.

Now, the biggest reason why laborers aspire to come to America is that they hear exaggerated stories told by people who have just returned home. And this man was certainly one of those. He had been living in the fields of Kishū where buckwheat flowers bloomed, but it happened that a man had returned from Hawaii after fifteen years and bragged about America where, as he put it, there were gold-bearing trees everywhere. So our man decided, on impulse, to go to this unseen paradise, particularly since he was told that women earned higher wages than men. So the couple undertook their trip to America—landing in Seattle, a city whose name they could not even pronounce—a land about which they knew nothing. On the wharf, the ship was greeted by employment brokers, agents from lodging houses, smugglers of prostitutes—all with sharper eyes than most, who used all their power to capture their prey and toss them into their nets. One such man who identified himself as a guide for an inn led the couple through dirty streets covered by huge wagons and evil-looking American laborers to an alley, pushed open a dark doorway, and, instead of going upstairs, took them to a dimly lit underground room.

Here, after they paid an exorbitant commission, it was decided that the wife would work at a laundry in the city while the husband was to be hired as a woodcutter in a forest on a mountain about ten miles out of the city. As he was taken to a lone house, dark even in daytime, in the forest, he found three other Japanese working as woodcutters. One of them, perhaps the leader, said, "We only have each other to trust in a foreign country. Let's be like brothers and work together from now on." Our man felt quite relieved and started working hard every day with this group under the supervision of a white boss.

[One day,] returning from work to this lonely log cabin, the fellows prodded the newcomer to tell them about his life. . . . As he did so, the leaderlike, strongest-looking man raised his voice as if taken aback, looking around at his other companions with flashing eyes.

"You mean you left your old woman behind in Seattle? What a stupid thing to do!"

"But, you know, once in this country, I have to earn money, so it's nothing to live apart from my wife," said the newcomer, sounding sad nevertheless, to which the other man responded, "That's not what I mean. Of course, you've got to be prepared for such a life, since you came here to make money. What I mean is that it's more dangerous to leave a woman alone in Seattle than to let a child play at the edge of a river."

"Oh? But why?"

"It's natural you don't know, since you just got here. But in Seattle . . . of course, it's not limited to Seattle, in America generally, they will never leave a woman alone, safely. If she is raped, that's the least of your problems. In the worst case, you may never be able to see your old woman again."

"That's true. You'd better be careful," another fellow added. The first fellow remained silent and cunningly scrutinized the newcomer, who looked as if he wanted to cry.

Puffing once at his large pipe, the leader said first, "In this country, any broad, as long as she is a woman, is a treasure chest worth a thousand *ryō*, I mean a thousand dollars. So, procurers called pimps are on the lookout for women, and sometimes they do pretty ruthless things. I'll tell you a true story. Once, while a couple were walking down a street, a guy came from behind, knocked the husband down, grabbed the wife, and disappeared. It's a big country, this America. Who knows? If you go far away and sell a woman as a whore, you can easily earn a thousand dollars. You too had better watch out before something terrible happens."

The newcomer's eyes were already filled with tears, but what could he do, given his situation? The first fellow then looked at the other two, and, after exchanging some glances with them and everyone seemed to be in agreement, he told the newcomer, "How about this? Why don't you bring your wife here?"

"But how on earth can I do such a thing?"

"Don't tell me you can't do it. True, I don't know how it would look, but there are only three of us Japanese in this isolated hut in the woods, so there is nothing to worry about. If she can agree to get over here, you'll be able to be with your wife every day, and besides, she can help with cooking and laundry. The addition of one woman wouldn't add to the cost of meals if the four of us share it."

Such was the proposal, but he had neither the strength to agree nor the requisite status to express disagreement, so that everything happened at once, the way the other fellow had suggested. That is to say, on the very next day, he and the other man went to the city and brought back the wife to the cottage in the woods.

The first four or five days were eventless, and he lived happily with his wife, but one day, which happened to be a Sunday, it rained from morning on and they were not able to get out for fun. So they began a party, drinking and singing, and before they knew it, it was already late in the evening. As it was time for bed, the man [leader] called back the newcomer, who was about to leave. Saying, "Hey, I just want to have a talk with you," he exchanged glances with the others.

The deep forest surrounding the cottage was roaring with the rain and wind.

"What is it?" The newcomer turned around impassively.

"I want to ask a favor of you."

"What is it?"

"What else? I want to borrow your old woman for the night. . . ."

"Ha, ha, ha, ha. You're pretty drunk, aren't you?"

"Listen, I'm not saying this because I'm drunk. It's not a joke or a jest. I just want to consult with you. How about it?"

"Ha, ha, ha, ha," came a forced laugh from the newcomer.

"Why are you laughing, when we are consulting you?" another man said this time.

"What do you think? This is among brothers. Can't you lend her to the three of us just for tonight?"

". . . ."

"Let's talk about it. How about it? You still don't want to do it? It's all right if you are against the idea, but think hard about it. Aren't you really bothered that on this mountain, where all four of us work together, only you are having a good time? If there is a mountain fire on a windy night, which happens frequently, we four will all have to die together . . . we can't leave one of us behind and run away; and if the worst happens, and no food reaches us from the main office, we'll have to share what we've got to eat. All men are brothers. Don't think that only you can have a good time. Listen, we've been in this America for five years, but we haven't even once felt a soft hand. We know your treasure is nobody else's but yours. So we aren't saying we are going to take it away by force and make it ours. Mind you, we are just begging you to lend it to us."

"The long and short of it is this. Since you have something we don't, we are asking you to share it with us."

"How about it? If you understand what we mean, why don't you answer us right away?"

The man turned dead pale and did nothing but shake his whole body violently. The woman fell at his feet crying, without any strength left to call for help.

A frightening dead of the night, with winds and rain still howling furiously, deep in the desolate mountains. Soon a woman's scream inside the cottage. . . . Hearing it, the man fainted and fell on the ground.

He did regain consciousness, but he had lost his mind and was never the same person again. So he ended up being taken to the insane asylum.

I was quite shocked, hearing this story. As for my friend, he had already pulled up his bicycle, which had been lying on the grass, and, stepping on the pedal, he said, "But it couldn't have been helped, could it? All we can say is that it was his misfortune to have met such a fate. We are simply helpless in the face of someone stronger than ourselves." He rode his bicycle for two or three *ken* [twelve to eighteen feet], and then looked back at me, following him.

"Don't you agree? It's impossible to resist something that is powerful. Therefore, we cannot resist Our Mighty God . . . that is, the Almighty God who is more powerful than we. We must always obey him."

He laughed cheerfully to himself and accelerated his bicycle at full speed through the meadows, which were being radiantly lit by the light of the evening sun that was about to set. Without saying a word, I pedaled away on my bicycle in order not to fall behind.

The sound of bells on grazing cattle's necks could be heard somewhere. A train heading south toward Portland was running along the edge of the fields.

(January 1905)

Atop the Hill

I

When I first came to this country, America, I decided to go to attend a certain college to practice my language, a college that had been built in a small town of less than four thousand people, about a hundred miles up the Mississippi River from Chicago, where I was then staying. As people already know, American colleges are mostly denominational schools, established in the scenic countryside, far removed from the cities that are full of temptation, and the teachers as well as the students lead an ideally clean religious life. The school to which I went was one of them, and at first I thought it would be most unlikely to meet another Japanese in such a remote place. Yet quite unexpectedly, I came across a Japanese who had been leading a strangely anguished life there.

For approximately four hours after leaving Chicago, wherever I looked, all I could see were cornfields. As soon as the train reached a tiny station standing in the middle of a vast prairie, I got off, and carrying a heavy bag, I walked all the way down a straight road of this provincial town, full of chickens and children at play, and called at the school, situated among leafy trees atop a small hill. The kindly-looking elderly principal greeted me, saying, even without looking at the letter of introduction given me by a Western friend in Chicago, and wrinkling his entire face in a big smile as if we were already good friends, "It is nice of you to come. Mr. Watano will surely be glad to see you. Ever since he came to us, he has not seen a Japanese for almost three years, so . . ."

I was at a loss, not understanding what this was all about, but the old gentleman, his face still all smiles, asked me, "Did you know Mr. Watano in Japan, or did you get to know him after you came to the United States?" The principal had jumped to the conclusion that because I was Japanese I must have come to visit my compatriot, Mr. Watano, at this school. This misunderstanding was soon dissolved in guileless laughter, and I was duly introduced to the person named Mr. Watano.

He must have been thirty-seven or -eight years of age. In an all but torn, threadbare striped suit and a faded black tie, he was dressed in a modest fashion one would hardly encounter in a flashy city like Chicago; as soon as I saw him, with his shiny black hair grown long the American way and his slender face with gold-rimmed eyeglasses, I thought he was a handsome man. His complexion was not so much white as pale, and there was something abnormally oversensitive about his large eyes.

Quite contrary to what the principal had told me, he looked neither particularly pleased nor surprised when he first saw me, and after shaking hands without uttering a word, he pointedly stared at the ceiling. Thus, since I myself was a rather unfriendly type with a gruff disposition, I didn't have a chance to find out what kind of background he had, other than that he was helping out with the collection of material in connection with the study of the history of Oriental thought in the school's department of philosophy, and would occasionally appear at lecture halls for Bible study.

However, it was on a Saturday afternoon about three months later [that I next saw him]. I had come to this place at the end of September when it was still warm; but the cornfields, which then looked like a green sea, were now a vast uninterrupted prairie under the dark, gray sky.

It was just after four o'clock in the afternoon, but the sun had already sunk below the vast horizon, and all that was left was a faint streak of crimson, low in a gap of gray sky. The air was calm, and the chill that penetrated the bones had been arising steadily from the bowels of the wilderness. As I climbed up the hill near the school on my way back from the post office located inside the railway station, I ran into Watano, who stood forlornly, with an indescribably sad face, on this hilltop with only a bare tree, gazing at the light of the setting sun, which was about to disappear, reflected on the face of the frozen wasteland. Noticing me, Watano just said, "What a desolate view," and looked at me intently.

Startled by his strange air, I was not able to respond right away. Watano cast down his eyes and then said, as if to himself, "People say that the sunset by a grave is sad, but it merely reminds you of 'death' . . . on the other hand, look at this sight; twilight by a wasteland brings to mind life's sorrows, the agony of existence. . . ."

We remained silent and climbed down the hill; suddenly, Watano called to me, "What do you think? Do life's goals lie in pleasure, or—" He stopped himself, as if he had become terribly fearful that he had said something thoughtless; then, eyeing my face intently, he added, "Do you believe in the Christian God?"

I told him that I wanted to believe and couldn't yet, but that I knew how happy I would feel if I ever were able to. To which Watano responded, energetically and swinging his arms, "So you are a skeptic. Very good." And then he asked quietly, "What sort of skepticism is yours? Of course, I myself don't have the kind of faith Americans have. . . . Let's hear what your views are."

So I freely explained my ideas about religion, life, and such matters. To my great surprise, he seemed to think my ideas had much in common with his; his eyes became animated as if to express his inner joy, and he ended up praising my abilities again and again.

Nothing is more pleasant than for two individuals, no matter who they are, to come together and discover that they share the same thought, even to a tiny extent. Such a coincidence also draws the two closer together spiritually.

After this encounter, we became close friends, talking together day and night, and I came to have some idea of Watano's background without directly asking him about it. It appeared that in Japan he had inherited a considerable fortune. About seven years earlier he had come to the United States and obtained a degree at an East Coast university, but after that he did not do any serious work and idled away his time in the New York area. But at a certain gathering he became acquainted with the president of this college, who told him that his school was looking for a Japanese who could help with the study of Oriental thought and customs. So he volunteered to come to this place. It was not, however, that he knew much about Oriental subjects; he just thought that he could at least help with the collection of research material. But his primary purpose in coming here was above all to see if his inherently skeptical views would give way to some deep faith so that he could attain a sense of security. For this reason, he told me, he had intentionally chosen to embrace religious life in this remote country.

Although he obviously had no need to work for a living, I could not but admire him for his decision, derived from a genuine spiritual anguish, not to return to his native land even after obtaining a degree but to live alone in a foreign land.

2

I spent a cold, cold American winter very peacefully and agreeably with this friend whom I admired so much. Then April came, and from Easter onward the warm sunlight returned from time to time, and the month of May for which we had eagerly waited arrived. How delightful were the skies of May, in contrast to the unbearably cold winter! Even the plains, which till yesterday had appeared utterly and incredibly lonely and unpleasant, suddenly transformed themselves into a boundless sea of fresh grass. How could we describe the sensation of enjoying soft green color all around us, under a bright blue sky?

I would roam about the orchards filled with apple blossoms, go to the meadows to lie down on soft clover leaves next to grazing cattle, or stand near a brook, getting drunk with the fragrance of violets and singing along with field larks; I walked at least three miles a day doing these things. Family members of rich farmers would wait impatiently for the afternoon and then set out in their carriages to enjoy themselves in the fields. Merry laughter of women and children could be heard everywhere. And yet, my friend Watano was an exception; even as the beautiful spring arrived, he became more and more melancholy, to such an extent that not once did he agree to go out for a walk with me and instead confined himself in his room.

How could I help but wonder what was going on? One evening, I determined to visit him in his room and ask him to tell me, even if against his will, whatever was bothering him so that at least I could try to comfort him. But once I reached the gate of the boarding house where he was renting a room, for some strange reason I could not quite go through with my plans. Actually, I really had not been able to form a firm idea of Watano's personality; and just as we combine a sense of admiration with some fear when we are face to face with a great man or a hero, so toward Watano I was not quite able to get rid of a slight squeamishness. In the end, I did not have the courage to knock on his door, not to mention asking him to tell me what was on his mind. . . . Thus I turned around and started walking here and there in this spring night, and before I realized it, I found myself on top of the hill where Watano and I had had our first serious talk last winter.

The lone leafless tree, which had been thin and worn out then, was now filled with snow-white apple blossoms, enveloping me in an indescribable fragrance. As I stood on the tender grass and looked around, I saw a hazy full moon over the vast prairie whose expanse made one realize that indeed here was a surface of the earth. Water puddles here and there caught the moon's pale light and reflected the dark colors of the sky. Behind me stood the college, where some music accompanying merrymaking by girl students could be heard; and the houses in the nearby town had all their windows lit with gentle lights. What a dreamlike spring night in a faraway land, as if conjured up by magic!

Right away, I fell under the spell of it all and lapsed into an inexplicably sad daydream, when all of a sudden someone came up to me from behind, tapped me on the shoulder, and called out, "You!" To my surprise, I saw it was Watano. He looked as if he had something to tell me.

"I was just at your place."

"My place? . . . Then we must have crossed each other," I responded, but I said nothing about my almost having knocked on his door.

"Actually, I wanted to talk with you, so I went to your place."

I was taken by surprise and said, "What is it? What sort of thing?"

"Let's sit here." He took the initiative and sat down first under the apple tree, but did not say a word. It was quite likely that he too had been struck by the mysterious atmosphere of the spring night veiling the vast prairie in this foreign land. But then, as if awakering from a reverie, he turned at once toward me and said, "I may have to say good-bye to you in a few days."

"What? Where will you be going?"

"I am thinking of going to New York once again. Or I may decide to go to Europe. . . . Anyway, I have decided to leave this place."

"Anything urgent?"

"Oh, no. You know I don't have any urgent business. It is just that I've been thinking about something," he said in a rather dispirited way.

"About what?"

To my question, he responded after a while, "Well, that's what I wanted to tell you tonight. We've known each other for less than half a year, but I feel as if I've known you for already ten years. So I wanted to leave you after telling you everything. But on the other hand, we may run into each other again since you tell me you will be traveling through America." Smiling sadly, he began in a quiet voice.

3

"Shortly after graduating from the University, I parted from my father and inherited all my share of his property, thus gaining an enviable status as a propertied new university graduate, able to move in any worldly direction I wanted. As I had majored in literature, I decided to organize a society, on the advice of my friends who gathered around me, and to publish a fine monthly dedicated to saving lives and reforming society.

"It so happened that my name was known at least to some people, since I used to contribute essays to journals and newspapers even while I was a student. So it was with a great fanfare that, backed up by the property I had inherited from my father, I made a grand debut into the world. The organization I represented consisted only of young university graduates who were entering the real world for the first time, but as soon as we advertised the new journal, even before its first issue was published, it came to be counted as one of the most important. Naturally, there were those around me who were not above obsequiousness, and I could not, indeed, hear anything but praises at that time.

"I was twenty-seven years old then, and still a bachelor. It may not have been true, but I frequently heard rumors to the effect, for example, that the daughter of a certain count had become lovesick after seeing me give a talk, or that a row had been stirred up at a girls' school somewhere as they argued about my person. Indeed, I even received some amorous letters.

"So, anyway, I could not help becoming conscious that I must have some power that subtly affected the feelings of the opposite sex . . . not only did I become conscious of it, but I felt an indescribable pleasure. This pleasure was even greater than the joy I had felt when I became aware that my argument or my character appeared to be taken seriously by society. How foolish of me! I really can offer no excuse other than to say that just at that moment, at that instant, this was how I felt.

"Having experienced such a pleasurable sensation, I felt like pushing this pleasure as far as possible. That's when I heard an inner voice saying something like, 'If that's what you want, then don't get married too soon. You men certainly know that there is no comparison between a married woman who is indescribably beautiful and a virgin who is less so in stimulating your fantasy. So it is with your own charm.'

"I became entirely enslaved to this voice. I would groom myself with care, visit the sitting rooms of young wives and daughters of peers during the day, and become intoxicated by the glitter of coquettish glances and bright smiles, while at night I would go wherever lights blazed and listen to the singing of beautiful women. In no time two or three years passed by like a dream.

"But one day, in order to avoid catching people's attention in Tokyo, I took as many as three beautiful women to a small quiet geisha house by the seaside. It was already twilight in winter. Waking up suddenly from an afternoon nap, I noticed that the geisha who was my favorite and who had been letting me rest my head on her lap was leaning against the wall behind her and dozing off. I had no idea where the other two had gone; the room was semi-dark, and outside, only the languid voice of tides in the distant ocean could be heard, as if something were crying out.

"I did not stir but closed my eyes again. But I started thinking, almost unconsciously: Who in the world would know that I was behaving like this, in such a place? Didn't everyone know me solely through my impressive title of social reformer? . . . Such thoughts gave rise to a disagreeable, helpless sensation. To be sure, this was not the first time that I felt this way. From the beginning, I knew this kind of pleasure seeking was not something good that was to be praised or encouraged, not something to be openly talked about like advertisements for charitable causes. That is, I had cleverly avoided public notice until now, keeping all this an utmost secret. It should be easy to continue to keep it; you cannot accomplish anything in this world if you cannot even keep such a secret. To that degree, indeed, I could be called a clever fellow. What came upon me now, however, was a question: What if I had no such secret, if I were innocent, so to speak? Would it be agreeable or disagreeable if I became a man of integrity, which was how the world imagined me?

"Of course it would be agreeable, I decided. Why? Because secrets are like relatives; they are equally cumbersome.

"At this point, I finally reached my period of penitence. I determined never again to lead a life of worldly pleasure but to marry a pure and wise woman who would help me avoid the dangers of a bachelor's life and carry out my resolution."

4

"What kind of a wife did I finally choose?

"It was a nurse.

"Just around that time, I came down with a severe cold and was tended to by a nurse whom I had hired upon my doctor's advice. The nurse was a twenty-seven-year-old virgin, not very short in stature, very skinny, and as for her looks . . . she was not exactly ugly, but she had neither the charm nor the air that would entice a man's heart. Her thin face, with its hollow cheeks, was just as white as snow, and she always kept her large, melancholy eyes downcast, as if she were constantly absorbed in some meditation. Apparently, she had been separated from her parents when she was little and had dedicated her painful orphan's life to the constant worship of God.

"While I was sick, I would often wake up in the middle of the night, and whenever I did so, I would always find her reading the Bible by the yellow light of a lamp. Her pure white figure, sitting erect as the night wore on, always gave me an indescribable sense of peace and of solitude. . . . Such an exalted sublime feeling, I could not help but think, emanated from someone above us mortals on earth. And I half-consciously asked myself how much I would be inspired if I married such a pious, saintly woman, and resolved that there was no other woman I would rather choose as my wife. So as soon as I recovered from my illness, I proposed to her.

"She seemed surprised, but, suppressing her emotions resolutely, gently declined my proposal. But I forcefully took her hand, confessed all my sins in the past, and told her that only with her sacred love would I be able to renounce worldly pleasures and sins and to start a truly meaningful life. . . . She listened intently and, moved to tears, began repeating some prayers under her breath. People may laugh at me or think that I was out of my mind, but at that moment I truly believed that she was a gift from Heaven, the only person who could save me.

"Alas, this was a big mistake—no, more than just a mistake, but the cause of my further wretchedness. I tried to turn to her as the helping hand of God and to love her from the bottom of my heart, but it was simply impossible to feel any warm and tender passion toward her. Merely a feeling of respect was aroused in me, but simply not the desire to combine two souls into one.

"One spring day, the two of us were alone, strolling in our garden, and I was trying to talk to her about this and that. . . . It was a dreamlike, beautiful spring day. The blue sky was glistening like a gem, cherry and peach blossoms were blooming in all their glory, and little birds were singing at the top of their voices. Is any season more conducive to setting ablaze one's youthful ardor than such spring? As we were about to sit down in a little gazebo underneath the blossoms, I held her hands tightly and kissed her on the cheek. She let me do as I pleased. But how strange it was to find that her white cheeks were not just pale but cold as snow; the chill my lips felt served completely to cool off what bodily passion I had forced to arouse in me. She was like a marble statue. Taken aback, I let go of her hands and looked at her face. She looked back at me and smiled sweetly and sorrowfully. . . . I shuddered in spite of myself. I didn't know why. But for no particular reason, a feeling of indescribable displeasure and repugnance swelled up inside me.

"I just left my seat and walked alone toward a clump of trees. She did not follow me but stayed where she was, looking up at the sky with her usual melancholy eyes, I supposed. Presently, I heard her sing a hymn in a low voice, but her tone at that moment sounded for some reason very disagreeable to me. I simply didn't understand why. Even when I was leading a life of debauchery, hymns that I heard outside the windows of a church on a starry quiet evening were music to soothe my heart, never something to arouse an intense feeling of revulsion. Why did this change now? I felt a little miserable and walked past the trees toward the backyard, my mind full of incoherent thoughts.

"This area had been turned into a fairly spacious vegetable garden where pretty flowers of melons and beans bloomed in profusion in summertime, and I particularly loved it when the evening moon shone above it. But this was just after seeding time, and all I could see was cultivated flat soil. At the same time, as nothing obstructed the spring sunlight that emanated from the sky, it was dazzlingly bright. I bathed in the light with my whole body, and I became warm as if I had been steamed, even perspiring slightly around my hairline. The hymn she was singing was no longer to be heard, and all I could hear were the cries of swallows flying past in the sky. In springtime it is sometimes even quieter during the height of the day than in the middle of the night. My confused thoughts had vanished somewhere, and, in a thoroughly dazed state, I turned my steps toward my house near the kitchen area at the edge of the vegetable garden, gazing at the clouds moving languidly at the corner of the sky.

"Peach blossoms in full bloom caught my eyes. It was as if a fire were burning. Then, all of a sudden, from among the peach blossoms, a female figure. . . . I halted in spite of myself. The peach blossoms were blooming in such profusion that they practically obscured the roof of the house, but just underneath the shadow of the trees, a woman was peacefully taking a nap, with her elbows placed on a low bay windowsill and one side of her face tightly pressed against them. With the whole place bathed in the spring light and the reflection of the peach blossoms shading the window, the charm of her profile displaying an indefinable deep red color was such that from the distance of ten steps, I thought it could not be anything else but a painting.

"She was a parlor maid, said to be nineteen years of age, who had come to our house to learn proper manners. I was not even thinking of such things but was just captivated by her beauty: her well-formed arms, her smooth cheeks, and what a complexion! All of a sudden a pretty butterfly fluttered over and alighted on the woman's lovely, crimson-tinged earlobe, as if mistaking it for a petal of some flower. What was the butterfly whispering into her ear on a spring day? . . . Whether you call it a pleasant or a sweet sensation, an indescribably exquisite fantasy welled up inside me and plunged me into an entrancing dream.

"I became completely oblivious of the world, myself, everything. Of course, at that moment I did not even ask myself if I loved her or not. All I can say is that the hot blood circulating within me told me to go near and touch her radiant cheek. I made my way toward her, but just at that moment, the woman suddenly woke up and, looking around, saw me, and for a while seemed not to know what to do. . . . She then covered her face and ran toward the next room.

"This was such a trifling incident. But to me it was a major event. From that day on, even if I was not conscious of it, I once again began recalling my earlier, pleasure-filled life. I could hear the sound of music and the whispers of beautiful women and see the fluttering red hems of dancing geisha. My previous resolutions had now completely vanished. And I became totally uninterested in the woman whom I had respected as God incarnate, who had redeemed me, and whom I had compelled to marry me. . . . I might have been forgiven if this were all, but what had come over me? I began disliking her more and more. I tried earnestly to fight such evil thoughts and at the same time made every effort to hide my change of heart from her. But apparently all was in vain. Although she never said anything or betrayed anything by her manners, her downcast eyes seemed to have noticed. I soon came to fear her and tried to keep out of her sight as much as possible. But, lo and behold, she seemed to see through all this and began shutting herself up in her room so as to make herself as scarce as possible. I didn't know what to say. I just felt like crying.

"On the other hand, I could not simply leave things like that. I told myself that, since I had chosen her as my wife, I had to care for her no matter what; but the more I struggled to get rid of my revulsion toward her, and I was really desperate, the more aggravated the situation grew, and in the end I felt as if I were losing my mind. One night, I lay asleep but was shaken awake when I thought I heard some sound. I sensed her presence, dressed in her snow-white nurse's uniform, somehow come to sit by my bedside; but then I thought I heard a voice somewhere, reading from the Bible. The voice sounded indescribably gloomy and spooky. Instinctively, I jumped out of bed, groped for a match by my bedside, and lit the light at once. But, of course, nobody was there; it was still the middle of a quiet, quiet night.

"From that moment on, almost every night I could hear the gloomy voice reading the Bible, and I was no longer able to sleep peacefully. I said to myself, What would happen if I slept beside her, as I used to do when we were first married? I tried this, but it made matters even worse. As the night wore on, I became all the more wide awake. Her body lying beside me felt as cold as stone, and it was as if my own body gradually lost its heat. If I slept by her even for this one night, I thought, I might never regain the senses that had taken such pleasure in looking at beautiful flowers and had appreciated the sweet taste of warm wine, so that, instead of my senses responding delicately to such sensations, they might steadily disappear. I tried to rub my body with my palm as hard as I could in order to regain some heat, but it was all in vain. If I closed my eyes and fell asleep now, I felt, I was sure to die. I would never be able to see the warm sun the following morning shining over the flowers in the garden or hear the birds beginning their songs. Such thoughts thoroughly frightened me, and I was unable to close my eyes.

"Then, as the night wore on, I became conscious of her thread-like breathing as she lay asleep. At times her breathing would seem to die away, but then it would come back, and I felt as if the soul inhabiting her body were gradually ascending toward heaven, the heaven she was constantly dreaming about, even as the night intensified its stillness. Unconsciously, I furtively put my hand on her chest. But she lay on her back, with her hands tightly clasped over it, and did not stir at all. . . . All of a sudden, I felt something ice cold. I instinctively withdrew my hand, but when I finally groped for that object again, I discovered that it was a cross she always kept on herself.

"So from then on, I could not sleep at all at night, and I grew physically exhausted, my only fleeting moments of rest taking the form of brief afternoon naps. I resolved that in order to preserve my life I had no choice but to take myself away from her. Since nothing was going to work so long as I lived with her under the same roof, I was forced to the conclusion that I should travel, and decided that I should go abroad.

"So without delay, I told my wife that I was going to the United States, ostensibly to study. My wife, as usual, appeared to understand perfectly what was on my mind and raised no objection, agreeing to my plans and telling me that she would in the meantime resume her life as a nurse. I gave her, much as she protested, one third of my fortune for her living expenses, and came to this country without much purpose.

"I don't have to tell you much about what has happened since then. As you know, the United States is a country where you can see both the best and the worst in society, so that it is possible for a person to go in either direction, following his inclination. So it is perfectly possible to indulge in an opium-induced dream, resting one's head on the shoulder of a naked beauty under crimson lights in a perpetually darkened room of a clandestine club, or to experience a religious life in the country, far from worldly glories, listening morning and night to the tolling of church bells echoing throughout a peaceful meadow.

"I have seen most of the United States, at least superficially, and have no need to remain here any longer. I can go back to Japan anytime to engage in whatever business activities I choose with even more flair than before. But I still have a question. That is: Will I not again feel nostalgic about worldly pleasures? Will I be able to go back to my country and live happily with my icy cold wife? . . . Of course, all people, in varying degrees, have some self-control, so that it will not be impossible for me to do so. But I won't be satisfied just with that. Instead of opening the Bible in the morning and using the same hand to raise a wine glass secretively in the evening, I would rather hold the glass alone (even if it is possible for me to refrain from doing so). Self-control has no meaning other than demonstrating your rather strong will. Convicts in jail are the greatest saints in this regard, since they do nothing wrong so long as they are imprisoned.

"Thinking like this, I have already spent nearly three years in this lonely Illinois country, but I still am not totally sure of myself. I am going to experience life in the city one more time and to see the bright lights in the city streets. And then I shall make a final decision as to my future.

"I am going to say good-bye to you tomorrow, but I make this promise. In order to let you know what I have decided upon, I shall send you one of three [sic] pictures. If I prove successful in totally eliminating my longing for pleasure, as I hope I shall, then you will receive my wedding picture with the nurse. Otherwise, I shall send you . . . well, some picture of an irresistibly seductive *danseuse*, let's say from France. That way, you will be able to guess what sort of life I am leading."

(March 1904)

The Inebriated Beauty

In the summer of 1904 I had a most ideal guide with whom to visit the World's Fair that was being held in St. Louis.

He was an American named S——, an artist with whom I had earlier stayed at the same boarding house outside Chicago, and we had become quite friendly as a result. He told me that his work was being exhibited at the Fair and so, knowing that he lived in a village in Missouri called Highland, which was not far from St. Louis, I first sent him a telegram and then boarded a train from Michigan up north. The trip would take fifteen or sixteen hours, and for scenery along the way, as is so frequently the case on this American continent, there was little else than vast cornfields, an occasional brook where cattle would come to drink water, or a hill with two or three farmers' houses with clumps of trees that appeared to be orchards. But I did not grow too weary and crossed the state of Illinois agreeably daydreaming all alone. Before long, the train crossed the famous East Bridge built from East St. Louis across the great Mississippi River.

By the time roofs in the outskirts of St. Louis begin to come into view, innumerable tracks carrying trains from all over the new North American continent can be seen converging like a spiderweb onto this midwestern city, their terminus. Amid whirling dust and coal fumes, our train enters the railway compound that is filled with all kinds of noise, combining into a roar. Many huge, mountainlike locomotives go back and forth, emitting black smoke, in the middle of which two rows of cars, perhaps heading east, cross our train, while along far-away tracks, a train is seen moving in the same direction as ours. Trains belonging to just about every railway company in the United States arrive at the platforms in this great central station.

I got off the train and walked with the crowd to the very end of the long platform. When we went out through the exit with a tall iron railing, there was a sea of men's and women's hats in a cement-paved square under a tall roof. But Americans are quite used to this sort of confusion, and my friend S— quickly spotted me and came running over. With a cheerful "How do you do?"—the standard Western greeting—he shook my hand.

Dispensing with formalities, I asked him what artwork he was exhibiting, and he answered, "Thank you," twice, as if very pleased. But he said we would talk about it at greater leisure later; as the city's hotels were too crowded and unbearable in this heat, he suggested that I come to Highland anyway. I let him lead me out of the spacious, stone-built station, under the glaring summer sun, and we walked for about two blocks on streets that were crowded with carriages and people. "We take that blue car for one hour, and then it will stop at a corner in Highland, just across from my house," S— said, waving at a streetcar about to overtake us. I jumped on with him, and thus we gradually left behind the crowded streets of St. Louis.

Passing the outskirts of the city—as everywhere, filled with shabby shacks, saloons, and cheap lodging places that mingle with large brick factories—we soon come to woods of maple and oak trees above bright green wild grass, appearing on both sides of the car tracks without interruption. How lovely are the sunlight penetrating layers of tiny leaves and the color of the blue sky that can be seen from time to time through tree branches! How gentle, friendly are these woods of Missouri, in contrast to the dark, damp, vast, deep forests that occupy the Cascades, the Rockies, and the entire Northwest Coast of North America, evoking only fear in men.

"I just love these woods!" I cried out, and S— looked very happy, saying, "I live in a small village in the middle of one of these maple woods. It has nothing besides bright green grass, ribbonlike streams, and a perpetually blue sky. But my landlady has nice cows and sheep, and I am sure she will treat you to delicious homemade ice cream."

So saying, he pulled out his watch and said, "We are almost there. We'll soon be in a village called Kirkwood in the woods. Once we pass it, we will be in Highland."

Even as he was talking, we seemed to pass the village he mentioned, with its large stone churches and people's homes looming, again amid bright green trees; after that, the road went up and down for a while, and then S— patted me on the shoulder and said, "Here we are!"

When I got off the car, I saw that it was indeed a quiet village where practically all one saw were the indigo-colored sky and green foliage; in contrast to St. Louis and other large cities where the fierce summer temperatures were over one hundred degrees, here it was cool, with breezes whispering among the tree leaves. In the meadows visible beyond the woods, cattle were mooing languidly in the summer afternoon, while in the fields at the back of nearby houses, hens were starting to cackle. It was as if I were in a dream, recalling the hustle and bustle of St. Louis that I had left behind only one hour earlier.

"It is a little far from the Fair, but we can get there in forty minutes by train. So why don't you stay in this area like me?" S— asked.

How could I object? In the villages around there, just about every farmer's house was making the best room available to rent to summer vacationers from the cities and, especially this year, to Fair visitors. So I decided to stay in a room two houses down from where S— was renting his own.

THE INEBRIATED BEAUTY

The very next day, we started going to the Fair. But before any sightseeing, I had first to visit S—'s exhibit.

Together with him, I take the train to the rear entrance of the Fair and, walking past a grove, we come right away to the art gallery in three separate buildings. The central building is for art from the United States, and he tells me his work is on display there. I ask him to take me in immediately. He goes ahead of me, passes through a number of exhibition rooms, and eventually enters a rather narrow, elongated room. "There," he says, stopping to turn back toward me and pointing to a painting of a nude hanging on the west wall.

He must have used a woman from Egypt or Arabia as a model. A buxom woman with black hair and black eyes is lying on her back on a couch, barely twisting her head toward the front and holding a half-emptied wine glass in her hand. Her large, bright black eyes appear already leaden from exquisite tipsiness, but they have an indescribable expression, as if she were gazing at something. For a while S— remained silent, facing his nude beauty, and then said, "I had so much trouble with those slightly tipsy eyes, of course. But I worked even harder on the skin color of a colored race, although people have not much appreciated this. I thought to myself, the whole body is permeated with the warmth of the wine, while inside her veins arise the passions of the so-called tropical climate. . . . The meaning of this I think I managed to convey not so much with the expression of her eyes as with the tone of her skin bathed by lamplight. What do you think? Don't you agree?"

I could not give a definite answer and continued to gaze at the painting in silence, but he resumed right away, "It may be that such a subject shouldn't be included in art. Actually, I thought of trying some such work when I heard a true story about a certain former French friend of mine."

He wanted to go on, but at this moment a group of several women entered the room, talking loudly, so he glanced at them and said, "Why don't we take a look around? In the galleries, some works by British and French masters like Millet and Corot are on display."

We walked in that direction. After viewing most of the exhibited works in the central pavilion, we entered the east pavilion and looked around at the paintings sent from England, Germany, Holland, Sweden, and other countries. Time passed amazingly fast, and soon it would be six o'clock, closing time. So we decided to come back on another day for the offerings from France, Belgium, Austria, Italy, Portugal, and Japan among them in the west pavilion, and exited the east pavilion with the crowd of people. Exhausted, we sat down on a bench at the foot of the grand concert hall [Festival Hall], in front of which cascades were overflowing from three staircases and a large basin.

This area has the most spectacular prospect within the Fair grounds, the circumference of which is more than seven miles. It looks down in one sweeping view over the far-off main entrance and the plaza with a tall monument and numerous statues. Among the huge buildings standing like castles, one can see a spacious pond, looking almost like a lake, into which cascades of water fall, running from the towering basins above us and down the tall flights of stairs. Even small ships and gondolas of various sizes that float around the tremendous water fountain can be seen from where we are.

This much is already an amazing sight, but wait till bells begin to toll somewhere in the Fair grounds and, simultaneously, the sun sets completely beyond the woods in the background; then every last snow-white building is illuminated in blue, red, and other colored lights, so that the many nude statues standing under the pale blue sky look as though, having absorbed these lights, they have just now awakened from a sleep of death and are floating out from around the staircases and roofs of various buildings, ready to start dancing to the band music that begins to be heard here and there.

An extraordinary nightless city! This surely is one of the magical worlds created by the wealth of the Americans.

I was simply dumbfounded and looked around as if in a daze, but as for S——, he was busily chewing tobacco and watching the crowd of people as they came climbing upstairs; whenever a particularly young and beautiful woman passed, he nodded to himself and closely watched her, even as she walked away.

"Is there anyone you could use as a model?" I asked, to which he replied as he spat out the tobacco unceremoniously, "Those are rather rare. But it is a lot of fun to watch buxom young women, even if they may be no good as models. This pleasure is a great privilege God has bestowed on us, so we men have a duty to devote our whole lives to the study of women. It's hard to beat a Frenchman when it comes to this. I had a very close friend, a journalist who had come from France. He was avidly studying how much pleasure a male body could receive from a woman, but he died a young man while in the middle of his research. He had sacrificed himself. This happened some time ago, but I have always wanted to express one of his experiences in my own work. That is why I finally made that particular painting. . . . Have I told you its title? The slightly inebriated naked beauty. It's called *The Moment Before a Dream*."

I have forgotten to mention that this S—— is very much a Francophile, but he has never been to France and doesn't know much of the language, either. But he believes, arbitrarily, that since his ancestors were pureblooded Frenchmen who came to the new continent about a century ago, and especially since his grandfather married an actress from France, it is certainly in his blood to become an artist. Moreover, he has concluded that strong-willed and excessively clearheaded Americans are not likely to succeed as artists.

Having spat out all his tobacco, he pulled out some cigars this time, and, offering me one, he continued, "That man's research was really quite valuable for us. Monsieur Mantéro was his name. When he first came to America, he was often grumbling that he could not stand such a drab and uncivilized country, that apart from some chic-looking women, all you saw were Jews with their pointy noses and Negroes with thick lips, or that there was not a single place where you could have a pleasant dinner. But strangely enough, soon he became infatuated with a woman of mixed breed, with some Negro blood in her.

"The reason was that, one evening, after he had had dinner at a restaurant in town, he started walking aimlessly and passed a dingy little theater. At the entrance there were various painted posters and photos, including a painting of a plump woman kicking her leg up high and dancing. In France, the birthplace of such pictures, one can encounter hundreds, even thousands of them in an hour in the streets, so M. Mantéro hadn't paid much attention. But instead of walking away, he bought a ticket and went in.

"It was the kind of vaudeville one sees in any American city. After some acrobatics, burlesque dancing, and rapid playing of vari-ous musical instruments, a woman with a substantial amount of black blood in her veins—one could see she must have been the subject of the poster at the entrance—dashed out from backstage and started dancing energetically, with her short hair parted in the middle and wearing a short costume exposing her upper torso. But to his eyes this was nothing unusual. He could barely stifle the yawn that was already welling up in his throat, but he could not just avert his eyes, so he con-tinued to look vaguely in the direction of the stage. But then sudden-ly he realized how plump her frame was—perhaps this was typical of a young black woman—and said to himself that it would be worth studying how such a frame differed from that of a white woman, something he had never given much thought to. . . . So he began pay-ing closer attention to the stage, where the woman, each time she came to rest after a dance number, would beckon passionately to the specta-tors with her large dark eyes. His interest was aroused anew. That look in her eyes, he thought, does not really belong to us civilized humans. Rather, it reminds one of a domestic animal begging his master for food. Thus thinking, Mantéro could no longer suppress his curiosity—or rather, as he was wont to force such curiosity out of himself, he did not hesitate to return to the same vaudeville show for three more evenings or so. And it was all too easy; they shook hands, and within less than an hour they were already arm-in-arm like old acquaintances and heading toward her lodging for fun.

"And here he readily discovered something: unlike a woman of a civilized country, this woman of mixed blood did not have the least desire to enjoy herself by trifling with men's feelings, using artistic gestures and manners or suggestive conversations with hidden meanings. Rather, from the slightest quivering of her eyelashes to the subtle movements of her fingertips, she seemed to be trying to feel all the pleasure she could obtain for her bodily senses.

"It so happened that this was a cold winter night, and she shut her room up completely as she built a big fire. She then drew up a soft sofa with velvet upholstery; the two of them stretch themselves on it while she warms the tips of her toes and the soles of her bare feet, already rid of shoes and stockings. Next she crosses her arms behind her head as if she were holding it, and as all parts of her body gradually warm up, she forcefully stretches herself and twists her body here and there; once she feels that all her muscles have been sufficiently softened, for one last time she flexes her whole body from her fingertips to the tips of her toes. Then, drawing a long breath, and already limp, she quickly throws down her upper body upon him and, as she slowly smokes a fragrant Turkish cigarette, she intensely watches its blue smoke, which hangs motionlessly in the light of a lamp covered with a pale red chimney.

"After a while, she finishes smoking a couple of cigarettes with him and empties in one gulp a glass of champagne, which to her is even more precious than jewelry. All at once, the blood within her whole body seems to boil with tremendous force, caused by the warmth of the wine inside and the fire of the hearth outside. Her eyelids look leaden, as if she is too weary to open her eyes even halfway. Still, she stares at him and around the room intently. But this lasts only a moment, and in no time she drops one arm from the sofa to the floor as though her body has lost all its bones, and she dozes off. That very moment of entering dreamland, she believes, is nothing short of earthly paradise.

"This curious discovery must have given great satisfaction to Mantéro, for he kept visiting her room for three months, without skipping a single night. But, as is usually the case with such a person, as soon as the weather changed he began craving something different. Now he made up his mind to see her for one last time and even told her unambiguously, before he took his leave, 'I am going to be busy with my work for a while and won't be able to come.' Yet the following evening, as he came out of the restaurant where he always had dinner, he noticed the lights radiating beautifully from the lamps above the city streets, and he thought the women passing to and fro seemed even more suggestive than during the day. He paused at a corner of an intersection for a while, but a strange sensation, something he had never experienced before, made him feel impatient and compelled him to walk fast, faster, to what destination he didn't know. But when he came to himself, to his amazement, he found himself in front of the house where that woman lodged.

"It is too late to turn back now. So he knocks on the door of her room. She greets him and, far from showing either surprise or happiness at seeing him after he had just told her the previous night that it was going to be their last, just takes his hand, as she has always done, and leads him to the sofa where they have been accustomed to sitting together. It is as if she had already known he would come.

"He recalls that the previous night, when he told her he would not be able to come again, she had not betrayed any sorrow at parting but had said, quite calmly, 'Oh, is that so?' Maybe this already suggested that she knew all along that he was destined to come back. That memory frightened him for some reason and, thinking he should dash out of the room, he was about to rise when immediately she grabbed his hand and threw her heavy body onto his lap.

"The woman's body is so hot that it is like a fire. He feels the heat directly with his hand she has clasped, and besides, within less than a minute, his heart starts to pound painfully, and he feels as if all his body heat is steadily being sucked away by her. At that moment, she looks intently into his face with her large, deep, dark pupils, and says in a calm voice, 'So you are not coming back after tonight?'. But he no longer has any energy left to respond.

"The eyes fixed on him seemed to express fierce and powerful emotions . . . as if to say, 'you may struggle to run away from me, but once I have marked you, I will never let you go.' He felt a shudder run through his whole body. And he could not help becoming aware of a sense of hopeless resignation welling up from the bottom of his heart, the feeling that there was nothing he could do, that he was this woman's prey—just like a mouse facing a cat, or a lamb transfixed in front of a wolf.

"Pity him! Mantéro had been so self-confident because he was a man, the master who had loved and flirted with her as if she were a docile domestic pet, but in time, consciously or unconsciously, he had come under the invisible power that enveloped her body and could never free himself from it. The story may sound familiar to you. For instance, in an old Persian or Turkish legend, the story is often told of an animal that is so infatuated with a young, beautiful queen that it kills her. Maybe this French gentleman too had become the object of infatuation of a Negro girl who had more animal than human blood.

"He became thinner and thinner, with only his eyes glaring; and the more desperately he struggled to get away from her, the closer he was drawn to her. It was, I think, about a year later that he fell gravely ill and so, in order to avoid the cold winter of the United States, he first returned to France and then proceeded to the warmer climate of Italy. But there he became sick from the febrile disease that is often brought with the southern winds. As he was so debilitated, it was more than he could bear, and he ended his life there."

S— finished his story, smiled at me, and continued, "What do you think? Mantéro died doing what he wanted to do, just like a warrior dying in war, so I applaud him even as I am saddened.

"It's getting late. Let's emulate his example tonight and savor as much tasty meat and tasty wine as the nerves of our tongues can take. If we are happy, so will be the God who created us. Which restaurant shall we choose? Come, let's be on our way."

S— stood up from the bench where he had been sitting a long time. I followed him, and we both went down the wide stairway step by step, underneath several large nude statues.

In the coolness of the summer night, countless couples were in the plaza, near the pond, and under the trees. The nightless city glittered with lights and stood amid the uproar created by every kind of music and joyous voices. (The end.)

Long Hair

Unlike in the countryside, where the coming of spring is heralded by blooming flowers and singing birds, in New York, which is made of stone, iron, bricks, and asphalt, one knows that spring is not far away by the latest models of women's hats being displayed inside the glass windows of the millineries.

As the windy month of March passes and April comes with its occasional afternoon showers, Easter Sunday is the customary day to change to spring clothes so that even if the weather is unpredictable and the day may be too cold, women of New York who have been impatiently waiting hastily discard their ornate winter garments and ride in carriages and cars in high spirits, fluttering the skirts of their chic thin garments.

I am one of those who love the fashions of this country, so rich in their variety of colors, so I decide to take advantage of the fine weather one day in order to watch the crowds of people. Around three o'clock in the afternoon, I take up a slender cane and walk, all alone, from Fifth Avenue to the tree-lined paths of Central Park. The sight of numerous carriages and cars, one after another, moving slowly in the serene spring sunlight is like Paris's Bois de Boulogne in the afternoon, which I have seen in pictures.

Onlookers of this grand spectacle are sitting on rows of benches on both sides of the tree-lined street, and I soon find a seat for myself.

Alone, looking at each occupant of the passing cars, I comment end-lessly on the person's choice of fashion and degree of tastefulness.

Before long, a carriage approaches from afar, advancing from the shadow of lush green trees; everything is deep indigo blue, from the four wheels to the driver's costume and even his hat.

This flashy indigo blue might not be so striking anywhere else, but here, it is in such harmony with the clear blue spring sky and the bright new green leaves that it cannot help but attract people's atten-tion. I too am curious to see what sort of people are riding in the carriage. As they approach, I notice a woman wearing a hat with ostrich feathers dyed in the same indigo blue color and a flashy cos-tume to go with it—she is, however, not very young. Riding with her is a young gentleman, from what country it is hard to tell, whose long, pitch-black hair hangs all the way to his shoulders just like that of men in the eighteenth century, sporting a short red moustache and pince-nez attached to a red ribbon.

People sitting on the benches were evidently struck by this curi-ous scene, and they murmured among themselves:

"Whatever country does the man come from?"

"Maybe Mexico."

"But the dark color of his hair must be of Spanish origin, so he is probably from South America."

The coachman wielded his whip, and the carriage passed in front of my eyes and immediately disappeared among the cars that kept coming.

The spectators' topics of conversation also kept shifting, corre-sponding to what passed before them, but I continued to look into the distance to see if I might still catch a glimpse of the indigo blue carriage that was just driving down the avenue.

This, however, was not because of the lady in the carriage. Rather, it was because I was convinced that the black-haired gentle-man was Japanese. To be sure, when I first saw him he struck me, as he did others, as bizarre, but when I carefully looked at him as he passed close by, the expression formed between his eyebrows and his eyes clearly proved that he was of the same race as myself, no matter how he dissimulated his appearance.

What sort of a Japanese was he? Was the blond lady who was riding with him his wife? Or was she just a close friend?

Fortunately, within less than a week I was able to satisfy my irrepressible curiosity. It so happened that I ran into a Japanese friend at a certain place who had recently graduated from Columbia University and now had some connection with a newspaper in New York. Whereupon, after chit-chatting for a while, I casually mentioned the matter to him, and he responded in a tone suggesting that he knew we were going to talk about it, "Is that so? So you saw that man? Don't you agree that he doesn't look like a Japanese at first sight?"

"What kind of person is he? Do you know him?"

"Yes, indeed. He came with me to America on the same ship, and afterward, when I entered Columbia University, we were again together. . . ."

Then he told me the following story.

That man's name was Fujigasaki Kunio. He is the eldest son of a wealthy count. He came to the United States to study and entered Columbia University, but he attended classes merely for appearance's sake and spent his days just having fun, devoting himself to lively and free relations with male and female American students, picnicking and horseback-riding in the spring and ballroom dancing and ice skating in winter.

One year, then two years went by, and the third summer recess arrived. As I did not have enough money for my studies, I earned a little during the summer by rearranging the books in the house of a certain lecturer, Dr. So-and-So. Kunio had no such need and spared no expense to undertake a sightseeing tour of the West, from the hot springs in Colorado, which could be called the Switzerland of the American continent, to Yellowstone Park, which is considered one of the seven most scenic spots in the world.

It was soon autumn. The university reopened and students returned from all over, but there was no news or sight of Kunio.

I thought perhaps Kunio had gotten bored with school. Given his personality, this was understandable. He had always preferred play to books—not so much play as spending his time in idle comfort. I had often seen him lying down comfortably on a long sofa in his living room or on the green grass in the shade of a tree, leisurely smoking a cigar or watching the drifting clouds in the sky, without thinking or doing anything; I often said to myself, there could be no lazier person in the world.

I knew it would be no use admonishing him, but wrote him a couple of serious letters anyway, thinking that perhaps he might decide to return to school. Since I didn't know if he had returned from his travels and I didn't have his current address, I mailed the letters to the house he had lived in before the summer vacation.

There was no answer. Feeling a bit disappointed, one evening I took a walk and stopped by that house. The landlady came out and told me that no sooner had Kunio returned, about two weeks earlier, than he moved to an address on Central Park West. Greatly encouraged, I headed for that address. It was a tall apartment building, about ten stories high, facing Central Park.

I accosted a Negro porter wearing a purple uniform with shiny golden buttons, and he told me that the Japanese gentleman had a room on the eighth floor. I took the elevator and rang the doorbell.

Since it was a large building, the outdoor noise was completely shut out; as the air in the corridor was cool and still, like the inside of a cathedral, the sound of the doorbell could be heard clearly as it echoed far away at the end of a room.

I waited for someone to appear for quite some time, but there was no movement. So I tried pressing the bell a little longer. Finally, I heard some faint footsteps, and a lady opened the door just a crack, showing only her face.

I bowed politely, removing my hat, and said, "I would like to see a Japanese named Fujigasaki."

Immediately the lady led me to the parlor, but as we walked down the narrow hallway, she anxiously stole a furtive look at my face.

The lady was, let's say, about twenty-seven or -eight, it seemed. . . . She had a round face with a short chin, and her clear, blue-green eyes with long eyelashes had the usual indescribable expressiveness typical of a Western woman. But to my eyes, she looked quite indecent and lascivious, perhaps because of the blond hair loosely knotted behind her neck, almost tumbling down onto her shoulders, and because she was wearing an ample indoor gown for afternoon use, exposing her plump shoulders and arms.

I was taken to the parlor and left alone, waiting for Kunio to appear. In the next room I could hear the lady talking to someone, presumably Kunio, and soon the door opened and he entered the room.

Exclaiming, "I am very sorry," he stole a glance at me and cast down his eyes, as if embarrassed. Assuming an air of nonchalance, I said, "Your travels must have been great fun, but . . . by the way, how about school?"

"Oh, school. I've simply missed a chance to go."

"But it's really a shame to quit now. If you just attend classes for one or two more years, you'll at least be able to get a degree."

"I don't mean to quit school for good, but somehow in the morning . . . I am late getting up in the morning."

So saying, he again looked down. I was lost for words myself and remained silent. Through the windows covered by mistlike, thin lace curtains, trees in the park that were starting to turn yellow provided a backdrop for the stillness of a sunny afternoon. All of a sudden, a sound came from the next room—someone playing the piano, or rather, toying with the keys as if to pass the time. It stopped abruptly in less than five minutes, and quiet returned.

Kunio seemed to be listening attentively without being conscious of it, but suddenly said, as if he had made up his mind, "I really appreciate your thoughtfulness. I have read your letters also. But for the time being . . . I may return to school someday, but for now I am going to take a leave."

"Is that so? In that case, I won't insist, but tell me, why have you come to such a decision?"

I asked the question casually, but somehow he seemed to take the word "decision" seriously; looking surprised, he gazed at me intently for a moment and then said, as if he had changed his mind, "It's not that I have come to a decision. It's just that I have been bored with reading, and would like to take it easy and rest."

I returned home without further ado, but after four or five days had passed, while taking a walk down the boulevard along the bank of the Hudson River on a fine autumn evening, I saw him and the lady of that house by chance, riding together in a carriage.

In this country there is nothing unusual about a man and a woman riding together, but it occurred to me, for no particular reason, that something was going on between the two of them, and that Kunio had given up school because of it. As always happens when one's curiosity is piqued, I wanted to find out if my suspicions were justified, and so I continued to visit Kunio.

These frequent visits must have been bothersome to Kunio, but for me they were very useful, and in time I learned that my conjectures were not altogether wide of the mark.

For instance, one day I came to their parlor, following as always the Negro maid who answered the door, and saw the two sitting tightly close to each other on a sofa by the window overlooking the park; on another occasion, I came upon them as they were sipping wine from the same glass.

LONG HAIR

It was at least clear that the two were in love. But I wanted to know how the affair had started and what her background was. When an appropriate opportunity came, I pressed Kunio, who was no longer as reserved as earlier and told me that they had met at a mountain resort during his summer travels. She, he said, was the divorced wife of a wealthy man.

"Why was she divorced?" I asked further.

"Because she was of loose morals," he answered and told me, perhaps against his will, all that he knew.

"In a word, you can say she is flirtatious. She says, for instance, that if she reads a novel and finds it interesting, she wants desperately to experience the same things. So it happened that within less than a year after she was married, she fell for a Polish musician with Tartar blood and had a tryst with him. Her husband found out about it and divorced her after a trial, giving her one fourth of his property. Once such a shameful event becomes public, you can no longer mix in respectable society. No matter how much money you have or how beautiful you are, you are a social outcast. When that happens, it is easy for anyone to give up and become desperate. This woman too started making playthings of all sorts of men."

I was startled and asked, "But you . . . you know that she is such a depraved woman and still love her?"

Kunio smiled in silence, as if to say, of course. I was still more astounded and continued, "Do you really think that the woman loves you, such a dreadful woman? . . . Even if she does for now, don't you think it is just a matter of time before she starts flirting with other men?"

"Of course, I can't be sure. But I don't care if this lasts just for a while, so long as this brief moment, whether five minutes or even one minute, brings me sweetness, not pain. In other words, don't you think you are that much ahead for having had a pleasant dream?"

He smiled again and looked at me as if to pity me, a bookish type, for simply not being able to understand anything except scholarly matters.

For a while I was utterly at a loss how to interpret this. How on earth could Kunio feel any affection for the lady, knowing full well her immoral background that was too dreadful to hear about?

Later on, reading Daudet's *Sappho* and other books, I came to understand that in certain circumstances men are capable of passionately loving women with such a background, even while feeling an intense aversion toward them. But Kunio's feeling toward this lady seemed to be of an entirely different kind.

I continued to see him frequently; each time I learned to look at the matter from a different angle until I finally got at the truth. The upshot was that, while at one time I felt revolted and even wanted to spit in his face, after observing the situation more deeply, I reversed myself and ended up shedding tears of pity for him for having been born with such an unfortunate nature.

Poor Kunio! In him there is not the slightest sense of bold, strong, manly love. The usual positions of men and women are completely reversed for him; although he is a man, his ideal is to be held in a woman's arms and spend a dreamlike life under her protection, to live the life of a so-called gigolo.

While in Japan, he had set foot in pleasure quarters from early on, even before he came of age, like many young men who are lured by them. He had money, came from a good family, and was also good-looking, so many women became interested in him. Among them were young beauties, but he didn't pay the slightest attention to them, finding satisfaction in becoming the lover of an older geisha who treated him like a younger brother.

There are many in the world who are driven by monetary considerations to seek an older woman's affection, but he was different, pursuing his rather singular desires even at the expense of his honor and status, which are even more valuable than wealth. Why on earth does he envy the lot of the actors who are kept as women's lovers or the good fortune of a *samisen* carrier who helps tie a woman's sashes? Even he probably could not explain.

His family accused him of having disgraced its name and practically disinherited him for a while, but this was more or less what he wanted, and he enjoyed a dissolute life reminiscent of the Edo era, for example by going to a bath house late in the morning, fluttering his mistress's short coat over his shoulders in the spring rain.

This was too much for the count and his family, and they finally decided the best solution was to pack him off abroad. That is how Kunio came to study in the United States. But alas, in what may be called a quirk of fate, our young lordship, having traveled several thousand miles, once again fell in thrall to a beautiful sorceress and forgot all about his home, even his country, not to mention himself.

It really was a quirk of fate, to repeat myself. It is now nearly two years that Kunio has been kept by that lady. It is not amusing but rather sad, and it brings tears to my eyes to see how hard he tries not to let her tire of him, not to be abandoned by her.

I know many stories like this that I can hardly bear to repeat. But I wanted to explain why the man whom you encountered in the park was wearing his hair so long.

Women generally tend to become more violent and tyrannical the more accommodating men are. Especially someone like her, rejected by society and living in adverse circumstances for so long, becomes overly sensitive and angry without cause. She does things like break her cherished implements or jewelry or even hit her lover though she loves him very much.

But Kunio endures everything. One day, for instance, the lady mercilessly tormented Kunio and, on top of that, began tearing at her beautifully arranged hair, removed the jeweled comb, and smashed it to bits and pieces with her feet. It was hard to tell what she was feeling, but it was as if she doused herself with cold water on a summer day. . . . That may have been it, for she asked Kunio to grow his hair long like the portrait of Henry IV.

Immediately, Kunio began letting his shiny and abundant black hair grow; it came to reach his shoulders, and he nicely curled its edges.

When you saw him riding in the carriage, you may have thought that his long hair indicated an excessively foppish taste, but in reality all it did was to give her some peculiar sensation by letting her tear at it whenever she flew into a rage.

Spring and Autumn

In a small provincial town in southern Michigan, by the train route running in a straight line from west to east between Chicago and New York, there is a university called K—— [Kalamazoo College]. Among its many students, both male and female, are three Japanese, two males and one female. One of the men, Yamada Tarō, is, like the female student, Takezato Kikue, a student of theology, both having been sent from their respective churches in Japan, while the third, Ōyama Toshiya, has nothing to do with religion but is registered in the political science department.

These three had come to the United States in the same year and happened to end up in this school. As a result, when they first met, they were so surprised that they hardly exchanged greetings with each other. But for Toshiya, studying law, it felt almost inconceivable that in this remote foreign country he should encounter a woman of the same race, with black eyes and hair. Whenever he saw Kikue in the school hallways, dining room, or wherever it was, he could not help but turn his head in her direction so that, within a month or so, he was able to recapitulate in his mind everything about her figure, from head to toe. Not that he admired that figure; actually, he was constantly critical of it. She seemed to be about nineteen, certainly not over twenty. Her hair was dark and glossy, but her forelock was frizzy and her hairline uneven. For a Japanese, her complexion was rather fair, but her only special features were her rather high nose and a charming, firm mouth. But what a round face, what small eyes, and what thin eyebrows! And what could one say about her narrow shoulders, which were clad in shabby clothes evidently made in Japan, and were too thick, or about her posture, bent over as if she were carrying some heavy load on her back? And her fat and short arms, or her shapeless fingers, which looked like green caterpillars. Thus commenting on her in close detail, Toshiya wondered why there were so many female students from Japan who were of this type. Some scientist should study the relationship between Japanese women's intellect and physiology; somehow, drawing a deep breath, he called to his mind scenes from the streets of Hongō and Kōjimachi that are frequented by female students. In no time, however, he found himself thinking of his own past.

He had, fortunately, been born into a family of considerable wealth and came to the United States when he found it difficult to find a respectable job after graduating, as was customary in those days, from a law school that had been renamed a university. Those were quite some days, he recalled, when every Saturday evening he would go to a beer hall or a *sukiyaki* restaurant and flirt with waitresses upstairs. Remembered too were the times when he engaged in heated discussion about female performers at a show, when he first went to Yoshiwara [one of the pleasure quarters in Tokyo] on the way back from a sporting event in Mukōjima, when he stayed overnight for the first time in a *machiai* [assignation house] after a year-end party in Ushigome, or when there was so much racket at a farewell party organized for him. . . . By contrast, when he thought of the present circumstances, he had to admit that, although when he had first come everything—from the classrooms, student meetings, street scenes, to the landscape of the fields outside the town—had been new and interesting, once he got used to them, life had become lonesome and extremely monotonous, that of "a stranger in a strange land" who can find no suitable pastime.

Every now and then, as Toshiya became tired of reading, he could think of nothing better to do than dropping in on Yamada, the student of religion. Yamada had been reading the Bible silently, as was his wont, but he closed it and said politely, "Do sit down. How are things? Don't you think English is a rather difficult language?"

Toshiya asked without ceremony, "Anything interesting?"

"There will be a lecture tonight," Yamada answered immediately, as if he believed this was the most appropriate response to the question. "Indeed this is a Christian country; it has been such a pleasure to hear good lectures by preachers. Tonight, an elder from Chicago named B— is speaking at the church downtown. So you too . . . how about it? He is quite a famous minister in America."

Toshiya was not in the least interested in religion, and so he said, "I don't think I'll be able to understand it . . . especially a theological lecture."

"That's not true," Yamada said rather earnestly, leaning forward his stocky torso, which was long in contrast to his short legs. "Tonight's lecture is not going to be on religion. I am told that he is going to talk about the evils of drinking and smoking, so anyone will be able to understand. All the students here are apparently going."

"All students . . . I wonder if Miss Takezato is going," asked Toshiya, for no particular reason but just to respond.

"Miss Takezato . . . I am sure she is coming. Female students are going there too."

"Maybe each male student is going to invite a female student. Why don't you also invite Miss Takezato and go there, arm in arm, American style? Ha, ha, ha, ha."

"Well, I cannot quite . . ." Yamada said in a stiff manner, and even blushed a little. Toshiya, on his part, while he was joking, all of a sudden developed an irresistible urge to take Kikue out and walk with her arm in arm like the Americans did.

Yamada continued to urge him to go to the talk; even if he decided not to listen, he said in a voice full of sincerity, just hearing the sound of the organ would greatly move one's spirit. Toshiya could now no longer refuse.

If I am going, then by all means I must go with Kikue— So as soon as Toshiya noticed Kikue that evening among the students, male and female, coming out of their respective dormitories to go to the dining hall, he quietly accosted her and asked, "Will you be going to the church downtown tonight?"

"Yes, I shall," was Kikue's only answer.

"In that case, as I am also going, may I pick you up? I hope this won't be an inconvenience for you."

Kikue, as he had anticipated, looked lost for words and bent her head, moving her hands restlessly.

"I gather that the students are all going there with their friends, so I thought it would be nice if Japanese students went there together. I mentioned this to Yamada, and he agreed with me entirely. What do you think, Miss Takezato? If you are going there anyway, this won't be too inconvenient, don't you think?"

It was not particularly inconvenient for Kikue, but she was aware of the Japanese custom that forbade socializing between the sexes and just felt uneasy somehow. But ultimately, she agreed to wait for Toshiya at eight o'clock that evening so that they could leave her dormitory together.

It was about a thirty-minute walk to the church. The night in mid-October was cold and quiet. Feeling uncomfortable, Kikue looked around and noticed, in front of and behind them, the college's female students arm in arm with male students and walking in unison, bathed in the light from bright street lamps, underneath rows of already yellowing trees, their shoes noisily stepping on the pavement. Some of them were whistling marching music. Toshiya drew closer to Kikue and took her hand.

"Look, Miss Takezato. They are all having a good time, aren't they?"

SPRING AND AUTUMN

Soon they entered the church. Yamada, the religion student, had arrived already, and all three took their seats at the back and looked around at the designs on the high ceiling, the pipe organ above the recessed flight of steps, and the stained-glass windows at every corner. Soon, there appeared the minister of the church, wearing a frock coat, and a church elder with a large bald head and a white beard, his eyeglasses perched at the tip of his nose. The minister introduced the subject of the night's talk to the audience, whereupon the elder called out, "Ladies and gentlemen," and began his lecture at once.

Toshiya was utterly uninterested in the religious man's talk, and from the start he scrutinized everything, from the looks of young women sitting near him, to their hats, jackets, hair, and even the way they tied their bows. But as the long lecture dragged on, he even became tired of this and turned his aimless eyes to Kikue, who was intently listening. Her face was the usual round one he was familiar with, but if only her small eyes could be a little larger and her eyebrows darker, she might qualify as a beauty to some people, given her high nose bridge and the loveliness of her firm mouth. . . . Thus analyzing one by one the shortcomings and special features of her looks, he then proceeded to indulge in a rather fantastic daydream—What if this woman loves me; how should I then behave?—when the elder on the stage raised his voice and banged the podium. Toshiya, startled at the sound, came out of his daydreaming. Then he realized that he was in a foreign country, where he only saw people of a different race. He had nothing he could claim as his except for what he was wearing on his back at the moment, so different from the situation in Japan where, from his second-floor lodging, he used to comment on the young girls passing by in the streets below. However, what a strange fate that here he should be sitting next to a Japanese female student. He must really prostrate himself in front of fate and accept gratefully what it offered to him. Thus thinking, Toshiya closed his eyes for a while and then looked at Kikue's face in the bright electric light.

The lecture was over in about two hours. Toshiya held Kikue's hand, just as he did on their way over, and they, together with Yamada, returned to their respective rooms. But even after he got into bed, Toshiya indulged in some idle thoughts. To imagine that Kikue and he had already become lovers seemed to enliven his otherwise lonesome life; he could vividly picture the two of them, on a Sunday afternoon, sitting and frolicking on the grass in the meadow. Suddenly, it even seemed possible that the following day could be a Sunday. Laughing aloud to himself, he rolled over in his bed and nodded as if to say he had decided on something.

Indeed, Toshiya had made up his mind. But then, a question arose in his mind as to whether his plans would succeed. This question, he said to himself, might be divided into two: would the plans totally fail, or would they simply be rather difficult to carry out? From past experience, Toshiya easily answered the first question in the negative but had trouble with the second; what did it mean that the plans might not easily succeed? The word had broad meaning, and he had difficulty answering the question. So he decided to set aside theory and explore some actual examples: for instance, how, when he was in Japan, a certain person managed to seduce some waitress or other working for a Western-style restaurant; how another person failed in his attempt on a woman *gidayū* reciter; how yet another person unexpectedly won the heart of a nurse. In addition, he tried to recall numerous instances of love affairs from the novels he had read and came to the conclusion that of all these examples, the one that held the greatest lesson for him was a short novel he had read in translation, although he had totally forgotten its author and title.

If he remembered correctly, the story began with the theory of magnetism and described a man who fell in love with a woman but for a long time missed a chance to approach her. One night, he awakened with a start, having unexpectedly dreamed that his love had been consummated. He was hardly able to control himself, and, as luck would have it, he soon saw her and impulsively dashed over and held her hand tightly, without uttering a word. To his complete surprise, so the story went, she meekly yielded to his advances as if she had long been his mistress. Toshiya felt quite envious and jealous of the protagonist of the novel and wondered what sort of temperament the woman he had won over possessed. Of course, if she was of a different race from Kikue, it might not help much.

The night had gone on and everything was quiet in the dormitories. All one could hear was the rustling of the wind among the trees in the athletic field and the rumbling of trains passing by in a faraway distance. After a great deal of deliberation, Toshiya reached a most mundane conclusion: since it was premature to send her a letter, he had first to try to be near her constantly so that they would become closer; and feeling frustrated and angry at himself, he kicked back the blanket with his foot.

Autumn is already nearly over. When Toshiya first came to this land, it was the middle of summer, and rows of tall maple trees formed a tent, covering both sides of the quiet street in front of the college with their large and broad green leaves. But now, their leaves are fast turning yellow because of the chilly mist in the morning and at night, and the slightest wind causes them to fall wearily with a rustling sound. When he looks out the window of his tall dormitory toward the fields in the back, he notices that all the trees in the orchard, which diagonally climb halfway up the hill, have shed their leaves, and the apples that remain are shining with the light from the setting sun and glisten like so many large coral beads. In the flat meadow, the wild grass is still thick and green, but the willow trees along the little brook running through it have now nothing left but thin branches.

Every Saturday and Sunday, Toshiya invited Kikue out ostensibly to enjoy beautiful nature and appreciate rustic charm, choosing quiet fields with as few people as possible. They took a walk together, but by now Kikue had gotten used to such outings and no longer seemed to fear having Toshiya hold her hand; she had learned that, unlike in Japan, the relationships between men and women in America were unexpectedly wholesome and platonic.

Around the second Sunday in November, Toshiya took Kikue out as usual to the edge of the meadow, and they sat down on the soft wild grass near the stream that quietly glided through it.

It was what you would call "Indian summer" in this country, with infinitely clear skies, the afternoon sunlight shining brilliantly, and yet the winds that wafted over the fields were quiet but already somewhat chilly. As one looks back at the hill in the background and toward the village with its windmills standing here and there, one notices the entire oak forest turning red, and on the tall roofs of farmers' houses peeking through the trees, flocks of numerous migrating birds may be seen from time to time, flying high in the sky, one group after another. They must know that winter is soon coming and are preparing to return to warm southern climes.

Kikue was intently gazing at this peaceful and poetic sight. Suddenly, somewhere the clanging of a quiet bell was heard, and a huge cow appeared out of the thick wild grass a mere four or five yards away, walking ponderously while shaking the bell around her neck.

Being a frail Japanese woman, Kikue was startled and instinctively drew closer to Toshiya. Taking advantage of the situation, Toshiya held Kikue's hands but said casually, "Don't worry. It must be a milking cow from a nearby farmhouse. They are used to humans, so don't worry."

The cow looked at them with her gentle eyes and, as if remembering something, went back the way she had come, again clanging the bell around her neck, and lay down lazily.

Watching this, Kikue finally breathed a sigh of relief but then was startled even more than before when she realized that her hands were being held firmly by the man's. She did not have the courage to shake off his hands and so looked down, with her face flushing red and breathing heavily.

Toshiya too could no longer suppress his excitement. What was he supposed to say? What should he say in order to make further advances?

He brought his mouth to the woman's ear, which was all red, and whispered something in English rather than in Japanese.

Kikue was not able to utter a cry but seemed totally frightened and bewildered. Her face became deadly pale and she was shaking all over; tears started streaming from her eyes.

Toshiya, as might be expected, was at a loss. But he never let go of her hands and said in a deliberately calm tone, "Kikue, Kikue, what happened?"

Kikue fell prone on the spot and continued to tremble and sob.

The same cow seemed to have started walking again; the clanging of the bell echoed across the grass in the quiet meadow.

Not discouraged by his first attempt, Toshiya eagerly waited for another opportunity to take Kikue out to the quiet fields. But whenever Kikue caught sight of him, she somehow managed to slip away.

The following Sunday came and went, and he waited patiently for the next Sunday, but it rained.

At the end of November, once the skies cloud over and it starts raining, it is entirely impossible to enjoy the autumn weather in the country. It becomes chillier and chillier by the day, just as the wind shaking bare trees grows more and more fierce. Soon ashlike snow flakes will come, mixed in the wind. Winter! Winter! The whole universe will be buried under the constantly accumulating snow for as long as three months.

And Toshiya's hopes too became buried along the way. However, the fire, once making his young heart ablaze, would not be extinguished even by the cold, sub-zero temperatures day after day . . . the cold air bearing down from the Great Lakes region in the north. He continued to send a letter to Kikue as if it were a daily assignment.

When, finally, he ran out of things to write, he once copied word for word a passage from a collection of poems sitting on his bookshelf and sent it to her. But he received no answer. How many letters he had written, Toshiya could no longer keep track. Thinking that this was too much, and out of desperation, at one point he just sent her these words in large English letters: "Upon your cold cheeks, my kisses a hundred times, a thousand times. . . ." Still no answer.

Toshiya was finally at his wit's end and became desolate. He laughed at himself. And he gave up writing letters as if he had never written any. And one morning, the sky was suddenly blue, the sun was smiling, winds from the south were blowing, and the snow that had been frozen harder than rocks began to melt.

Before one knew it, winter was over and spring had come.

Just like last year, wild green grass starts to grow thick in the meadows. In the orchard up the hill apple and peach blossoms are in full bloom, and in the oak and elm woods glittering with young leaves, robins begin to sing. Nothing is greater than the contrast between the winter and spring in a northern country.

And lo! Young men were again going to the fields to pick flowers, holding young women's hands. But as far as Toshiya was concerned, it was as though he had completely forgotten even Kikue's existence.

One evening, returning from his usual walk after supper, he noticed a letter had been placed on his desk. Perplexed, he opened it.

"Good heavens, it's from Kikue!"

He crossed his arms as if to recall something from the distant past and began to read the letter. After repeatedly apologizing for not having answered the numerous letters he had sent her since last year, she said at length that she could no longer restrain herself when she thought of his passion and his letters coming one after another. The power of love was stronger than anything else, she wrote, and she was now ready to "throw myself into your arms."

Receiving such an unanticipated response at such an unexpected moment, Toshiya was for a time dumbfounded and wondered if he were dreaming. No, it wasn't a dream, no it wasn't. After rereading the woman's letter two or three more times, Toshiya wrote his response immediately.

Once again, he held Kikue's hands when, the following afternoon, they went to the bank of the same brook in the meadow where, toward the end of the previous autumn, they used to sit together.

From then on, every afternoon Toshiya would walk with Kikue through the village paths, the orchard on the hill, or the cemetery not far from the college. When the night fell in the woods and stars started to shine atop the old trees where squirrels squeaked, Toshiya even held her tightly under his overcoat to protect her, ostensibly, from the cold evening wind. Kikue no longer had the strength to resist him. On another occasion, as they went picking violets blooming in the fields, he offered to pin a bunch of them on her collar; bringing his face close to hers, he impulsively kissed her on the cheek, but even this just made her blush bashfully.

So, in less than a month, Toshiya became as happy a man as he had long dreamed. This happiness was of the kind that only newlyweds enjoyed in secret gratefulness to God and to fate.

Two years passed, and as the summer preceding his senior year arrived, Toshiya left the campus to travel, as he said, to the New York–Boston area during the vacation. But he never came back in time for the start of the academic year in the fall.

All he did was send a letter to Kikue to the effect that "due to certain circumstances, I have switched to an eastern college; I intend to obtain a degree here and then go back to Japan next year. I thank you deeply for your numerous kindnesses in the past. . . ."

A year passed, then another year.

Toshiya had returned home and become a promising employee of a certain company. One day, at the Shinbashi station, he ran into a theologian, Yamada Tarō, his fellow student during his early days in the United States.

Yamada held Toshiya's hand in a friendly gesture, but what a story he had to tell!

He was now a minister and was married to Kikue. According to Yamada, Kikue had completely lost her senses when she realized that she had been forsaken, or rather used as a temporary plaything, by Toshiya. And one winter night, during a frightening snowstorm in Michigan, she wandered about the woods trying to kill herself, but was rescued by Yamada by chance and confessed everything. Yamada felt deep pity for Kikue for having been victimized by a demon and did everything he could to care for her in order to save her from her dark despair and to restore her to her former happy self.

Upon receiving his degree, he returned to Japan with Kikue and, after consulting the elder of a certain church to which both belonged, entered into holy matrimony in front of the Cross.

"Mr. Ōyama. I am no longer blaming you for your sins at all. She and I have been saved from our earlier sins, Kikue through the mercy of God, and I through the power of love, and she has become once again a gentle lady, and I the master of a good family. So I hope you too will express your sincere thanks to God."

Since this encounter, whenever young people of his firm argue among themselves about the merits and demerits of Christianity, Toshiya has been given to saying, "Well, at least it is clear that Christianity never causes harm to society. . . ."

So saying, he always gives a puff at the cigar he holds in his mouth.

SPRING AND AUTUMN

Lodging on a Snowy Night

Whenever Japanese men in America come together to indulge in idle talk, without fail the first topic of discussion is what they think of the United States—from its politics and business to general customs and manners, but most of all its women as they have observed them.

Western women—especially American women—are educated and strong-willed, so unlike Japanese women, they are rarely deceived or corrupted by men . . . thus concluded one of the men who were at this evening's gathering.

To which another immediately objected, "But even in the United States, not every woman is so strong-willed. I have heard many incredible stories. . . ."

"Tell us. Are they true stories?"

"Of course they are. If you don't believe me, I'll introduce such people to you anytime!"

He took his glass of beer, slowly drank from it, and began.

It was December last year, before Christmas, in the evening when it had snowed for the first time.

However, in the early evening, even though the sky became overcast, there was little wind, and it was not yet that cold. I had been invited to the theater by a family I knew, and so as soon as I returned home from my company, I quickly shaved, washed my face, combed my hair again, and put on my jet-black dress coat, an opera hat, a snow-white tie, and pure white gloves. Just before I was set to depart, I stood proudly in front of the mirror and took one last look at myself. . . . How good it made me feel!

The play we saw was one of those musical comedies. The female star was said to be from Germany. She had a better voice than looks.

The show once over, like everyone else on his way home after the theater, we entered the corner restaurant, Shanley, to have a bite.* We spent so much time in idle talk that by the time we came out it was past one o'clock, and the streets were completely white. It was a heavy snowstorm; we had no idea when it had started.

At the nearby subway entrance I parted with the family who had invited me, as we were going home in different directions. I turned the corner onto Forty-second Street in order to take the elevated train, but the snow was blowing so hard in my direction that I had to pull my hat down over my eyes as I walked with my head bowed, without looking ahead. In no time, I bumped into someone coming toward me.

The person must also have been walking without looking; before I said anything, "Oh my, I am sorry," uttered a female voice, in an offhand, coquettish manner. Startled, I looked up.

"Dear me, it's Mr. K——. Where have you been? It's such awful weather."

It was a woman I knew. I don't have to tell you what sort of things she did . . . the kind of person who could be walking on Broadway past one o'clock at night.

"Where have *you* been yourself, in this heavy snow? Take it easy with your sweethearts, otherwise you could lose your life."

Trow General Directory of New York City (New York, 1915) lists Shanley restaurants at 117 West 42nd Street, 1204 Broadway, and 1493 Broadway. See p. 2578.

"Ha, ha, ha, ha. My sweetheart is right here, and I don't need another one," she said, snuggling close to me. "Seriously, Mr. K—, we haven't seen each other for a long time. I was thinking that you must have gone back to Japan without telling me."

"Rather, you were thinking that you had finally gotten rid of the Jap . . . but then this happens tonight. Too bad about that."

"What are you saying? I'm not going to let you talk like that." Through the veil she was wearing, the woman pretended that she was angrily glaring at me.

"Let's go. I can't really bear this cold. See, it feels like ice." Thus saying, she pressed her cheek against my face.

"Where are we going? To have a drink to stave off the cold?"

"It's too late for bars. Let's go to . . . my house. It's really been such a long time."

She decided all by herself and took my arm, resting her plump body against me.

I couldn't resist such an attack. We walked toward Broadway, from where I had just come. It was much better there, as the buildings on both sides of the street sheltered us from the wind.

For a while we stood at the corner, arm in arm. You should have seen the sight of the snow at midnight in Forty-second Street, the theater district that could be called a nightless city!

From the tall Times building and the Astor Hotel up north to the opera house and the faraway Herald Square with department stores like Macy's and Saks Fifth Avenue in the other direction, the rows of buildings are all clad in snow and loom like clouds or shadows, their blurry tips completely buried in the dark sky. Only from the windows, higher up and lower down, lights are shining like fireflies or stars. Here and there, at the entrances to theaters or the doors of bars and restaurants, bright lights of various colors still glitter, as they did earlier in the evening. But some of those farther away are covered with the driving snow and look like lanterns on a spring night.

The sidewalks on both sides are all covered with white snow and particolored like so many ribbons—blue in places, red elsewhere—by the colored electric lights. Men and women who are only now leaving the pleasure quarters go to and fro, arm in arm, some boarding the streetcars that approach noiselessly parting the snow, others hailing a nearby automobile or carriage. Gradually people disappear, one couple after another.

Looking at the sight, I really felt that the theater district late at night was at its best blanketed in snow. Maybe this is because a profound harmony is produced by the combination of the lights that look tired in the depth of the night after so much merrymaking and the snow that arouses in everyone a sense of inviolable quietude.

Prodded by one of the coachmen who were waiting for hire in the streets, I helped the woman into his cab and we rode away, although our destination was not that far off.

Even in Japan, there is something romantic about riding together with a woman on a snowy night; all the more so when you are in a comfortable horse-drawn carriage with rubber wheels. Holding each other's hands, leaning against each other, and flirting with abandon as if we owned the whole world, soon we reached the woman's house.

It was a flat house [sic] with a huge front door, and her place was on the third floor. She took out a key from the muff she was carrying, opened the door, and led me to the parlor at the end of the hallway.

On the walls hung two or three nude prints in color. On one side of the room was a piano, and on the other a cozy corner partitioned off with some cheap Turkish woven fabric. Here we sank down, drinking, singing, then kissing and tickling each other. Gentlemen! If you want to have a really good time, indulging in all kinds of tomfoolery, reserved Japanese women are no match for Western women.

After a while, there was a light knock on the parlor door, followed by a voice, apparently belonging to the madam of this house.

LODGING ON A SNOWY NIGHT

"Bessie, Bessie, please come over for a moment."

My Bessie, quite irritated, answered in a shrill voice, "What do you want?"

"I need you just for a second. The girl is being difficult again."

"Don't bother me, I am too drunk," she said, but nevertheless stood up and left the room.

In the room next door, a man was saying something in a deep, grumbling fashion. Bessie and the unfamiliar voice of another young woman could be heard. Evidently, there was some trouble.

The man with the deep voice—apparently one of those amorous and jealous types not uncommon in such a place—must be leaving, although the others tried to detain him, for after a while I heard the madam's voice, followed by the sound of the door being opened and shut . . . and then the entire house was quiet again.

"I'm really sick and tired of this. Why on earth did our madam get stuck with such a woman?" Bessie was muttering as she came back. She immediately sat next to me and said, "I'm sorry. I shouldn't have left my precious darling. . . ."

"It sounded like a lot of trouble."

"Yeah. But it couldn't be helped. The girl came here only four or five days ago."

"You mean she jilts her customers?"

"Not even that, she simply doesn't take them in. But then, she didn't come here because she wanted to. I mean she was tricked into coming."

"Tricked . . . ? By a man?"

"Yes, from the country. She was tricked by one of those bad characters who want to make money by ensnaring women."

"Then she wasn't exactly cheated by her lover?"

"No. Things like this happen all the time."

"Is that right? So that means there are pimps in America too," I said, intrigued by this discovery. "But how do they manage to lure them away? Just because they are women doesn't mean they would be cheated so easily, does it?"

"Sure, but you see, these bad characters will try everything, depending on time and circumstance." Bessie became more and more eloquent. Striking a match on the sole of her high-heeled shoe and puffing out cigarette smoke, she continued, "Take Annie, for instance . . . who came here . . . she used to live in the country miles out of Buffalo, working in a pharmacy or some such place. But she met a man boarding for a while in a house near hers, who said he was an official of an insurance company in New York. One day he managed to persuade her by saying, 'Why don't you come with me to New York to see the sights?' You know, anyone living in the country would want to see New York at least once. So I guess she fell victim to temptation and let herself be brought to New York. She had thought that he would help her look for a nice job, but in fact she was like a mouse caught in a trap. As soon as they arrived at the station, he took her without warning to one hotel after another before finally bringing her to this house. And then he disappeared into thin air. She had no money to go back home; as you know, if you hang around in this house, sooner or later you have to join the business."

"It may work out that way, but what if she is a chaste woman who would rather die than degrade herself?"

"You won't find many women like that," Bessie immediately contradicted me, being one of those jaded creatures.

"In the beginning, everyone is virtuous. Even I once made an honest living. I come from New Jersey, from a respectable home that is still there. Coming to New York, I worked for a while as a salesgirl at a department store on Thirty-third Street. But how can you live on a measly wage of only five or six dollars a week? I couldn't. Of course, that was just enough to eat, if that was all I wanted. But it was like living for the sake of not dying; how could a young person idly watch the hustle and bustle of New York? You would want to wear fashionable clothes others are wearing and go to the theater just like everyone else. I wanted to experience such luxury and so first I willingly became the mistress of a man who worked at the same store, and following that steadily slipped into a shameful life. Of course, at times, being human, I would become anxious about my future and tell myself that I shouldn't be doing things like this, that it would be better to go back to the country. But the thing about New York is that once you are exposed to its winds, you can never leave this place, even if you end up dying in the street. For the young, New York is everything, like it or not.

"So with Annie, just wait and see. Even if she had worked at a respectable house, it wouldn't have been the end of it. Once you are in this New York, it is inevitable that sooner or later you say to yourself, 'I might as well have some fun while I am young!' "

Sure enough, Annie changed each time I visited Bessie after that night. First she would come and drink with us, then she would start cracking jokes . . . and she became more and more blasé. Her transformation never ceased to amaze me.

Today she is quite something to behold: the way she smartly holds up the rear hem of her skirt with one hand and clicks the narrow heels of her French-style shoes on the pavement of Broadway. How about it? If you like, I can introduce her to you.

Everyone laughed, drank more, smoked more, and then resumed the conversation.

In the Woods

Travelers who have been sightseeing in boisterous northern cities such as Chicago and New York will be surprised by what they see when they come to the capital of the United States, Washington. On the one hand, the whole city is like one large park, with beautiful deep clusters of maple trees covering the streets, and on the other, there is a large number of ugly Negroes wandering all over the city.

I too am a wanderer in the new continent. One autumn, I arrived at this capital and for two weeks saw just about everything one is supposed to see: first, the official residence of the president, the White House, the Capitol, various government offices. And, having also paid my respects at Washington's grave in far-off Mount Vernon up the Potomac River, I began visiting several places in the suburbs to enjoy the colors of the fall season at their peak in this foreign land.

I can never forget the twilight over the meadows of Maryland that I saw yesterday.

About half an hour after sunset, the fiery evening glow gradually fades and leaves only a faint rosy hue around the edges of the white clouds floating in the sky. The vast grass-covered surface of the fields turns into a misty blue sea, and at the distant horizon it is difficult to tell where sky ends and earth begins. On the other hand, the whiteness of certain objects—the pure white walls of the farmhouses here and far away, the white skirts of four or five women who are probably driving cattle across the fields, the treetops tinged here and there with yellow leaves, or the flowers of some unknown plants—is truly striking as it reveals itself, perhaps reflecting the rays of light from the sky, against the surroundings that are slowly growing darker. As I watched these objects, I had a strange sensation that they were gradually moving toward me.

What a mysterious sight. It evoked in me, not just in my eyes but from the bottom of my heart, an indescribably pleasant feeling. I could not help but remove my hat and wave it intently as if to beckon those moving colors, until it became completely dark around me. What a mysterious sight it was.

The following day, wishing to savor this beautiful twilight dream once again, I waited till sunset and left—but this time for the woods across the Potomac. I was already in the state of Virginia as I crossed an iron bridge at the foot of a cliff at the end of the city.

As soon as you cross the bridge, you come to a little train stop made of wood, and behind it there is a thicket of trees spreading their branches. This is the departure point for the train bound for Arlington, where there are the large public cemetery, military drilling grounds, army barracks, and officers' residences. Most of the people waiting for the train now are U.S. soldiers in khaki uniforms, but there are also Negro maids who are probably employed in the officers' houses, as well as middle-aged white women who must be returning home from their shopping in Washington.

I never feel more depressed than when I see soldiers and sailors. They all have excellent physiques and youthfulness, but all their passions are constantly oppressed by military rules and regulations. The physical agony of this oppression is somehow reflected in their suntanned faces and bloodshot eyes, making them appear fearsome and at the same time pitiful. They wait for the train in threes and fours, some leaning against the railing of the bridge in order to sober up, others spitting out tobacco and walking on the bridge with loud footsteps, while still others gaze wistfully in the direction of Washington across the river, as if to ruminate over the women they visited in the afternoon.

I too leaned against the bridge railing and looked around. Just then the evening sun was about to go down, setting the whole sky afire. It was shooting its pointed rays of light directly toward Washington, making the colorful treetops throughout the park along the Potomac look like an opulent Turkish hanging. Above it, standing erectly, was the 555-foot Washington Monument, that amazing marble structure, which now looked like a column on fire. The round roof of the somewhat distant Capitol and the various white office buildings that towered here and there were equally dyed in deep red, and all the windows in the city's tall hotel buildings glittered like colored electric lights.

A splendid, expansive panorama. I stood aimlessly in the autumn wind and reminded myself that this was the capital that ruled over the entire Western Hemisphere. As I looked beyond the river and far into the distance in the shadow of the setting sun, certain abstract thoughts arose in my mind like so many layers of summer clouds: humanity, humanism, nations, governments, ambitions, fame, history. And yet I did not have a single coherent idea that I would convey to others. I simply felt as if I were vaguely pursuing the shadow of something large, while at the same time my head was weighed down at the nape by some powerful majesty.

After a while I raised my head and looked around once again, but by then the soldiers who had been walking on the bridge and the groups of women waiting for a train seemed all to have gone. Another group of two or three people was already gathering, to wait for the next train.

I walked along the train tracks, and after a couple of blocks made my way aimlessly into the woods whose trees were spreading over both sides of the road. . . .

IN THE WOODS

The woods consists mostly of oak and maple trees. The maples of this country are easily affected by the night dew, and the leaves tend to start falling even before they turn yellow. As a result, the winding path was everywhere covered with large fallen leaves, making it undiscernible. But the oak woods was at its peak foliage season. The light from the evening sun penetrated the trees' thickness and shone upon every leaf. It was as though a golden rain were pouring down. But the autumn light in the dusk shifts rapidly; even as I watched, the bright treetops far away became covered by a shadow, while the dark ones nearby emerged in the light. In the bright areas, little birds that had already gone to bed began to chirp again, while in the newly darkened treetops, squirrels chattered loudly.

I kept walking aimlessly, but unconsciously straining my ears, when all of a sudden I heard a cry—not a bird or a squirrel, but unmistakably a woman sobbing.

No sooner had I stopped abruptly than I discerned two people amid the fallen leaves. One was a soldier clad in khaki, and the other, at his feet, a quite young Negro girl, perhaps half-white, with her hands clasped together on her chest as if in prayer.

A soldier and a girl—it was quite easy to guess what was going on.

"Please, please . . ." the girl's voice echoed from the depth of her bosom, her clasped hands pressed against it.

"You are still talking such nonsense," the soldier looked away in evident disgust, spitting out some tobacco, and he seemed about to leave.

"Don't!" The woman clung to the soldier's hand as she sank to the ground. "You really are asking me to break up our relationship, aren't you?"

"What? . . . Me asking you? No, I am not asking you to break up. I don't care if you break up with me or not. I am breaking up our relationship," the soldier declared spitefully and also haughtily. He was a respectable American, but she was the daughter of former Negro slaves. He must have taken no small offense at the woman's presumption that he was asking her "to break up."

Unable to answer, the woman just sobbed over the man's hand to which she clung. The soldier watched her for a while and then addressed her, as if remembering something, "Just think about it, eh, Martha. Don't you remember? From the beginning, it wasn't me who asked if we could become lovers. It was this spring, while I was stationed as a valet at Colonel M——'s house . . . that one evening when you came out to the backyard and I happened to run into you . . . I was drunk then . . . ha, ha, ha, ha. Well, never mind the details. But the next evening, didn't you tell me you wanted to see me on such and such a day at such and such a place? How could I refuse? . . . But this time, no." He broke off.

The woman sobbed even harder.

"It's no use offering excuses, but the long and short of it is, everything has a beginning and an end. Just like the seasons."

I could no longer bear to eavesdrop on this cruel and brutal live scene. Just then, the last deep blood-red shaft of sunlight struck my feet. I was also worried that they might see me, so I hastily left the scene without once looking back.

I was thinking, of course, not so much about love as about the long-festering problem of the relationship between the black and white races in this country. Why are Negroes so despised and hated by whites? Is it because they are ugly, or because they are black? Or is it simply that fifty years ago they were slaves? Is there no way for a race to avoid persecution unless it organizes itself as a political body? Is there a need for states or armed forces forever? . . .

I came out of the woods and walked back to the foot of the bridge. The evening sun had completely gone down and the bright red hue of the sky had faded, while across the river, in Washington, electric lights could be seen among the trees in the parks and in the windows of tall buildings. Once again, I leaned against the railing of the bridge and looked over the city, which was steadily growing darker.

On the bridge, as earlier, several soldiers were walking while they waited for their train. Amid the din of loud talk, laughter, and whistling, I chanced to look back and recognized the soldier whom I had just seen in the woods, tormenting the Negro girl. I had no idea when he had come back, but he was right by me and saying something to a friend wearing the same kind of uniform. My curiosity aroused, I listened to their conversation. The one who first asked a question was that soldier.

"How was it? Did you come across a pretty girl?"

"Oh, no," responded the friend. "I had a terrible time today."

"What happened? Did you lose money at gambling?"

"That would have been better. Instead I went to the usual C Street and lost all my money."

"Ha, ha, ha, ha. You mean you have to spend your own money to have a woman? You aren't very good at that, are you?" So saying, he spat out some tobacco. "What do you think? If you really are so desperate for women, I can procure a young one for you."

"Hey, that sounds great."

"There is a catch, however. If you don't mind. . . ."

"Oh, it doesn't matter. Nothing beats having a woman of your own without having to pay for it."

"Of course, it's a good deal," he nodded. "But the catch is this: the girl is a nigger, not bad looking, though."

"I don't care. I am not about to worry over such details."

"Good for you, Jack! I just wanted to tell you that this girl works at the house of Colonel M——, where I once did valet duty. She is still awfully young but crazy about men. As soon as you say some sweet words to her, she falls madly in love with you."

"Is that right? But there could be trouble if she became too crazy about you."

"Exactly. And I know it. The girl really loves men, loves to fool around with men. So after you've had your fill and gotten tired of her, just pass her on to somebody, it doesn't matter who, so that he will take your place, and then you can simply run away. As long as you find her a substitute, she will soon become attached to him and won't chase your ass forever. See, she is not the type to fall in love, but she's just crazy about men. Don't think you will find anything as convenient as that anywhere."

Just then, at some distance a train appeared from under the trees with a loud sound.

"Here is the train. Let's talk some more on the train."

"All right!" was the sole answer.

The soldiers ran toward the train stop whistling a popular tune— "I'm [a] Yankee Doodle sweetheart, I'm [a] Yankee Doodle joy."

The forests, woods, and water grew steadily darker. Red lights were being lit on the small craft and fishing boats moored under the bridge and under the trees on the riverbank. The lights of Washington began to shine brighter and brighter each moment, as did the stars in the sky. Alone, I crossed the bridge to walk home, but various ill-formed, undefined, yet very grave thoughts somehow seemed to keep occurring to me.

I never saw that Negro girl again while I lived in Washington.

(November 1906)

Bad Company

I

Not long ago, when the issue of discrimination against Japanese schoolchildren arose in California, there was much speculation in the press in New York and elsewhere in the country that Japan and the United States might go to war. Quite naturally, whenever those of us Japanese who were living in New York came together, the topic of conversation was very often developments on the Pacific Coast.

One evening, at a certain place, we were engaged in our usual discussion of such topics as the race question, the yellow peril idea, internationalism, Roosevelt's personality, justice, and humanism, when all of a sudden someone seemed to remember something and asked a totally unrelated question: "Is it true that there are a lot of Japanese prostitutes over there?"

That topic spread in all directions like a shower cloud arising rapidly at the edge of a swelteringly hot sky, and drove away grander discourses on public affairs. Some even pulled up their chairs, as if to suggest that an even more serious subject had been introduced.

"I hear that over there they not only have Japanese prostitutes and *samisen* but also Japanese-style bath houses and even archery grounds."

"There is hardly anything they don't have: *shiruko* [sweet red-bean soup] shops, sushi restaurants, *soba* joints. Even in Japan, if you go to a remote region, you won't be able to enjoy such convenience. On the other hand, most Japanese there are laborers from Kyūshū and the Chūgoku area; for those of us from Tokyo their food as well as their women are totally unappetizing."

"Maybe that's the case."

"I've visited many parts of the Pacific Coast, from San Francisco to Portland, Seattle, Tacoma, and on to Vancouver in Canada, but the situation is more or less the same everywhere. Oh, yes . . . I did run into just one half decent looking woman who had apparently come from Tokyo . . . and was working as a barmaid in a whorehouse in Seattle."

"Did you have any interesting experiences?"

"Oh, no. I only went there a few times to have a drink. You have to assume that a woman like that is already claimed by a scoundrel. Lower classes might not mind trying, but we have to be on our guard. Especially since I found out that her husband was a famous thug in the Seattle area who had graduated from college and spoke English. . . . I am told on that coast there are really disgusting characters who make a living by kidnapping or smuggling women . . . so-called pimps."

The young man paused in his speech and took a puff from his pipe. Someone seized the moment and spoke up from a corner seat, saying, "I think I've seen the woman you just mentioned. . . . Do you know the name of her thug of a husband?"

Everybody looked at the questioner, surprised, for he was always known to be a serious man who never paid attention to talk of women and drinking.

"Mr. Shimazaki. That's amazing. Who would have guessed that you were familiar with such things," two or three startled voices could be heard simultaneously.

"Oh, no. I am as uninitiated as ever, but I do know about that woman because of certain special circumstances. Wasn't she about twenty-six or -seven years old? With a slender face and tall in stature. . . . Yes? Then it's certainly the woman I saw. This is indeed a coincidence, but the husband of that woman was once my brother's . . . my dead brother's close friend."

The man addressed as Shimazaki began his story by request.

2

It was exactly three years ago, for the place where I disembarked when I came to the United States was Seattle.

We arrived at the pier on a fine day at the end of October, just as the sun was setting. But we were told that the immigration officials would not appear till the following morning, and so from the handrail on the deck I kept looking at the waters and mountains, the first sights of this foreign land, till late at night. The next day, I went ashore without a mishap but had no idea where I was. Together with a couple of others with whom I had become acquainted during the voyage, I wandered about, getting lost, but then we met a man, about fifty years of age, who said he was the desk clerk of a Japanese inn looking for guests. We followed him and got on a train for the Japanese quarter. We ended up at a dingy wooden inn at the corner.

It is no wonder that Japanese are misunderstood in that part of the country. The inn is located in an area that is at the extreme point of the city where the bustling streets lined with stores are gradually deserted, just as though people are falling upon bad times. The only buildings around there are shipping companies, communal stables, and such, and the streets, which are covered with horse dung, are monopolized by carts and laborers.

Sticking my head out the window of the inn to which we had been taken, I was able to see the backs of the city's buildings far away and, closer, a tall, dark, and huge gas tank standing like Asakusa's Panorama

Building [in downtown Tokyo]. The street became suddenly narrower near that area, cramped with dirty, wood-frame little houses, through which a thin alley penetrated and then disappeared. Apparently, it ultimately led to the sea, for one could see, above the rooftops of people's houses, steel roofs of the warehouses that stored ship cargo, as well as numerous masts. There must also be a railroad yard there: tremendous black smoke was gushing forth incessantly to the sound of locomotives' bells, covering everything with soot, from roofs to streets; depending on the direction of the wind, there were times when you could not see very far. This alley, these squalid wood-frame houses, these made up the den for the Japanese and the Chinese, the Oriental colony, and also the place where unemployed Western laborers and poor, oppressed Negroes found shelter.

Just the sight of the coal fumes distressed me. Thinking that perhaps I should move to a hotel somewhere that was for Westerners, I actually went out to the street with my suitcase. But since I was a student, my travel money was limited; besides, even if I had enough money, a hotel for Westerners immediately conjures up the image of something like the Imperial in Tokyo, which makes one feel unwelcome unless one is wearing a silk hat. For no particular reason, then, I hesitated and told myself that I was not going to stay here long, that I was to leave for the East Coast within a week with a friend who was arriving from California. So although I had left the hotel, I returned to it sheepishly. But I could not stand being cooped up in a room at the dingy hotel and so from the very day that I landed, and even before I had had enough rest from the voyage, I walked from morning till night all over the city; not only the city, but I also went to the huge lake to the north of the city and to the thick forests nearby. But wherever I went, children would jeer, crying out "*sukebei*" [lecher]. It was amazing that this word that had come to mean something special in the mouths of Japanese prostitutes had from them spread throughout the lower classes in the United States.

BAD COMPANY

Indeed, how shall I describe the view from the inn's window at night, looking down at the streets below? Before I left Japan, I had spent one night walking around in the pleasure quarter, saying to myself that I needed to observe Oriental social customs, as I would not be back for a long time. The night life I was witnessing now was similar, yet it made a far stronger impression on me. Perhaps this was because I was a newcomer to this country so that everything, good and bad, had a freshness.

The riffraff who hung around in the area during the day were joined later by laborers who were finished with their day's work at various piers and construction sites and came out of nowhere to gather together on the sidewalks. The result was that the air, already abominable, now seemed to have the added smell of alcohol and sweat. Accompanied by the sound of heavy shoes and abusive shouting, rows of soiled torn shirts, torn trousers, and torn hats steadily moved like dark shadows toward the brightly lit alley of the Japanese quarter. And from that alley one heard a constant Babel of voices accompanied by the noise of band music sounding like the clanging of a circus, probably produced by gramophones in bars and shooting ranges. There was also the sound of *samisen* everywhere, echoing "chinten, chinten" as if in response to one another, followed by women singing and men clapping their hands. . . .

Just imagine. Against the surrounding American view, you have on one hand the noise of "the West" presented by the whistling of ships, the bells of trains, and band music played by gramophones, and on the other, long-trailing, howling, moaning, and sleepy country songs from the Kyūshū region, accompanied by the brief, intermittent sound of the strings. No music is sadder, giving rise to such a discordant, unpleasant, and complex, even if monotonous, sensation.

One evening—I think it was the night before I was to depart for the East Coast—I found myself unable to sleep, as the sound of the *samisen* was still ringing in my ears, so I joined the line of laborers and started walking toward the alley on the other side. Once inside the alley, I noticed huge crowds of Japanese everywhere, from the large archery grounds and billiard parlors to various restaurants and even the sidewalks. But they all seemed self-possessed, as if to say that this was their turf, so that even Western laborers were looked upon like foreigners. In the meantime, from the windows of wood-frame houses, women's faces could be seen on and off, drawing the curtains aside and spying on what was going on outside. Some of them were calling out to others in shrill voices. All of them were women from the western part of Japan, with flat noses, narrow eyes, and flat faces. Their hair was swept back in a bun at the back with bangs at the front, and they wore what appeared like Western-style gowns. But for me, just a glance at them was enough to make me feel satisfied—or rather, queasy—anyway, I could not bear to get closer to them.

Still, I stayed at the street corner for a while and watched as laborers from East and West kept going in and coming out of dark entrance ways that were gaping like holes in between small shops selling tobacco, fruit, and other wares. Suddenly, I noticed a gentleman of fine appearance coming out, mingling with the laborers. He was wearing a heavy gold chain shining on his vest as well as a derby hat slightly hitched back; he looked drunk, with his face all flushed, and a small toothpick was sticking out of his mouth. Struck by the incongruity of the scene, I instinctively looked at his face.

He somehow looked familiar, so I gazed after him as he walked by, but then the gentleman stopped in front of a tobacco store a few feet away, revealing his profile by the store's lights. . . . A profile is often a good indicator of one's facial features. Thus it helped me suddenly remember what had happened about seven years earlier.

This sudden sensation must have moved me, for despite my customary timidity, I ran after him and called to him.

BAD COMPANY

The gentleman was none other than the close friend of my late elder brother, who used to come to see him quite frequently.

3

His name was Yamaza. He had graduated from the same school as my brother, and they were working for the same company. As my brother was the eldest son and ten years older than I, the youngest, with two sisters in between, I naturally had no opportunity to speak with the man. But I used to hear a great deal about him from my parents and others.

It all goes back to the time when I was about to graduate from middle school. My brother had frequently caused our father trouble by leading a dissolute life and as a result, together with Yamaza, borrowing money at high interest. As if this were not enough, he, Yamaza, and a few of his sort swindled money out of people by using their company's name. In no time their action was discovered and they were all arrested. However, my brother escaped punishment when my father sold the property he owned and indemnified the company. Yamaza too somehow managed to get acquitted, thanks to his uncle who was an army officer of some rank or other. Thus, only the remaining two, neither of whom had any such help, were to experience the most dismal of circumstances. But at that time I did not fully grasp the meaning of criminal acts, so all I felt was some vague fear.

After this incident, my brother idled away his time for about two years, becoming the focus of the whole family's fear and aversion, as if he were an ill omen incarnate or a plague. But then he unexpectedly contracted consumption and died before the winter passed. Just as suddenly, my father and mother stopped badmouthing my brother, and on every occasion they would say that it was all because of that bad company, Yamaza, who used to frequent the house. . . . The maxim that goes "Who keeps company with the wolf will learn to howl" particularly became my parents' favorite quotation. Not just my parents, but even my eldest sister (who was two years my brother's junior and was already married to a graduate of law school) would say, whenever she visited our house and came across some pictures of my brother and Yamaza as she turned the pages of the family album, "My, doesn't he look foppish! Just like an actor or a comic storyteller!" I still remember her gazing at the pictures intently and sometimes even hitting his face with the point of her ornamental hairpin.

One year came and went, and then another. And every year, whenever the cold month of February arrived, the month when my brother had died, Yamaza's name would be mentioned anew by my parents, and the old maxim and numerous moral lessons would be repeated to me. But no one in my family knew where this dreadful Yamaza had gone, or what he was doing.

4

"So, you are the younger brother of Chiyomatsu . . . indeed, I've never forgotten. At that time you were just a mere kid, weren't you? It must be already seven or eight years . . . perhaps even longer ago."

Yamaza had just lit his cigar in front of the tobacco store, amid the laborers jamming the streets; he did look surprised and stared at me for a moment, but then changed his tone.

"Why did you come to the United States? To study? . . . But this is no place for young men like you."

"I'll be leaving for the East as soon as my friend gets here, perhaps as early as tomorrow," I answered calmly. "And how about you? Are you engaged in some business?"

"I?" he broke off and studied my face for a while. "You'd be shocked if I told you. Ha! ha! ha! ha! One does change a great deal."

"Maybe some immigration business?" I was led to ask, judging from his appearance, showing off a fine moustache and an ostentatious array of golden items like rings and chains; his somehow vulgar manner of speech; and the special conditions of this region.

At that, he burst out laughing and said, "You can indeed say it's a kind of immigration business. Sure, it's something the immigrants need. . . ." He fell silent for a while and puffed away at his cigar. "Why don't I take you to a Japanese restaurant? Once you are in the East, all you get to eat at first will just be Western food."

I didn't decline his offer and was led to a Japanese restaurant in the same alley, which had a paper-covered lampstand saying SAKU-RAYA, if I remember correctly, sticking out of the second-floor window. The dark entranceway was similar to that of the brothels I had observed, and as we climbed upstairs, I noticed five or six painted doors on both sides of a narrow hallway where a lone naked gaslight was flickering. It was dim, but one could hear noises inside the closed doors created by the voices of many men and women and the sound of *samisen*, and the smell from the cooking of *sukiyaki* was lingering.

Yamaza looked around as if this were his own house and took me inside a room. As he pushed a bell button, a woman appeared, with a face thickly painted white, looking like a maidservant at a post town in Japan and wearing a Western-style dress plus Japanese-style indoor sandals. Behaving as if they were on quite friendly terms, she said without ceremony, "Do you want something to eat?" and leaned wearily against the nearby wall.

"Doesn't matter what. Just tell Oyuki and bring over something nice."

The woman did not even respond but simply nodded and headed down the hallway, her sandals flapping.

Abruptly, from some room came the sound of merry *sawagi samisen* [boisterous *samisen* to enliven the party], along with the tapping of teacups to keep time. It somehow reminded me of the noises created by boatmen at a tea house on the wharf one evening some summers back in the Bōshū area [to the east of Tokyo]. All of a sudden, the feeling of loneliness from having come to a foreign land a long way from home welled up in my heart, making me a little sad. Then the door opened. Another woman entered, carrying pickled vegetables and *sake* bottles; but she didn't treat Yamaza as a guest, either, and sat down close to him, saying, "What happened last night? Don't you think it was too much? Don't carry your jokes too far."

Taken aback, I looked at her face. She was about twenty-seven or -eight, and judging from her way of speaking and her slender face, she was the type of woman one saw frequently among the maids at small restaurants or *sukiyaki* houses in the Asakusa area.

Even Yamaza looked a little embarrassed in my presence and, repeatedly puffing cigar smoke, he said, "What's the matter with you, talking silly nonsense as soon as you arrive? Can't you serve some *sake* to our guest right away?"

The woman poured me some and took the opportunity to turn to me and say, "I can't help complaining once in a while, can I? He brings me all the way to America and then flirts around every night. . . . Please straighten him out a little."

Finally, it came out, and I must say it was stranger than ever. Yamaza let the woman go, telling her to hurry the kitchen. As if determined that he should no longer hide his secrets, he said, even before I asked him anything, "You must be amazed, yes? Aren't you flabbergasted?" He laughed and then told me what had happened to him.

Around the time that he learned about my brother's death from the newspapers' obituaries, he left his country, where he had been unable to make a living any longer, for San Francisco in search of some good fortune. After experiencing the kinds of hardships and disappointments of most immigrants to the United States, he came to the conclusion that the best way to make money in America was to live on women. So he went back to Japan and immediately returned to

America with a maid from a *sukiyaki* house, namely Oyuki. Settling down in Seattle, he told me, he had been making a living as an intermediary in smuggling prostitutes and by gambling.

"Once you take one step in the wrong direction, it's all over; you can't reverse course midway. No matter how repentant you are, the world won't forgive someone who has been tainted. The only choice for you is to push as far as you can in the direction of evil. Take your brother, Chiyomatsu. He wanted to turn back halfway in order to become respectable, but he worried so much about such things that he contracted tuberculosis and ended his life. It's the same with everybody. Scholars who don't know the world seem to think human beings will continue to fall if let alone, but don't worry. They might fall halfway, becoming neither good nor bad, but to settle down in the bottomless pit beyond that point is hard work for anyone who has any measure of education. You have to completely subdue that creature called 'conscience' that sticks its head out from time to time. That's far more difficult to do than to say. There is nothing unusual about a guy born to a family of beggars becoming a beggar. And it takes no effort for someone born into a good family to become an ordinary good citizen. The problem is what comes next, whether to take another step and become a great figure, or to retreat a step and move to the wrong side of society, neither of which is easy. The efforts and training involved in either course are the same, though they are as different as night and day. So the choice boils down to whether one wants to become a Napoleon or an Ishikawa Goemon [a notorious thief in the sixteenth century]."

He was discoursing in a grandly exalted tone of voice, drinking cupfuls of *sake*, as if he were back at a time, ten or twenty years earlier, when students used to aspire to serving the country, accomplishing great deeds, or achieving fame—unlike today when we are more accustomed to talking about life or mysteries. I decided it was best to listen to his words as an expression of some eccentric satire coming from the aching heart of a man with an injured past, and so I didn't contradict or ask him questions but just pretended to be absorbed in his speech.

Outside, the *sawagi samisen* had not yet stopped, but another party's *samisen* and the singing of "*Shinonomebushi*," a song popular in Japan three or four years earlier, began to be heard.

The very next day, joined by my friend who had arrived from the south, I departed for the East Coast on a Great Northern train.

A little later, in a letter to my mother, I casually mentioned my encounter with Yamaza, to which she responded saying that everything, whether good or bad, was now but a dream; Mr. Yamaza had been a close friend of my elder brother's, and so as a token of her good wishes, she had sent under separate cover a can of *yakinori* [toasted seaweed], which she wanted me to deliver to him when I had an opportunity.

The parental thoughtfulness, the motherly affections, of an elderly person who had no idea that New York and Seattle were separated by three thousand miles: thinking of her moved me to tears in spite of myself.

(June 1907)

Old Regrets

I was discussing opera with Dr. B——. We talked about the enchanting and passionate Italian school, the discreetly tasteful and beautiful character of the French school, and eventually about the sublime, imposing, and mysterious Wagnerian opera of Germany.

The great *Das Rheingold* and the trilogy that follows it, the sacred *Parsifal*, the sorrowful *Tristan und Isolda* [sic], the beautiful *Lohengrin*, the profound and melancholy *Der Fliegende Holländer* . . . among all these immortal works bequeathed to us by the great genius of Bayreuth, somehow the story of *Tannhäuser* was unforgettable to my amateur's ears. . . .

"Dear sir, what are your views about that opera's ideals?"

As I asked the question, Dr. B—— heaved a deep sigh as if he had been stabbed in the heart and gazed at me silently for some moments. Then he said, looking down, "Unfortunately, I am not qualified to pass scholarly judgment on that opera, for whenever I recall the time I heard *Tannhäuser*, I am struck by an uncontrollable emotion. . . . Shall I tell you the story? It happened nearly twenty years ago. . . ."

As I drew up my chair, he began.

"It was already twenty years ago. My wife, Josephine, asked me, just as you did, the meaning of *Tannhäuser*.

"At that time, I was touring Europe with her on our honeymoon, and one evening, while we were staying in the capital of Austria, we went to its famous Imperial Opera House. (As he spoke, he pointed to a building in a photograph on the wall.) That evening's opera was none other than *Tannhäuser*.

"I still vividly remember everything, from the appearance of the inside of the opera house, the faces of the singers who performed that evening, and the musicians to the faces of the numerous members of the chorus who appeared as retainers in the hunting scene or in the procession of lords and pilgrims.

"Soon after my wife, Josephine, and I took our designated seats in the hall filled with beautiful gowns and jewelry, the long-haired conductor appeared at the podium at the foot of the stage and marked out three beats with his baton; all at once the brilliant lights went out and the huge audience fell silent, enveloped in the darkness of the spacious theater. The orchestra starts with the sad and solemn tune of the pilgrims and moves on to the passionate music of Venusberg, then to 'the hymn of Venus,' concluding the long overture that may be said to summarize the whole meaning of this opera. . . . The curtain rises, and it is the scene of the goddess Venus's mountain.

"As you know, at the left-hand side of the stage, Tannhäuser, the *Minnesinger*, slumbers at the foot of Venus's bed, still holding a harp. Numerous nymphs dance, and apparitions float in the air, suggesting Tannhäuser's dreams, and finally the singer awakens; he says that, having been inebriated for many years by all imaginable pleasures through Venus's love, he now misses the world and wants to return to it, bidding Venus farewell. The goddess tries to dissuade him, saying that if he goes back to the world he will surely recall the bygone dreams and regret the decision; he should forever play his harp of love and sing songs of joy with her. But Tannhäuser is unmoved, and as he sings a hymn to Saint Mary, he is awakened from his dreams of the bewitched world. Venus disappears into darkness, along with her mountain. Alone, Tannhäuser stands by a mountain path near his native place of Waltburg.

"On a rock by the mountain path, a lone young shepherd is playing on a pipe and singing with a clear, innocent voice. Soon, from beyond the mountain, sad voices of pilgrims on their way to Rome begin to be heard, and their procession moves down the path and away.

"Tannhäuser pays rapt attention to these songs, and suddenly he is filled with dread as he recalls the sinful pleasures in which he indulged; he is so shaken that he throws himself down, sobbing.

"Listening to this, I could not help but heave a deep sigh and closed my eyes.

"Ah! what must have gone through the *Minnesinger*'s heart as he awoke from his long dream of pleasure and lamented his sins. From his aria, from his music, I suddenly recalled my own forgotten dissolute life before my marriage, my own dreams of pleasure that had vanished for a while. It seemed as if Tannhäuser on stage was a satire of my past ecstasy, anguish, and shame, and Venus, the beautiful heathen goddess, the goddess of pleasure, could only be Marianne, the young actress who was once my mistress.

"Ah! Is there anything more delicious in the world than a forbidden fruit? The fear of sins, the apprehension of poison, these merely enhance its magical power. I shall tell you everything now. . . . (The learned man cast down his eyes slightly, as if embarrassed.)

"All men seem entranced at least once by the attractive make-up of this type of woman, yet I daresay few have been as bewitched as I. For some reason (let's just say it was my inborn nature), I always found attractive and desirable comediennes or actresses in beautiful costumes, dancing or singing with affected looks and gestures in front of footlights on a stage, or the type of woman one meets in restaurants, theaters, dance halls, even in the streets and in carriages, whose particular air and appearance draw people's attention. Dumas [fils] described this kind of woman as 'neither a duchess nor a virgin,' and indeed she possesses an indescribable beauty, a magical power. Even if she is not the type of beauty an artist dreams of, there is an irresistibly seductive power in such a woman's cloudy, drowsy eyes, her unhealthy, thin fingertips, or even in her sometimes awfully vulgar-looking mouth. That is to say, her eyes suggest that she is ready to fling herself at your mercy, yet her mouth seems to sneer and pout, as if to say, watch out, or you'll pay dearly.

"Once a man's fancy is tickled by such mysterious, magical power, soon to his enchanted eyes cultured and virtuous wives and young women begin to look like cold puppets of morality; he becomes intoxicated with the unrestrained poetic sentiment of the song, 'Love is a vagabond, a child of Bohemia,' losing all sense of family or country and enslaving himself to fervent desires with little thought of the future.

"Even before I finished my education, I would often imagine silly things and wonder, while smoking a cigar at the window of my study on a peaceful spring day, whether I would ever in my life be loved by a woman of that kind.

"Ah! What a silly, vulgar dream. After all, I was better educated than most and was also well read. I knew such desires were vulgar and foolish, yet no matter how hard I tried, I could not suppress them. I would often read French and Russian novels of the naturalist school—depicting a gentleman of fine character ruining himself for the sake of such a despicable woman—and be moved to tears like a hysterical female, thinking of my own situation, and throw myself into an abyss of self-doubt, wondering if such was to be my fate.

"In this way, the more reason and wisdom berated me, the stronger my desires grew. As soon as I graduated from school, I joined a club consisting entirely of playboys and spent evenings wherever there were brilliant lights and perfumed women, from theaters to dance halls, from billiard parlors to restaurants; when I look back on those days, I can only say I was insane. To be sure, during the day, while the sun was shining, I retained proper judgment and trusted my own willpower, but once the mist rose in the evening and streetlights began to flicker, that was it. The streetlights turned my conscience, sense of shame, and hope to ashes, while the women who went to and fro under those same lights appeared to me to be nothing but symbols of pleasure.

"I still remember the scene at Broadway around midnight during a snowstorm, when shows were concluding at various theaters. At that time and in that place it is impossible to feel the cold even during a winter evening in the hustle and bustle of numerous people and carriages. Brightly lit with colorful streetlights, the city is like a dream in an enchanted world as far as one can see. Inside the glass doors of hotels' grand halls and restaurants standing side by side, bright lights shine on many couples, with women baring white shoulders and men with neatly smoothed-down hair, while at the tall second-floor windows here and there, you can see silhouettes of men holding billiard cues in one hand as they tirelessly play their late-night games; in the meantime, women constantly enter and exit the painted doors of nearby bars and saloons, trying to seduce men. As I intently watched the scene from the vantage point of an intersection, I would often wonder if there was anything more precious in life, in which any enterprise, any genius, is fated to perish, than such frenzied joys of youth.

"It was while I was leading such a life that I came to know the vaudeville actress named Marianne.

"One evening, after the show was over, two fellow libertines and I entered a restaurant that was frequented by female night birds, and as we looked around with hungry bachelors' eyes, two women at a table recognized one of our group and hailed him.

"We seized the good chance and sat at the women's table and indulged in our usual merrymaking, engaging in silly conversation. At times, however, I would unconsciously shudder at some shockingly vulgar talk, producing within me both swelling self-disgust at my failings and, at the same time, a pervasive sense of emptiness, with the result that I alone would tend to lapse into silence.

"Marianne noticed all this and apparently concluded that I was a novice at pleasure-seeking.

" 'Why are you so gloomy? You should laugh more heartily,' she would say from time to time, as if feeling sorry for me.

"Our merrymaking lasted till past two o'clock at night, and then it was decided that we should take the two women to their homes, as we usually did, but by the time we got out to the street to catch a carriage, by chance my two friends became a threesome with the woman named Nelly, while Marianne and I got on another carriage, just the two of us.

"She said she lived in an apartment near the Hudson River, so we drove up north on Broadway for nearly half an hour, away from the center of the city; the loneliness one felt past midnight was almost frightening, the sound of the horse's hooves echoed in the distant sky, and the night gleam slanting into the carriage window cast a pale, dim light on the woman's powdered face.

"By now Marianne was helplessly resting her head against the backrest, perhaps because she was exhausted from keeping late hours every night; she occasionally opened her heavy eyelids with an effort and glanced sideways at me, forcing a smile on her rouged lips. But she had apparently no energy left even to make an attempt at small talk.

"I remained silent and gazed intently at her profile, deeply inhaling the scent of her face lotion.

"She was perhaps twenty-one or -two years old. She was of a small build, with a long neck, a round face with a pert, pointed chin and large round eyes, and small, firmly set lips that suggested some mocking, ironical air—she was by no means a beauty, not a model for a large oil painting, but she reminded one of a cartoon drawing done in one stroke. Such 'imperfection' or 'incompleteness' is sometimes much more attractive than 'perfection'!

"I lightly pressed my lips on those of the woman, who was dozing off with her head almost tilted back. Her soft, warm breath immediately penetrated my body.

"Marianne opened her large eyes even wider and looked at me for

OLD REGRETS

a moment, but she dozed off again. I saw from the carriage window the silhouettes of the trees lining the street as they moved backward and heard the sound of winds blowing in the faraway sky, but my mind was already wandering in a dreamy state, and once again I brought my face close to hers—when suddenly the sound of the hooves stopped, and the carriage halted in front of a brightly lit entrance.

" 'Marianne!'

"At my voice, she seemed to wake up, as if for the first time; rubbing her eyes with her white muff made of mouse [sic] fur, which had been lying on her lap, she said, 'I was having a nice dream . . . but was it you who kissed me?'

"Ashamed of my impulsive behavior, I looked down without responding, but Marianne laughed merrily and hopped down through the carriage door as the driver just then opened it.

"I saw her to her fifth-floor room, but did not stay there even for five minutes that night and, taking my leave right away, returned home.

"Then the following afternoon, a letter was brought to me by a messenger boy; opening it, I found—oh, what a fragrant whispering of love!—these words:

I have moved to a hotel on — Street to be near you; the other place uptown was inconvenient for love's secret talk. I fell in love with you at first sight. Our love is just like this, and please do not ask why. Ah, until we meet again this evening—*Au revoir* (the ending was written in French). From your loving M.

"My dream of all these years had finally become a reality! My resolution must have been even quicker than hers. Without a moment's delay I rushed to the designated hotel that evening, where we were to live for about a year and a half as if in a dream.

"Determined to savor as many pleasures as are available to humans, sometimes we would kiss each other without interruption except for bringing water and bread to our mouths just to stave off hunger, as if any food or drink might diminish the flavor of our sweet kisses; at other times, we would even embrace each other throughout a wintry night with the windows open, in order to savor the warmth of our youthful blood.

"Yet in this life, even the most fragrant of dreams or the deepest of intoxications in time fades away. Ah, when I recall those times, it is still a mystery, and I cannot explain why I decided to part with her, when we had loved each other so much. It may well be that my educated intellect had gradually awakened me from my bewitched senses, or that the search for fame that is innate in men steadily grew stronger than the dreams of love, or that, just like in the Tannhäuser story, I became weary of the magical charms of the land of pleasure and longed for the purity and lightness of green mountains and streams, or that, having been intoxicated by the heavy scent of a warm room, I wanted once again to feel the crisp coldness of the fresh air outside. . . . Whatever the explanation, I rejoined the world, abandoning Marianne, who begged me to stay.

"I vowed that I would never again indulge in the foolish dreams of my youth, convincing myself that there was something nobler and more permanent in our human destiny than wallowing in pleasure that would vanish with our earthly lives. I must first become a good citizen by starting a proper family! Fortunately, I was from a family well known in America and possessed not a little inheritance from my father, so when I went out among polite society, the world being both small and large, no one knew of my past, and soon I married Josephine, the daughter of a certain judge.

"Thus it was that we spent our honeymoon in Europe and listened together to an opera. . . . I was trying to suppress the tears of sweet memory deep in my heart listening to the *Minnesinger*

Tannhäuser on stage, whose song of lamentation was also my own, while Josephine, who had no way of being aware of it, appeared to be listening attentively in an artificially cultivated attitude of art appreciation without any viewpoint, which is common among women of the upper classes.

"But as you are already aware yourself, the music of the great genius, Wagner (here he glanced at me for a moment), is different from all other music in that it has a mysterious power that never fails to make a strong impact upon its listener.

"Thus it was that as the first act was followed by the large Hall of Song scene of the second act, then by the return of the pilgrims in the third act . . . as we heard all three acts of the opera, I could see that my wife had fallen into a rather pensive mood, as if trying to collect some tangible impressions from her disturbed imagination.

"On my part, I was preoccupied with my own thoughts, so we left the theater, before we knew it, without talking much, and as we did not feel like going to the usual late-night café, we got into a carriage right away and returned to our hotel.

"We were both tired and sank into the chairs in front of the fireplace; after a while my wife looked up at me and asked, with her cheek resting on her hand, 'Really, what was the meaning of that opera?'

"We were in one of the rooms of a large old hotel, where only a lamp with a green shade was lit on a small table at the corner, and not a sound could be heard outside the window. To us Americans, it seemed as if, in this quiet night in an Old World city, we could hear the voices of all sorts of people from the past centuries coming out of nowhere; I looked around in amazement and felt a chill, as if from the walls of an old cathedral, noticing the heavy, dark velvet curtains hanging over the windows and the doorway, matching the dark decorations of the walls and the ceiling and silently draping over the silk carpet.

"I stood up and tried to turn on the beautiful electric light hanging from the ceiling, but my wife stopped me, waving her hand.

Perhaps she thought it would be better to keep the room dimly lit in order to have an intimate conversation. As I returned reluctantly to my chair, my wife asked in a melancholy voice, 'Dear, it really doesn't make sense. I can understand Tannhäuser's feelings as he parts with Venus and returns to his homeland, but why is it that after returning home he should recall his affair with Venus, which he has already repented, and right in front of Elizabeth, the lord's daughter who loves him? I don't understand that kind of feeling.'

"All of a sudden, Tannhäuser's fierce aria, 'Goddess of love, Venus, only to you I speak of love' (*Die gottin der liebe* [sic]), began to sound in my ears, and simultaneously, Marianne's face appeared deep down in my heart. I looked up at the dark corner of the ceiling beyond the reach of the light and answered as if engaging in a monologue in a dream.

" 'That's what life is. No matter how hard we try to forget, we never can. Knowing it is all foolish, we still yield to temptation and agonize over it. In all situations, life would be so much happier but for such contradictions, such irrationalities as the agony of reason versus emotion, or, going a step further, the struggle between body and spirit, the collision between reality and ideals. . . . But this is an unattainable dream, and it seems to me that such agony is life's inescapable, miserable fate.'

"While talking, I felt as if not just my own weak self but the fate of every human being living on earth were so fragile, and I almost wanted to cry aloud like a child.

" 'Isn't that why we turn to God . . . to rely on religion?'

"The voice of my wife sounded as if it came not from a living woman, but from somewhere far away. I answered in a quavering voice, 'But there are times when neither religion nor faith can give us any consolation. . . . For instance, take that Tannhäuser; he goes on a pilgrimage to Rome barefoot, persuaded by the saintly maiden Elizabeth, but he is not forgiven by the Pope and so determines once again to go to the mountain of the heathen goddess Venus. . . . Doesn't that passage satirize religion, which has failed to give hope to someone who has twice erred? Yet in the end, even Tannhäuser, who has been led astray by love in the world of evil, faints in agony at the sight of the chaste maiden Elizabeth's lifeless body, and at that very moment a song announcing his salvation resounds far away. . . . It was Elizabeth's love, the love of a chaste maiden, that redeemed Tannhäuser's soul from Hell.'

"Having finished, I gazed at my wife's face. She was wearing an eggshell-colored evening gown, in décolletage, revealing her white shoulders and broad chest, so that her still figure, looking as if it were floating in the dark room against the pale green light, gave the impression that some noble glow of feminine virtue was going to emit from her.

"Carried away momentarily by a deep emotion, I flung myself at her feet, held her hands with all my might, and shed warm tears on her lap as I exclaimed, 'It is the love of a chaste maiden that redeems us from eternal damnation. Josephine, you are my Elizabeth!'

"To which my wife responded, with a slightly puzzled look and casting her eyes down on my upturned face, 'You mean you too, like Tannhäuser. . . .'

"Ah! Like a Catholic Christian who kneels down in front of the confessional, I felt driven by a suffocating need to confess, and, without thinking of the consequences, confided everything to her about my past.

"And what was the result? Did my wife possess as noble a love as Elizabeth? No way! As soon as she heard my story, her eyes flushed with flames of violent jealousy, a sharp light of rebuke, like a bolt of lightning. . . . Alas, that terrifying glance!

"I came to myself immediately and regretted my rashness in revealing my unsavory secrets on the spur of the moment; I apologized, consoled, and did everything I could, but none of this was sincere, merely an artificial device to cover up my failings, and so the situation grew worse.

" 'How could you have deceived me like this until now?' With these last words, my wife shook off my clinging hands and went into the next room.

"Our honeymoon, life's happiest occasion, now became a most miserable one. The following day we left Vienna for Germany and immediately departed for home from the port of Hamburg, but all through the trip, whether at the dinner table, by a train window, or on the deck of the ship, my wife would not utter a word to me.

"Nevertheless, I continued to entertain the faintest hope, with all my courage and patience, that someday my sincere feelings would get through to my wife and induce her to dissolve her anger. But a woman's heart, once closed, will never open again. Day by day, her face became gaunter and her eyes began to glitter almost frighteningly, so that by the time we reached New York several days later, she looked a totally different person from the Josephine with whom I had set out on our journey.

"So at her request, I reluctantly agreed to a temporary separation, but shortly thereafter she wanted a formal divorce; four years later, I received word that she had remarried. Ah, my Josephine! I have, as a result, been living a life of solitude these twenty years or so. . . ." Having finished his story, Dr. B— stood up from the chair, walked around the room two, three times shaking his hands, then ran, staggeringly, toward the huge grand piano at the corner of the room and immediately began playing, with trembling fingers, the pilgrims' music from *Tannhäuser.*

As the base notes resounded, one, two petals fell down from the white roses in the vase on the piano.

I listened intently with my head bent.

(January 1907)

Rude Awakening

Mr. Saburō Sawazaki pursued fame and fortune by daily promoting himself in his company and was rewarded by being appointed business manager of the New York branch of Company X. So, intoxicated by the vain-sounding words, "going to the West," and swayed by the greedy thought of a certain sum of dollars for living expenses, he left alone for the United States in high spirits, leaving behind his wife and children at his home in Tokyo.

However, there is a difference between what one sees and what one hears. For the first month or two after arriving in New York, Sawazaki virtually lived in a complete daze, but once he became somewhat accustomed to the way the branch office functioned and reached the point where he could walk around the city without a map, he gradually began to experience intolerable boredom.

It is all right so long as he works at his office from nine in the morning until five in the afternoon, but once he goes outside, there is no place to go to but his dreary boarding house, despite the fact that New York is such a big place. It would be all right for the young clerks right out of school to divert themselves by chatting idly through the night, but for someone with some social standing and consciousness of his outward appearance, it is no longer appropriate to exchange pleasantries with just anybody. Of course, he knows that in order to understand a foreign country, it would be useful to socialize in various clubs and hotels where Westerners amuse themselves till late at night, but this option is simply unavailable for financial reasons. Maybe he could try some reading, but alas, for someone who has been exposed to the ways of the world for so many years after leaving school, curiosity about new thought or new knowledge has steadily diminished, and he does not even have the energy to try to understand a foreign country, although there was once a time when he was intrigued by it.

So as the days go by, followed by three more months, then half a year, he is more and more given to feeling the inconvenience of daily life as well as the loneliness of his lot. There are times when he desperately wants to take a morning bath in a Japanese tub or eat grilled eel with a shot of warm *sake*; anyway, his thoughts run to his homeland. Back home he has a wife who willingly does everything he asks, and there was also a time when he secretly kept a mistress; once he starts recalling these things, he feels utterly foolish for having ever left Japan at the mature age of forty, when life had been so comfortable. Every now and then, while he is busy at work or lying exhausted at night, some meaningless thoughts occur to him like a shadow, like smoke, and as soon as he comes to himself, he feels desolate, as if all his strength had suddenly left him.

He is ashamed of his own weakness and also vexed by it; at times he downs a quick whisky or tries to turn his attention calmly to office work, but the sense of forlornness simply will not go away. He feels as if a big hollow had opened up in his heart and a cold wind were blowing into it.

However, Sawazaki neither knew the cause of this sensation nor wanted to know it. To begin with, his wife was merely someone he had married as if hiring a maid, according to common custom; and his home was just a gateway for show, his children, ones to bring up primarily because they had been born. . . . That was all there was to it, and it felt quite unmanly and cowardly to worry about wife or home.

Especially since he had received his education during a transitory period, when it was believed that it was shameful for a man to turn his mind to inward thoughts such as anguish or contemplation; so in the end, he decided to have a hearty laugh, mocking himself and concluding that the vulgar cause of his strange frame of mind was, in short, that he was missing women. So he felt slightly satisfied with himself and with his willpower.

Indeed, it is true that he has been short of women. Ever since he came to New York he has occasionally slipped to the red-light district on his way home from a dinner party with fellow Japanese, but he would always be looked down upon as a "Jap" and so would be unable to linger on beyond the perfunctory, cash-on-delivery service; so his plight is to have nobody but himself to warm up his bed every night. What draws his attention nowadays, wherever he goes in New York, is no longer the twenty-story-high buildings that used to astonish him when he first arrived, but the figures of narrow-waisted and large-hipped women with their breasts pushed up by corsets; from the way they walk to the way they talk, they appear to him irresistibly inviting.

Every day he has been commuting by subway between the business district commonly known as downtown and the quiet, exclusively residential uptown in order to go to his company's office, but the crush in the cars is extraordinary; around nine in the morning and five in the afternoon it almost seems as if all the young men and women from all over New York come and go at these hours.

Men and women, in heaps on the platforms of the station, rush inside the cars like a flood when the train has barely stopped, scrambling for seats, and those few who have managed to sit down immediately start reading the newspaper they have brought with them without a minute's hesitation. Those who have failed to get seats either cling to straps or lean against others' shoulders, pushing or being pushed; no longer having the leisure to mind gentlemanly or ladylike manners, they vie with one another for a chance to grab a seat, by force if necessary.

Following the example of these busy Americans, Sawazaki always holds a newspaper, but when young salesgirls or office girls sit without ceremony very close to him on both sides, not only pressing their soft bodies against his whenever the train jolts as it stops and starts again but also gradually transmitting their body heat, the fine print of the paper simply disappears, and he suddenly feels a slight spasm in his toes, an itchiness at the roots of his hair, and a sort of agony all through his body. Being underground, the air is all the more oppressive, with the smell of sweat characteristic of a meat-eating race added to the crowded condition of the car intoxicating him like a bad wine, compounded by the constant and subtle quivering of the train. Sawazaki falls into a trance as if he were running a fever; what usually happens is that at precisely the moment when he begins to lose self-control, feeling he cannot stay another fifteen minutes in the car without unwittingly grasping the hand of the woman sitting next to him, the train fortunately arrives at the stop where he has to get off, so he rushes out of the car and draws a long breath in the cold air outside.

He repeatedly tells himself that something must be done, but there is no immediate solution. At his boarding house there is a young daughter of marriageable age and also a passably pleasant-looking maid, but the long and short of it is that he does not want to complicate matters. To join the young clerks in the office and to frequent the red-light district is too foolish. Matters have stood thus for almost one and a half years, and it is already the second spring since he came to America, and the month of May when robins gather in the woods.

He has never felt the force of spring so strongly. Gentle breezes penetrate his lungs as if they were tickling him, while the soft sunlight pierces his skin and inflames his blood. All women walking in the streets under the clear blue sky seem without exception to have shed their heavy winter coats, barely concealing their splendid flesh under thin summer clothes as if to torment him, and to expose deliberately their thin silk stockings from the raised light back hems of their skirts in order to mock him.

That morning, being particularly apprehensive of the crowded subway, he went to his office by the elevated train, which was usually less crowded, taking the trouble to make a big detour; as he entered the manager's office where his desk was located, he noticed with a pleasant thrill that an unfamiliar young Western lady was sitting in a corner seat as if waiting for him.

He had completely forgotten about it. It so happened that the old lady, close to fifty years old, who had for a long time worked in the office doing chores like answering the phone, had resigned for personal reasons, and they had hired this young woman through a newspaper advertisement; she was to begin work that day, and that was why she was waiting for his instructions and explanations as to what she was expected to do.

He told her that all she had to do was answer the telephone and, if she had time, help with filing letters written in English, but as he explained these things to her, he felt strangely happy that from this time on he would be able to keep this young woman by his side and have her assist him in his office work. In contrast to the time when that wrinkled, gray-haired, and bespectacled old lady had worked here, it felt as though the whole office had brightened up.

He could not take his eyes off her profile even for five minutes while working in his office. She must be at least twenty-six or twenty-seven years of age. Plump and not tall, and of passable looks, her general appearance, with her black hair parted in the middle and rolled up around the crown as if she were wearing a sports cap and neatly clad from head to toe in off-the-rack clothes bought at some emporium, emanated strong magical power because of its very lack of grace and dignity; she was, in short, an example of the type of women who are remembered for a long time by men who have just happened to pass by them on the street. Sawazaki tried to break the ice and become better acquainted with her by starting a conversation on one pretext or another, but unlike the stereotypical office girls who stuffed their mouths with candy throughout the day and spent their time laughing with anybody, she was exceedingly reticent, probably feeling ill at ease about everything. After all, this was her first experience working in a Japanese company, and all she was willing to let out was that her name was Mrs. Denning and that she had been living in a boarding house by herself since she was widowed about a year ago. Sometimes she even sat pensively with her elbows on the desk.

Three weeks went by, without her showing the least sign of having become familiar with her new surroundings. Then she started arriving late for work in the morning, and toward the end of last week, she began to stay away from work—due to some illness, he was told. Sawazaki felt somehow disappointed. She had told him she was ill, not that she was going to quit, but all the same, he suspected that perhaps she did not want to work among unfamiliar Japanese. . . . She would soon send word one way or another, he thought, and he waited all day the following Monday, and again on Tuesday, but he did not hear from her.

On the evening of that day, he had just started walking along Amsterdam Avenue after dinner to run some errands; it is a broad street but actually more like a seedy boulevard lined exclusively with tenement houses and unattractive retail stores. It was twilight in stuffy, windless late May; even though streetlights had begun to be lit, the surrounding areas were still bright, enveloped in a purple haze. From wide-open windows and doorways here and there slovenly housewives with uncombed hair and the faces of prettily made-up young girls, in contrast to their shabby clothes, could be seen, and along the streets where greengrocers, fruit merchants, and such kept stalls, little boys and girls were playing noisily.

Recalling the street scenes in Yanagichō or Akagishita [in Tokyo] for no particular reason, Sawazaki just happened to stop in front of a stall, when a woman came out from a nearby doorway. It was—most unexpectedly—that Mrs. Denning.

Taken completely by surprise, Sawazaki accosted her, calling her name without ceremony.

The woman, not a little surprised herself, stood still on the spot, obviously reluctantly, as she could not run away and hide herself. But she averted her face and was quite afraid of speaking out.

"How is your illness. . . . Have you already recovered?"

"Yes, thank you."

"Do you live around here?"

"Yes, I rent a room on the third floor here."

"How about coming to work tomorrow?"

"I am so sorry; you must have been so busy."

"It cannot be helped if one is sick. . . . By the way, you were just going out for a walk? If you don't mind, let me accompany you part of the way."

Approached this way, she could not quite refuse his offer, and so she walked aimlessly next to Sawazaki toward wide, tree-lined Broadway. This far north on Broadway, only quiet apartment buildings stand on both sides, and the traffic is not very heavy. The water and the trees of the Hudson riverbank can be seen through the buildings.

"Let's walk up to the riverbank. The deep green color of the leaves of those trees really suggests the summer has come, doesn't it?"

They walked about one block and sat down on a bench under some trees. For a while they sat quietly, watching the river as it changed its appearance from twilight into the beginning of the evening, but then Sawazaki said abruptly, as if he had just remembered, "You will be coming to work tomorrow, won't you?" The woman remained silent, as if she had not heard him, but then she seemed to have made up her mind and said, "Actually, I was thinking about leaving."

"Why? Are you not happy with the work?"

"No, no. It is not that," she protested emphatically. "It is simply that I don't feel up to it, perhaps because of my illness."

"What kind of illness?"

The woman seemed at a loss for an answer and looked down without a word. Sawazaki pressed on, "Is this the first time that you have worked at an office?"

"No, not really. For a long time before I got married I used to work for various stores and companies."

"Then you must be accustomed to office work."

"I am afraid not. For three years or so after I got married, I simply didn't go out and stayed put at home, so I guess I became rather lazy. After my husband died, it became necessary for me to go back to work but . . . well, what can I say, I seem to have lost my staying power," she said, smiling sadly.

"But the work you do at my office isn't really strenuous. Besides, you are the only Western woman, so you don't have to socialize. . . . Couldn't you somehow put up with it?"

"You are quite right. There isn't a nicer place than your office anywhere in New York. That is why I really wanted to be employed by you, but somehow every morning . . ." The woman unwittingly closed her mouth and blushed.

It was already night all around, the kind of summer night that is dark even though it looks as if it holds light, and light even though it seems dark. Realizing that the young new leaves of a tall linden tree standing behind the bench intercepted the starlight and streetlights, casting a dark shadow upon the couple, she seemed to have become somewhat reassured and glanced furtively at him.

Even though poetry and song were alien to him, the mere fact that he was sitting there, on a bench with no other people, close by her even if he was not holding her hand, in an indescribably poetic night of beautiful young leaves, made Sawazaki feel so happy that choosing a subject of conversation was the least of his worries.

"What did your husband do?"

"He worked for an insurance company."

"You must miss him, for many reasons."

"Yes, of course. . . . For a time I was totally at a loss as to what to do."

Whenever the river breeze gently caressed their hair, the young new leaves whispered all around. The sound of the piano being played in a house nearby could also be heard. The woman became steadily more relaxed; for no particular reason, she felt as if she wanted to talk to someone, just anybody, about personal things that she would not discuss during the day even with her closest friends. Maybe this was a case of confiding one's life under the gentle stars of a summer night. . . . She leaned one elbow against the back of the bench and said, as if in a monologue, "It was so much fun while my husband was living!"

Sawazaki had been in this country for more than a year and was used to Westerners' talking uninhibitedly about intimate matters. So he responded, assuming an all-serious air, "I can see that," and asked, "How did you get married?"

"Well, he and I commuted to work on the same train every morning, and so we got to know each other and began meeting on Saturdays or Sundays. . . . Soon we decided to live together. He at first insisted that both of us continue to work until we had accumulated some savings, but I really hated the idea of getting up early in the morning and sitting properly in a chair till evening. . . . Actually, that was why I had wanted desperately to find some kind person to take care of me, and so I managed to have my way. For me, there is really nothing more painful than getting up in the morning when I am still so sleepy. I do think it is criminal to force people to get out of a warm bed to wash up and get dressed, especially in cold weather.

My husband, seeing this, gave up and left me in bed as he went to work every morning. But in return, I never insisted, like other New York women, that I must go to the theater simply because it was a Saturday night, costing so much money.

"Once you are home all day long, after getting up late in the morning, it is such a hassle to take the trouble to change and do other things in order to go to the theater; I would much prefer lying on a couch, reading some novel. So in the end my husband said it was nicer this way, as it didn't cost money."

Even though a bit put out by this exceedingly open talk, Sawazaki kept throwing in words of agreement in order not to interrupt the conversation. The woman, a typically talkative Western lady, became bolder and said, "That's not all; my husband would tell me . . . 'you look your prettiest all mussed up than with neatly combed hair or properly dressed up.' . . ." Laughing, she continued, "When I got mad at him for making fun of me, he would tell me earnestly that I was not like a typical American woman who was made for work. He said I was more like a Turkish or Persian beauty wearing a gauzy dress and daydreaming with a faraway look, listening to the water falling in a fountain in a large house."

She kept on like this, uttering one silly trifle after another, but presently stood up, asking, like an afterthought, "What time is it now?" Sawazaki did not want to detain her and said, "Maybe tomorrow. . . . Do come to the office. I'll be waiting for you."

There they parted, but when the following day came, he waited in vain for the woman, who sent him a telegram saying that she really had to resign because of her illness.

How impertinent . . . treating me like a fool because I am Japanese! As was the wont of the Japanese in America, Sawazaki became angry, reacting with a peculiarly patriotic defensiveness, but it was not something to fight about, and soon he hired an office boy of fifteen or sixteen to replace her. Yet as a week, and then ten days, passed, the event of that summer evening, when they had talked sitting together on a bench by the Hudson River, began feeling like fiction, something that could not have happened to a person like him. Especially when he put together the fact that she had personally complained to him about her lonely life after her husband's death and had ended up telling him openly about how she would look right out of bed, things that a woman would normally consider private secrets, he could not help wondering if the woman had not been dropping hints in order to entice him. Realizing that perhaps he had missed a golden opportunity through his ignorance of it, he felt all the more regretful, and in no time he began feeling jittery as if his insides had been torn up. So one night he stole his way to the aforementioned Amsterdam Avenue, climbed up to the third floor of the familiar building, and knocked on a likely door.

Someone stuck his face out, a big man who looked like a workman, around fifty, wearing only a vest without a coat; he had apparently been having his supper, for he was chewing something with his mouth closed, and bread crumbs were visible at the edge of his beard.

"Does Mrs. Denning live here?"

Hearing the question, the big man looked around toward the hallway and loudly called out the name of a woman, probably his wife.

"Hey, here's someone again looking for that broad. Say something to him, will ya?"

This time a bleary-eyed old hag with a protruding chin appeared on the scene and peered at Sawazaki suspiciously, but finally said, "I'm sorry, but that woman is no longer at our place. Yesterday morning we evicted her. Are ya also some relative of hers?"

He couldn't understand why, but her tone was extremely spiteful. Sawazaki was perplexed but said, barely keeping his cool, "I am the manager of the company that hired her."

"Indeed."

"She kept saying she was sick and wouldn't report to work, so I came to see what was going on. . . . What do you mean, you evicted her?"

"Sir, I guess you were also taken in by her," said the old hag, and abruptly changing her tone, started talking at great length without being asked.

"Sir, she is the most brazen creature around. When she had a husband they lived just above here, on the fifth floor, but she was slovenly, looking like a rotten prostitute all day long; while the young married wives in the neighborhood all worked hard in stores or did side jobs at home, that woman alone was a lazy bum, not even cleaning her own place. Then, after her husband died from a sudden illness, just at the end of the year before last, she became quite helpless. Complaining that the rent for her room on the fifth floor was too high and that the room was too spacious for one person, she moved into our place, as we happened to have a vacant room. For the first half-year or so, she punctually paid at least her rent, maybe because she had some savings, but then she gradually became cunning and started asking for a postponement again and again; not only that, whenever she got a decent job, she would tire of it in two or three weeks and quit, so we were worried that we would never be able to collect the rent if matters continued this way. But we couldn't just turn her out, as we had known her from the time she was married, and we didn't know what to do."

"But then, it was two nights ago," continued the workmanlike husband who had been standing by. "Two nights ago, she must finally have run out of money, for she brought in a man from somewhere and turned our house into a fine whorehouse. Actually, even before that, we had suspected something like it, but we didn't say a word since we didn't have any proof. But the night before yesterday, it was one, two o'clock past midnight, so it couldn't have been just one of her friends, and I said, our place here, it may not look like much, but at least it is the home of a workman who earns money with his own hands and I refuse to house a whore. The following morning we drove her out, telling her we didn't want the overdue rent . . . we just kept some of her valuable clothes and appliances as security."

"Do you know where she went?" sighed Sawazaki despite himself.

"How do I know? Maybe when evening comes she'll be hanging out in some bar around here."

With a heavy heart Sawazaki climbed down the stairs and went outside, but now that he had found out the woman's story of depravity, he regretted even more that he had not gotten the hint the last time and missed a golden opportunity; he stomped his feet on the pavement and gritted his teeth.

There is nothing in the world that has a more vexing and bitter aftertaste than a missed chance. As time went by, he would on occasion remember the woman, but he never had another opportunity to see her.

In the meantime, three years passed since he came to America, and the moment of his return to Japan was now only a couple of weeks away.

He was drinking Masamune-brand *sake* in a room at the club with a few Japanese with whom he used to play cards, and who perhaps wanted to give him a send-off party, getting drunk and engaging in endless talk, when a gentleman, an enthusiastic collector of nude photos despite the fact that he had daughters and grandchildren back home, showed off a few samples, saying they were true masterpieces he had obtained lately at a certain place.

Sawazaki casually took a look at them and realized that, even though the poses were all indecent and she looked different, the face was that of the unforgettable Denning woman.

Ah, so it meant that the woman didn't care how she made money so long as it was done easily, and would occasionally even pose for a photographer. He trembled with the renewed sense of intense regret, but unfortunately he never saw her again before returning to his country.

From this time on, whenever people would ask his opinion of the United States, Mr. Sawazaki would always conclude his remarks with the following pronouncement: "There is no country as morally corrupt as the United States. Because of the difficulties of earning a living, it can be said that there isn't a single chaste woman; it is not a country fit for a gentleman to live in for a long period of time."

(April 1907)

Ladies of the Night

I

Broadway at Forty-second Street: it is where people have fun every night till the small hours of the morning, in large and small theaters, hotels, restaurants, clubs, even in saloons, billiard halls, and cafés, all within reach of the New York Times building, which soars above them like a tower. Even for those who are tired of such ordinary pleasures, there are not a few places to go to indulge.

There is a small theater called the New York that always displays many billboards of alluring dancers in leotards at its entrance and is known for having sellout crowds even during the hot summer season when most theaters close. When you turn its corner, you suddenly hit upon a quiet alley.

This is the back street that connects Broadway to Sixth Avenue, where elevated trains are running, and you immediately notice the stage entrance to the Hudson Theater, which stands next to the New York, back to back. Diagonally across is the entrance to the not unattractive Lyceum, and a little distance away, there are two or three spiffy hotels where actresses and dancers bring their customers late at night and stay over, each having an entranceway with a glassed-in roof and a huge potted plant. Otherwise, apart from three or four modern, tall apartment houses like those you see uptown, both sides of the street contain only five-story rental buildings built in the style of sixty or seventy years ago; almost all their windows have small signs saying LADIES TALOR [sic], PALMIST FROM INDIA, MUSIC LESSONS, etc., together with advertisements for rooms for rent and an occasional red lantern of a Chinese restaurant.

This alley is almost deserted during the day, but from dusk onward, women begin to appear, walking back and forth, showing off their high-heeled shoes beneath the hems of their long lace skirts and suggestively swinging their hips like waterfowl; past midnight, the area is filled from one end to the other with small carriages occupied by couples.

Every young member of one club or another knows that amid this row of rental buildings there is a place for fun.

To be sure, the city police of New York are said to be strict, so there is nothing at the entrance to draw attention; however, some know by word of mouth where it is by the street number on the door, and those who don't can be taken there, even if against their will, by drivers of stagecoaches in the main street, in anticipation of a generous tip.

It is, after all, an old rental building, so its outward appearance is dilapidated, but once you enter, the first room you find is a large guest lounge consisting of three rooms, each divided by velvet curtains; both the floor covering and the walls are dark lobster-red, and the ceiling is a slightly lighter shade with a gold-colored arabesque pattern. The chairs and sofas are of the same heavy lobster-red velvet upholstery; over them hangs a large gold-colored floral lamp, with the result that all together it looks somewhat solemn, like a scene from a provincial theatrical performance suggesting the palace of a certain duke.

Covering the entire surface of the wall of the front lounge is a huge painting of many women, stark naked, embracing each other as they are about to fall prey to wild animals in a scene depicting the persecution of Christians in the Roman era; in the next room, there is

LADIES OF THE NIGHT

also a huge painting in which four or five naked nymphs, almost life-size, bathe in a stream under some trees, frolicking with a swan. And at each corner of the rooms, artificial palm trees are planted in pots and spread their green leaves like real trees.

The Madam of this establishment is a Mrs. Stanton. Nobody knows where she came from, but it is rumored that from early on, while she was working as a maid at a whorehouse, she learned the tricks of the trade even without realizing it; she then became the so-called housekeeper for the whole household. She saved a small fortune through working at one whorehouse after another in Chicago, Philadelphia, and Boston, then came to New York and started the present establishment single-handedly, where she has been engaged in this business for over thirty years.

She is very fat, and her waist, for example, looks almost as enormous as a marble column in a hotel lounge. She has a square face with a large mouth and small eyes, and her hair is completely white, but she always powders her face and sometimes even pencils her straight eyebrows.

She boasts that, while she has liked men since her youthful days, she hasn't spent any money on them, her hobby being to collect jewelry. Indeed, she has rings on all five fingers, and while talking with others, she has the habit of placing her hand squarely on her lap and polishing the jewels incessantly with her handkerchief. Besides the rings, what Madam cherishes as much as her life is a pair of diamond earrings, said to be worth two thousand dollars; but it draws too much attention to dangle them from her earlobes every day. Once, on her way back from a dance, she was followed by a hold-up man on three separate occasions so that, frightened out of her wits, she has since kept them at the bottom of a double-locked trunk. There is not a single woman in the household who doesn't know this famous story.

The room facing the street on the second floor serves as Madam's living room as well as bedroom; from its ceiling hang a Japanese-made parasol and a round red lantern, and near the doorway there is a double screen with a golden pheasant embroidered on black fabric, which also is apparently made in Japan; all these shades of Oriental colors create an amazing incongruity against the old-fashioned agalmatolite mantelpiece and the large brass bed.

At the center of the room, there is a small table on which the *Journal* and an illustrated newspaper called the *New York Press* are always on display, as well as a magnificent parrot cage. The parrot inside has resided in this house for ten years already and has learned every vulgar word that is used only in this society; from morning till night, it pecks at the perch and screeches shrilly, while in the armchair near the cage, Tom, the pet dog as small as a mouse, wiggles his ears and waits for someone to come and hold him.

Every afternoon after one o'clock, Madam finally wakes up; first she picks Tom up and kisses him, then she scolds the screaming parrot, has her breakfast that is brought in by the Negro maid, reads the papers, and spends the rest of the day caring for the plants near the windows, waiting for the arrival of six o'clock in the evening. That is finally the beginning of the day for this household. As soon as the maid gives a signal by sounding the gong, Madam slowly and deliberately goes down to the dining room in the basement, holding Tom; she sits down with an air of importance at the head of the table and is joined by women who noisily emerge from their rooms on the second, third, and fourth floors where they have been sleeping and come downstairs, wearing sandals and loose gowns, looking as if wondering what time it is; they, five in all, then take their seats.

To the right of Madam are, first, Iris, then Blanche, and then Louise; to her left are Hazel and Josephine.

Each of the five has her own history and personality.

The first one, Iris, is of Irish descent and is said to have been born in Kentucky. Perhaps around twenty-three or -four years of age, she has a round face with a short chin that is typical of her race;

her blue eyes are small, and her hair is shiny blond. Her sloping shoulders suggest something frail about her, but her beautiful shape from her waist to her legs is a matter of pride, and she produces as evidence the fact that she has twice been an artist's model. According to her, her family is quite well-to-do in the country, and she attended a Catholic school till she was sixteen or seventeen; sometimes, when least expected, she is heard humming a hymn, as if she is remembering something. By and large she seems to be of a subdued personality; she neither becomes particularly boisterous while drinking with a man nor looks too depressed even when stricken by sickness or anything else.

In contrast, Blanche, who sits next to her, has neither parents nor siblings and is a naturally loose woman, having been brought up in the gutters of New York in the company of dogs. She is said to be already thirty, but she is quite small, so that once she applies heavy make-up to her emaciated, sallow complexion and wears a red ribbon filled with false hair around her forelock, she transforms herself into a young girl of sixteen or seventeen and can easily fool a man in darkness. She is a boozer and, what is more, light-fingered, having, it is said, once pinched a customer's money and been sent to jail on "the Island"; they say that she even has two Negro lovers, one a vaudevillian and the other a hansom carriage driver. Thus she is disliked by her coworkers all the more because of their feelings as white people.

Now, the third one, Louise, is a plump Parisienne with dark hair and eyes; although she is said to be well along in years, she always looks young, perhaps thanks to her indigenous skill in make-up. Two years ago she came to the United States with her lover, having heard that this was a country of money; she is willing to do anything for money, even become a plaything of men, but on the other hand, she apparently does not spend her own money, not even on a bottle of wine, which explains why her companions don't speak well of her either.

As for Hazel at the left, she is a sturdy, big woman from British Canada; from her bosom, which looks as if it held a couple of balls, to her stout upper arms and shoulders, she gives the impression of extreme fleshiness so that when you approach her, it is as though you can feel the smell of her skin and the heat inside her body. Her round face is disproportionately small for her body, her mouth is slack, and her eyes are dull, as if she might once have been engaged in milking cows in some pasture, so that all the girls look down on her as a good-natured dupe; but once she gets drunk with whisky, they become fearful of her strong arms and try to humor her, half teasingly.

The last one, Josephine, is probably the best in the house for both her figure and her looks. She is just over twenty years of age. Her parents emigrated from Italy's Sicily island and are said to be still operating a roadside greengrocer in the Italian section on the East Side. Her full cheeks are pink and evoke the beautiful women of Southern Europe, her eyes have a moist luster like black gems, and her long eyebrows are as if they had been drawn.

From the time she was fourteen or fifteen, she began to sing popular songs at vaudevilles and beer gardens on the East Side to great acclaim; then she became a chorus girl and for a time appeared on Broadway, but she fell ill from debauchery and lost her precious voice. She did recover it after she left the hospital, but by then she had given in to laziness and steadily sank into the world of prostitution. Still, she has not yet experienced the kind of trouble that would induce her to look more deeply into the grim realities of life, nor has she fallen desperately in love with a man; rather, she just loves wearing pretty dresses and fooling around with young men, and for someone her age, for whom anything wicked is fun, her current frivolous life is a rather ideal situation. Except when she is sleeping or eating, she continues to sing popular songs day and night, as she once did professionally, or else screams with laughter over nothing in particular and wanders all over the house.

Not a single day passes without these five having a fight, but, like the passing of a storm, after an hour or so they forget everything and become friends again and spend the day backbiting the others.

After finishing their dinner, which always consists of roast beef or else roast pork, potatoes, cranberry sauce, celery, and afterward a pie wedge or pudding for dessert, each of the company returns to her room and spends a long time making up her face; then at ten o'clock, as Madam rings every doorbell in the house, they all come downstairs to the parlor and wait for their prospective customers, thus beginning what they call business hours, as befits women of a mercantile nation.

At this appointed hour, the five housemates are joined by four or five women who come from elsewhere through special arrangements with Madam, so that all together more than ten people take up various positions in the parlor, some dressed like respectable women in white waists wearing accessories around their necks, others in long evening gowns trimmed with an abundance of lace and even holding fans, as if they were at a nobleman's ball.

2

Past eleven o'clock, shows are ending at nearby theaters, and the streets become momentarily very noisy with people's footsteps, the roar of carriages, and the cries of drivers, but in no time quiet returns; it is between midnight and one or two o'clock that people leaving restaurants, clubs, and billiard parlors file in. Just now, a party of three young men, probably clerks from a shop somewhere, has been taken upstairs to various rooms on the second and third floors by Blanche, the light-fingered one, French-born Louise, and Flora, who is the wife of a streetcar conductor who has two children already but comes to work only at night to make money by mutual agreement with her husband; then, just after that, the doorbell rings again.

Marie, the Negro slave-servant,* opens the door. A fat, gray-haired man who looks like a manager is followed by three who are probably country merchants. Sensing that they are promising customers, Madam herself greets them and shows them into the front parlor.

The managerlike man pretends to be above such things at his age, as if he is doing this for the sake of friendship, but as he looks around with deliberate composure at the group of women before even sitting down, his eyes quickly catch sight of Josephine, the young ex-performer. Thinking he has stumbled upon a major find, he immediately discards his sense of shame, advances toward her to sit on the same sofa, draws the woman's hands into his lap, and says, "Let's have some champagne."

The other three from the country appear to have been flabbergasted to see, as soon as they entered the parlor, the huge depiction of the persecution of nude Christians hanging on the front wall—a religious painting, of all things, in the least expected place—and sit down in a row, silently gazing at the picture for the moment, as if they were visitors at an art museum. Besides the women who are already there, two or three others come out from the adjoining rooms, drawing the curtains that divide the rooms on one side, and they sit down in chairs surrounding the three; the Negro slave brings out two large bottles of champagne and pours it out into glasses all around.

"Here's to our happy occasion." The white-haired manager raised his glass first, took a sip, then pressed it to Josephine's lips and let her gulp it down.

Madam lingered around, holding her glass, then, looking toward the three, began, "If any of them suits you," to find out if the customers had decided, but the three were a bit self-conscious and merely smirked. . . . Just then, someone was saying, "Good-bye, see

---

*In later editions, "Negro slave-servant" is changed to "Negro servant."

you soon," in the hallway outside the parlor. Following the sound of kissing, three women entered the parlor, having sent off their second-floor customers. Blanche was humming a tune and swinging her hips, Louise was mindful of some loose locks and smoothing down her hair, and Flora was looking down in an affected manner.

The latter two proceeded to sit down in chairs at the far corner, but Blanche, seeing that there were customers, disregarded her colleagues, approached one of them while still humming, and abruptly sat on his lap. Saying, "May I?" she eyed him seductively and, taking a puff from the cigarette held between her fingers, slowly blew the smoke into his face.

At this, the man, who had finally gotten bolder after gulping down a glass of champagne, took the cigarette from the woman's mouth with one hand and puffed at it, while grabbing her waist with the other so that she would not slide off his lap.

Watching this, one of the other men, although still sober, no longer hesitated and leaned his shoulder against the blonde Iris, judging her to be the most docile of the women. The remaining one, apparently a rapacious type who wasn't particularly choosy, was gazing from right to left and then from left to right, not at the woman's faces as much as at the women's raised bosoms hidden underneath their dresses and at their white shoulders exposed by their ball gowns, and apparently indulging in indecent thoughts.

At this point, judging that the company had reached a definite decision, first Hazel, the large woman from Canada, and then the others left their seats and one after another withdrew to the adjoining parlor beyond the curtain; but as soon as she sat down, Hazel venomously blurted out, "I don't believe it! That thief Blanche. . . . She comes in late, and she has the gall to sit in the lap of someone who isn't even her regular customer and fool around. I'm thoroughly disgusted." The woman beside her agreed, saying, "Well, what do you expect from a shameless slut who has nigger lovers?"

Every night it is like this, starting with a scramble for customers, which continues into the following day and becomes a subject of gossip, resulting ultimately in a heated quarrel as the object of the gossip will not remain quiet.

For now, however, gossip in the adjoining room was happily drowned out by the heavy laughter of the intoxicated man. Blanche seated herself astride the man's lap, dangled her legs in silk stockings, grabbed his shoulders with both hands, and, swaying her upper body as if rowing a boat, urged him, "Let's go upstairs now," as if wishing to settle the business quickly.

"Time is money" being the maxim that sustains the lives of women in this mercenary capital, in order to make as much money in as little time as possible, they should not waste their time at the whim of a single man. For Madam, however, money spent on drinks becomes all her income; thus any customer who looks like a drinker must be detained as long as possible to sell him liquor. The result is that some conflict of interest cannot be avoided between Madam and the women who constantly complain . . . for instance, "Thanks to me, five bottles of champagne were uncorked last night, yet Madam tells me she cannot even wait a single week for my rent."

Madam had just poured a second round of champagne and begun playing the piano to keep the people entertained; then she called on Josephine, the Italian, who had for some time been keeping company with the gray-haired manager on the sofa. "Josephine, sing something for us." The former chorus girl, being young and not so greedy, liked to make merry with anybody, and so she began singing at the top of her voice to the clapping of her hands, and the manager sang along as well.

> I like your way and the things you say,
> I like the dimples you show when you smile,

I like your manner and I like your style;
.......I like your way!

Blanche became a little impatient and, for someone who was a hag over thirty years of age, said in an affectedly sweet voice, "I'm drunk and feel awful," and she pressed her face against her client's face and took a big breath, while Iris, imitating this, grabbed her man's fingers and said, "Let's go upstairs and talk, all right?"

The manager, watching the scene, said, "Look, they are getting pretty chummy over there. As for us, Madam, shall we open one last bottle?"

Madam leaped at the opportunity, jumped away from the piano, and called out, "Marie, quick, our guest is asking for champagne."

Even Blanche gave up hope at this point and said feebly, as if she were resigned to her fate, "You are so energetic," while the manager, pleased with himself, puffed out thick smoke from his cigar and said, "I'm always like this if I have wine, women, and money. . . . Josephine, won't you sing that song again for me?"

I like your eyes, you are just my size,
I'd like you to like me as much as you like,
I like your way!

At that moment, the doorbell rang again. Marie, who had just brought out the last bottle of champagne, rushed out to the hallway, asking Madam to excuse her and to serve the champagne herself.

One could hear a number of customers noisily entering the adjoining parlor, followed by the large Hazel and the French Louise with her funny accented English . . . then a husky male voice shouting, "Got no money for champagne," could be heard.

3

There was a steady flow of customers till, past three o'clock in the morning, it stopped for the moment.

All the women, though accustomed to staying up every evening, look a little tired around their eyes; as they have had champagne, beer, or highballs indiscriminately, their heads feel heavy from a hangover that has crept up on them. Even Josephine, the cheerful one, no longer has the strength to sing popular songs and is slightly yawning, with one elbow resting on the piano, while Blanche in a corner pretends to be pulling up her stockings but is probably trying to figure out how much money she has stuffed into them.

Iris, Hazel, Louise, and Flora are all sitting on the sofa in a row like so many birds bunched up close together, and lean against each other's shoulders; they look as if they have completely exhausted any topic of conversation or gossip. It seems that they are even tired of their incessant smoking; they look at one another, and if one of them blurts out, "Oh, I'm starving," this is not followed by somebody else proposing, "Let's go and buy something."

All of a sudden, the doorbell arouses the household from its collective fatigue.

As if to enliven the company, Madam goes to the door herself, without waiting for Marie; two men appear in silk hats, fur-lined coats, and white gloves holding canes, unmistakably suggesting gentlemen of fashionable society, so Madam leads them reverentially to the front parlor and calls out, "Everybody, we have visitors."

The large Hazel stood up first and, before stepping into the next room, took a peek from the dividing curtain to see if these were promising customers, as was the girls' wont, but then immediately turned around with a perplexed look and shushed them all.

"Is that it?" They apparently understood right away and looked at each other, while Blanche stepped forward, looked through the curtains, and, saying, "Yes, it is," stealthily returned to where the rest were. "They are detectives. And wearing evening dresses, for heaven's sake. . . . Doesn't Madam notice? I remember their faces very well."

At these words the women—although they were used to a life of prostitution, they had been burned once or twice when the New York police sent their detectives, disguised as customers, to catch culprits engaged in selling alcohol without paying taxes and in prostitution at least once a month—fled on tiptoe, coolly and calmly, from the hallway to the basement dining room; some slipped into the neighbors' yards from the rear garden, while others lingered on at the basement entrance, ready to escape into the streets if it became necessary.

Madam called them twice, but nobody showed up, so, typical of this society where people are quick to understand, she sized up the situation. When one of the men ordered champagne, she picked up a large bottle, poured it out, and, saying, "Stop playing jokes . . . it's not nice," laughed as she grabbed as much as a couple of twenty-dollar bills from her stocking and thrust them into his pocket.

The two detectives now appeared satisfied and stood up, saying, "Ha, ha, ha, ha. We are just doing our job. See you soon."

"Do please."

Exchanging such odd greetings, Madam finally sent them off and banged the door shut. Dropping her heavy body on the parlor sofa like a trundled keg, she shouted in a loud voice, "God damn it!"

For a while after this, the whole household remained quiet, but pretty soon Tom, the pet dog, stuck his head out from between the curtains, tinkling the bell that was attached to his neck and eyeing Madam with a worried look. He was followed by Blanche, who came up from the dining room, peeped into the parlor just like Tom, and called out, "Madam."

But Madam was apparently too distressed to answer.

"Madam, at least they went away without making too much of a fuss."

"Of course," said Madam irritatingly. "I let them have three or four twenty-dollar bills."

"Three or four twenty-dollar bills . . ." Blanche, very nimble-minded, was certain she was exaggerating and said, affectedly, "I am so sorry."

At this moment, those who had fled to the backyard noisily ran back into the parlor, thinking the danger had passed and shouting, "It's so cold, we could freeze to death," at which Blanche said, again exaggerating, "Madam says she has let them have seven or eight twenty-dollar bills."

"Oh, my God." Everybody looked at Madam's face.

Madam seemed to have become all the more disgusted by the women's expressions of sympathy and amazement; she abruptly raised her reclining body from the sofa in a resolute way, and told them, looking at all of them, "It's nothing to be surprised at. I've been in this business for fifty years. A glance is enough to tell me if a guy will leave quietly for just five dollars, or if he will shut his eyes for ten dollars. . . . You need proper training to figure these things out. I told you, I've been doing this for fifty years, since when President Roosevelt, even President McKinley, were mere kids."

"Fifty years," someone repeated, and another asked, "Wasn't even Carnegie a penniless laborer then?"

"Quite possibly. Even I didn't have a single ring on my fingers in those days."

The company was at a loss for words. Madam then haughtily straightened herself up and started recounting her past. "Indeed, fifty years ago I didn't have a single ring . . ."; then, looking as if tremendously proud of her current success at having overcome life's hardships, she quietly stood up and went upstairs, giving the women a contemptuous look.

The swishing of her skirt had hardly disappeared when Josephine, the simple-minded one, no longer able to contain herself, started laughing, tumbling about on the sofa.

"Since when President Roosevelt was a mere kid," Blanche mimicked Madam's speech. Hazel added, "Not a single ring fifty years ago . . ." and everyone burst out laughing.

The clock chimed in some room. Flora, the streetcar conductor's wife, listened and, turning to Julia, who also came to work from elsewhere, said, "It's already four o'clock. It's been such an unlucky night. I'm going home."

"True. Let's go."

The two of them went to the third floor, threw off their night attire, changed into neat street clothes, put on their hats, straightened out their veils and scarves, and lightly knocked on Madam's door, saying, "It's past four, so we are going. See you tomorrow evening. Bye."

They pattered down the stairs and, calling out from the hallway, "Good . . . bye . . ." stretching the words, went out to the street; there they bumped into Louise's lover, who had come from France with her and worked as an automobile mechanic.

"Good evening," he greeted them, removing his sports cap with a strange European gesture. "How is Louise?"

"She's in the parlor. Going to have a good time, are you?"

Every night around five o'clock [A.M.] is the time when these lovers file in, and the beau climbed up the stone steps and rang the doorbell.

"Oh, it's so cold!" Flora and Julia shivered in a theatrical manner and started out toward Sixth Avenue. It was already the middle of December, and although the sound of the city's streetcars, which ran throughout the night, could be heard incessantly, coming and going like waves that dash against the shore, some profound sadness permeated their bodies; Broadway, spread out beyond the theater at the corner, was still brightly lit, as earlier in the evening, but its streetlights looked paler than the moon, chillier than water, making the great city appear more lonesome now than at any other time.

The two drew closer together as if by common consent and walked for thirty feet or so, when from behind two or three carriages waiting for customers in front of the aforementioned hotel where chorus girls and others stayed overnight, a man appeared, with a large pipe stuck in his mouth.

"Aren't you rather early tonight?"

Julia recognized him against the flickering light in the area and said, "Well, it's been a long time."

The man was Flora's husband, the streetcar conductor, who always waited for his wife in this area, still wearing his regulation cap and uniform, at the end of his shift at four o'clock. Flora lightly kissed him and said, "There was a police raid, so we thought it was a bad omen and decided to call it quits at four o'clock."

"Is that right? But was the business good?" asked the shameless husband. The wife, equally unperturbed, replied as she looked back at Julia, "Well, it wasn't much, but still we were all pretty busy, weren't we?"

"Yeah," she nodded. "But the best one's still Blanche. I can't do like that."

"Flora, you'd better learn from her."

"Don't tell me, it's none of your business."

"I'm telling you out of kindness."

"You are?" Flora hit the man in the face with her muff.

"Ha, ha, ha, ha. Don't be angry."

They reached Sixth Avenue and stopped in front of a bar that was unlit outside but kept open all through the night.

Julia's husband was a waiter at this bar. As Flora and her husband said, "Well, so long," and started to go, Julia stopped them, saying, "You don't have to hurry, do you? Can't you come in and see my darling for a change?"

"Oh, sure."

They pushed open an inconspicuous door at the back, with a sign marked FAMILY ENTRANCE, and went in, Julia leading the way.

There would still be time before daybreak on a winter night. From a deserted straight road, one could hear the baritone voice of a man, singing either because he was drunk or because he wanted to overcome the chill:

> . . . I wish that I were with you; dear, to-night;
> For I'm lonesome and unhappy here without you,
> You can tell, dear[,] by the letter that I write.

All of a sudden, the sound of an elevated train shaking and assaulting the city. Somewhere, a dog started barking.

(April 1907)

January First

As was customary every year, on the evening of January first a *zōni-mochi* [vegetable soup with rice cake] party was held at the official residence of the manager of Tōyō Bank's American branch to celebrate the coming of the new year. Nearly twenty people came, many besides the gentlemen of the bank, since everybody was living the bachelor life in boarding houses while in the United States and had no other opportunity to taste even a glass of *toso* [spiced *sake*] for the occasion.

Extremely busily waiting on the guests are Kitty, the maid of German extraction who has been working at this official residence for three generations of managers; a male student said to be a distant relative of the manager's wife; and at times, even the wife herself.

"Who would have thought that we would be treated to such a feast in America?" someone gravely expresses his thanks, stroking his moustache, while another says to the wife with a broad grin, "This has finally cured me of my homesickness," and someone else takes another drink and mumbles an excuse, "It's been two years since I celebrated New Year's like this."

Unlike at a dinner with Westerners, they don't have to worry about making noise while having their soup, so in the spacious dining room with all the windows shut, noises begin to resound from the large crowd chewing *mochi*, slurping the soup, and before long crunching *gomame* [small dried sardines], herring roe, and seaweed;

after a while, shouts of "How about a drink?" are heard as people pass cups of *sake* from various tables that are beyond others' reach. All of a sudden, in the middle of this chattering whose uproar echoes like the croaking of frogs, a drunken voice could be heard—"Kaneda hasn't come again? He's become too Westernized"—sounding as if in need of an adversary.

"That Kaneda, he's a strange man, he never shows up at a party serving Japanese food. He is said to detest nothing as much as Japanese *sake* and cooked rice. . . ."

"Detests cooked rice . . . that's really strange. Is he also from your . . . bank?" someone asked.

"Yes," said the manager, the host. "He's been in the United States for six, seven years . . . and says he wants to spend the rest of his life abroad."

The whole company's noisy conversation immediately focused on this odd person. The manager, as might be expected of an elderly gentleman, contributed a mild, noncommittal comment, "He may not be very affable, but he is a reserved, gentle person, and is indispensable for our business because of his knowledge of the United States," then drank from his *sake* cup.

"But he doesn't seem to know much about social life. After all, even if he doesn't like *sake* or cooked rice, he is still a Japanese, especially on a night like this, on January first," grumbled the drunken one who had first spoken.

He provoked a response from a new voice coming from a corner of the room, as someone who had not spoken said quietly, "Well, I wouldn't criticize him too much. Rather, let's be more tolerant because people do have unexpected reasons; I learned just the other day that there is a good reason why he dislikes *sake* and cooked Japanese rice."

"Is that right?"

"I've become quite sympathetic toward him."

"What on earth do you mean by that?"

"The story isn't exactly fit for the New Year," the new speaker prefaced, but then went on:

"Just the other day, it was two or three evenings before Christmas. I had to choose presents for Westerners and decided I should ask Kaneda, as he has been here a long time; so he showed me around various stores on Broadway, and on the way home, I casually suggested that since it was getting late and I was hungry, we might go to a nearby Chinese restaurant, to which he responded that Chinese food was all right, but he hated the sight of cooked rice. . . . So I let him take me to a French restaurant. Likes wine, that fellow. He quickly emptied two or three glasses and, a little drunk perhaps, was intently fixing his eyes on the reflection of the electric light on his glass half filled with bright red wine; then suddenly he asked, 'Are both of your parents well?' Thinking what a strange fellow he was, I answered, 'Yes, they are,' whereupon he bowed his head and told me, 'My . . . father is still healthy, but my mother died just before I graduated from school.'

"At a loss for an answer, I killed time by having a drink of water, though I had no taste for it.

"'Does your father drink?' he asked after a little while.

"'Not really; he drinks beer from time to time. Nothing much.'

"'You must have a peaceful household then. Alcohol does so much damage. I intend to avoid it altogether but can't quite do so, maybe from heredity. One thing, though . . . I simply cannot drink Japanese *sake*; just the smell of it makes me sick.'

"'Why?'

"'Because it reminds me of my dead mother. Not just *sake*, but cooked rice, *miso* soup, every Japanese dish immediately brings back a memory of my deceased mother. Would you care to hear the story?

"'My father may be known to some; he was a justice of the Supreme Court, though he is retired now. He was educated before the [Meiji] Restoration and was not only a scholar of the Chinese classics but also wrote Chinese-style poems and was adept at tea ceremony in the Kyōto style. He was a connoisseur of calligraphy, paintings, and curios, as well as of swords, *bonsai*, and *bonseki* [miniature landscapes], so that the whole house was like a gardener's yard combined with a second-hand curio shop. Almost every day, bald curio dealers, always wearing glasses, and a train of strange, sycophantic officials of the kind rather rare nowadays, and court clerks would come over and never leave till past midnight, talking and drinking with my father. And my mother alone had to wait on them and keep the *sake* bottles warm. To be sure, we had as many as two servants, a housemaid and a kitchen maid, but my father was very fussy about food, as is often the case with a tea connoisseur, so that my mother simply couldn't leave the maids in charge. She prepared all three meals for my father, warming *sake* and even cooking rice. Even so, his taste must not have been entirely satisfied, for he never lifted his chopsticks for his three meals without complaining about the food. Even when he had his *miso* soup in the morning, he would grumble about the flavor of the San-shū *miso*, or about the amount of salt, saying things like: What a way to slice the *takuan* [pickled *daikon*]. It's stupid to serve *shiokara* [salted fish guts] on this plate. What happened to the Kiyomizu ware I bought the other day? Did you break it again? Be more careful, for heaven's sake. . . . It was just like a caricaturization by a *rakugoka* [storyteller], enough to give you a headache just by listening to it.

"'My mother not only had to be an eternally unappreciated cook, but also had to take care of fragile objects of art and curios as well as *bonsai*, with regard to which he would always find some fault, just as with her cooking, instead of thanking her. So the first sound I ever heard in my life was my father's grumbling in a husky voice, and my first view in memory was my mother with her *kimono* sleeves always tucked up with a *tasuki* [sash cord]; before anything else, my innocent child's mind was impressed with the idea that fathers were always to be feared, and mothers always to be pitied.

" 'I was practically never held on my father's lap. True, from time to time he would call my name in a gentle voice, but I cowered like a cat and was too frightened to come near him. As I told you already, what he ate was never suitable for a child, so I didn't have a single meal together with him. As I grew from an infant to a boy, my sentiments toward my father steadily grew less and less affectionate and, on the contrary, I began to consider him a ruthless and tyrannical demon, while my mother seemed to be leading a life completely devoid of amusement or pleasure, although I must admit this may have been more a reflection of my hatred of my father than what my mother really felt.

" 'From these surroundings and with these preconceptions, I eventually advanced to middle school; there, as I read English texts with depictions of happy family life or the life of innocent children, as well as journals and other readings available in those days, I became strongly impressed with Western thought that was filled with words like love and home. At the same time, an extremely defiant spirit steadily and firmly established itself within my bosom, deeming Confucianism and *Bushidō* [way of the warrior], which my father used to talk about, obstacles to a happy life. As I grew older, I could not even engage in small talk with my father without disagreeing with him, and so, upon graduating from middle school and entering a vocational school, I left home and lived in a dormitory. Occasionally, on the way back after visiting my mother, I would often dream of the time, three years hence, when I would graduate, leave my father, establish my own home, and invite my mother for a happy meal. . . . But alas, life is but a dream, and my mother passed away in the winter before my graduation.

" 'What happened apparently was that one night, it suddenly began to snow close to midnight, and my father told my mother to wake up the housemaid or somebody to bring the pine-tree *bonsai* he had recently bought into the house; he had placed it on a stepping stone in the garden, and its shape would be damaged by the weight of the snow if it were left there on this snowy night. But my mother knew that, unfortunately, the maid had a slight cold that day and was not feeling well, so she didn't have the heart to ask her. She opened the sliding shutters and went out into the garden by herself, wearing only her nightgown, to carry back the heavy pine *bonsai* in the snow. . . . She caught a cold that night that soon developed into acute pneumonia.

" 'I received an utterly bitter blow. From then on, whenever I went to a *sukiyaki* house or other restaurant with friends and heard them complain about the way the *sake* was warmed or the rice cooked, I would immediately be reminded of my mother's miserable life and feel like crying; likewise, whenever I observed people buying garden plants at a fair or some such occasion, I would feel as if I were witnessing an extremely tragic event and couldn't help trembling.

" 'Fortunately, however, once I left Japan and came to this country, everything completely changed, and since nothing reminded me of those miseries, I felt incredibly at ease spiritually. I hardly know what homesickness means. Some Japanese frequently find fault with American homes or women, but for me it is enough to witness a scene by the dining table where the husband slices the meat and puts it on a plate for his wife, while the wife in return pours tea and slices a piece of cake for him; it doesn't matter if these are superficial, hypocritical formalities, because such a scene makes me feel so good, and I don't want to dispel the lovely impression by inquiring into what lies below the surface.

" 'I rejoice each time I see a young woman taking a big bite out of a sandwich or an unpeeled apple at a spring picnic in the fields, or married women drinking champagne and chattering away at a restaurant late at night after the opera or the theater with little regard for their husbands or the other men in the group, or other even more extreme examples; at least they are enjoying themselves, having fun, and are happy. Because I never saw a mother or a wife in a happy state, such scenes are so soothing to me.

" 'Now you understand, I hope, why I don't like Japanese food or *sake*. Only Western wine, which is produced in a country that has nothing to do with my past, and only Western cuisine, which is totally different in form and taste from what used to torment my mother, enable me to experience the pleasure of a meal.'

"Such was Kaneda's story, and he proceeded to order a couple of bottles of champagne over my protest, saying he wanted to thank me for listening to his life story. As might be expected of someone knowledgeable about the West, he is quite well acquainted with the brands of wine and champagne."

The speaker finished and picked up his chopsticks to resume eating the *zōni*. Silence fell upon the company for some time, except for the clear sound of the manager's wife sighing; it seemed that women's hearts tended to be more sensitive toward all things.

(May 1907)

Daybreak

Coney Island, the summer playground built at the west-projecting end of Long Island, is a frequent topic of conversation among men and women not only in New York but throughout the United States. It is like Okuyama of Asakusa and Shibaura [west of Tokyo Bay] rolled into one and magnified to an amazingly large scale, and can be reached from New York in about half an hour, either by land via the elevated train running through the streets of Brooklyn, or by water on a steamboat down the Hudson River.

There is probably not a more vulgar, crowded place in the world. You can tell from the statistics in newspapers that on Sundays tens of thousands of men and women go there. There are scores of large-scale shows using electricity and water to astound the crowd; some contain useful information on history and geography, while some are naturally more disreputable, in dance halls and obscene vaudeville houses. Every night there are bright displays of fireworks. On a clear night, when one gets on a riverboat and looks at the wide bay of New York City, one is amazed at the lights from electrical lamps and illuminations brightening the entire sky as if it were daybreak; and beyond the sea, numerous buildings stand both tall and low, looking like the Ryūgū [legendary dragon] palace.

Among the many games in this vast Coney Island is *tamakorogashi*, Japanese Rolling Ball [sic], one of the most popular. It is nothing fancy, just like shooting or rolling games at Okuyama, where you win one of the prizes that adorn the whole store by rolling a number of balls. But because it is run by Japanese, and hence exotic, and also because it is like gambling, where you may win a valuable prize if you are lucky, it has become quite popular. No one knows since when; certainly it has been thriving even more since the Russo-Japanese war, and every summer there are more and more such rolling ball shops.

You can tell that most Japanese owners of these shops are over forty years of age, determined to make a killing from this popular enterprise. Their appearance and manners somehow suggest their situation in life as labor bosses, desperados, or hooligans. They have come to the United States after experiencing many hardships in their native Japan and, having tried just about everything in America, have reached the stage where they say it's no big deal to live in this world, you won't die even if you eat dirt. On the other hand, those working for them who, every day, count the number of balls rolled by customers and hand them their prizes, are either unemployed people who have not yet been hardened by failures in life but somehow hope to succeed their bosses or young men who have impetuously come to the United States to work their way through college.

I was one of them and had become a scorer at one of the ball-rolling shops, for no particular reason other than that I wanted to work at whatever was available in order to get money together for a trip to Europe. My pay was twelve dollars a week. The boss told me something like this: other shops might give you fifteen or sixteen dollars, but there you'd have to pay for your own meals, whereas at his place, it's twelve dollars plus three meals, and besides, you can sleep in the shop if you like; in other words, you don't have to spend a penny out of your salary, so work hard.

As soon as I was hired, I stood there, like the others, by the ball-rolling table installed at the storefront, waiting for customers to come, but till after three or four o'clock, the sightseeing crowd was rather thin and the wooden roof of the large beer hall across from us shone brilliantly with the light of the hot, hot summer's setting sun. To the right of the beer garden was a shooting gallery where a woman with a face completely covered with white powder looked in our direction from time to time, yawning with a mouthful of food, and to our left was a large show place with a billboard proclaiming FLYING TRIP AROUND THE WORLD. Sitting in a chair on a raised platform at the entrance was a buxom young woman, her face likewise plastered with powder, counting tickets and small change since there were very few customers. By her side a vulgar-looking man wearing gaudy patterned clothes was constantly calling out, "Come in, come in," in a loud voice two or three times even when no potential customer was passing by and then, just as frequently, eyeing and whispering to the female ticket vendor.

It was probably around five o'clock that electric lights came on everywhere. The sky was still blue, and the summer sun would not go down for a while yet, but the atmosphere in the area somehow grew livelier. Various sounds played from gramophones and shouts of barkers began to echo here and there, and in the beer hall across from us they were showing movies at a spot visible from the street. Somewhere nearby, there must have been a vaudeville theater or a dance hall, for you could hear a band playing the drum as well as a young women's chorus. From this time on, male and female visitors steadily increased like an ocean tide, and during the peak hours between eight and twelve o'clock, the streets became jammed with people and little space was left for walking. It was two o'clock in the morning when the shop's owner, noting the gradually quieting streets, finally declared, "OK, how about closing the doors." By the time we washed our sweaty faces at a roadside water faucet and lit cigarettes, it was already nearly three o'clock.

The oldest of the hired men, about forty years old and looking every inch a peasant, said with a Tōhoku [northeast] accent, "Well,

I'm going to go to bed. I won't last if I try to keep up with you. You young fellows go ahead and enjoy yourselves all you like. The night is still young. . . ." He then brought out a blanket that had been shoved away under the ball-rolling table, spread it out, and flopped down on it, spread-eagled on the table, wearing only a grimy shirt.

A man who looked like a student, with his hair neatly parted, then responded, "Are you going to sleep on the ball-rolling table again tonight? Do you think you will have nice dreams that way?"

"The bed in the back room is infested with bugs. You'd better practice sleeping on a wooden board a little. Every night, you seem to be thinking of nothing but sneaking into a woman's bed."

"Don't forget I am still young," said the student, followed by one of his companions who asked, as if to help out, "Hey you, old man, what are you going to do with the money you are saving? Don't tell me you have children or grandchildren back home."

"Oh, sure. I've got a sixteen-year-old mistress waiting for me there. I don't understand why you guys let whores in America fool you and cheat you out of the money you've earned with your sweat. Just think about it. If you take home the money you are throwing away in one night here, you'll be able to have as much fun as a lord till the morning sun shines on the folding screens. . . ."

The student workers, apparently thinking it was no longer fun teasing him, went outside, complaining about the heat. I too went out, from the side door, in part because the house did indeed become unbearably hot with its doors shut, in part because I didn't know where to sleep, having just today been hired. I found the hired hands gathered in a cool spot under the eaves, chatting.

All around, it is strangely, almost eerily quiet, considering the hustle and bustle a mere hour ago. Now that the lights from the illuminations have been turned off, the multitiered buildings for large-scale shows are just standing there, soaring like white clouds floating in the sky. The rather narrow street is almost pitch dark, dimly lit here and there by electric lights. In this dark shadow, like a dream, like phantoms, strange white-powdered women pop in and out of shuttered show places. A man wearing only a shirt with the sleeves rolled up goes after them up and down the street, followed by a woman's scolding voice, sounding like, "What the hell are you trying to do?" and by some screaming, laughing voices. They are all people who had been shouting and dancing in the show places and now, for the first time, have come out in order to breathe freely in some fresh air.

From the wide beach at the end of the street, with an indescribably chilly wind, the sound of waves reached one's ears, beating against the shore as quietly as rain—what a tired, lonesome sound. It must have been because I was not accustomed to staying up late and was dead tired that I felt as though this desolation after a night's noisy and frenzied merrymaking, this lonely, tired sound of the waves, were piercing deeply into my heart. As I gazed unconsciously at the stars vanishing one by one, far away in the summer night's faded-gray sky, I could not help wondering at the way some people lived, like those women of dubious character who had been making intermittent sounds of flirting and frolicking. It was as if I were confronted with life's mysterious puzzle.

The hired hands at the ball-rolling place were busy sizing up or commenting on the women passing by right in front of them.

"Hey, what are we going to do? Let's not just stand here forever. If we want to go, let's go right away."

"Where are we going? It's almost daybreak."

"Let's try the bar at the corner. Many women from the evening shows go there to drink."

"How much? Can you do it for two dollars or so?"

"Depends on the woman."

"If they are charging two dollars, we should go to Chinatown instead where it will be cheaper."

"Speaking of Chinatown, do you remember that plump girl with dark eyes who used to be on Seventeenth Street . . . Julia? That Julia is now working at the dance hall of the beer hall. She may be having a drink at the corner bar."

"Forget it, she already has a guy."

"A Japanese?"

"Yeah, a magician from Brooklyn, and she is like his wife."

"Who cares if she is a wife or a daughter. She'd be yours if you paid her."

"It'd be so businesslike. . . ."

"Don't be so choosy. Remember, this is America."

"What about America? Who says they won't fall for a Japanese? A Japanese may be too good for them."

"But I don't like the idea of having fun for money."

"Then you might as well rape somebody."

"I'm not that desperate yet. I'll wait for the right moment."

"So you're discouraged."

"No, not discouraged. Wait till I make you envy me."

"Don't get caught by the police loitering in the park or somewhere, muddying Japanese reputation."

Just then, two dubious-looking women who had been constantly walking passed us and, seeing we were Japanese, said "Hello," half teasingly.

"There they come!"

"Not bad."

"But they are skinny."

"That's because they are for summer use."

"Follow them!"

Two or three of the group went after the women. The rest watched the scene, quite amused, saying, "Those good-for-nothings. They would make their parents and siblings back home cry."

"It's lucky for all of us that there's a big ocean called the Pacific.

You know, we didn't come to America at first expecting to end up like this."

"Look! They are turning toward the sea. Are there still people at the swimming place?"

"Just go and look now. There'll be dubious characters all over on the beach."

"Let's not just hang around here. Let's stroll over and bother them."

"Nonsense! Don't be jealous."

"But the sea breeze'd be good for you."

"What are you talking about? If you stay up every night like this, nothing's going to do you any good, medicine or no medicine."

"Well, it looks like we're going to do the usual things somewhere. We'd better go to Chinatown; we know it better, and we wouldn't have a chance at the beach."

The company divided into two. One group left for the swimming area by the sea, the other for the train stop, as the trains were running all night. I was left alone; I didn't want to go back and sleep on the ball-rolling table, but I had nowhere else to go.

The stars have disappeared altogether, but the evening sky before daybreak is of an indescribably gloomy color as if entirely covered by a light fog. It is a sign that tomorrow will be terribly hot and humid.

I crouched under the eaves and dozed off before I knew it, but then I came to, hearing someone calling me close by; it must have been one of the guys who had gone away toward the sea. A young man, about my age and looking like a student, was standing with a cigar in his mouth.

"What happened? If you want to sleep, there's a bed in the store," he said, looking down at my face. But then he seemed to recall something and added, putting the cigar back in his mouth, "You don't seem to have gotten used to this sort of life, have you?"

"What happened to everyone?" I said, deliberately rubbing my eyes to hide my embarrassment a little.

"Just as always, they are looking for whores and other women of dubious character."

He crouched down beside me, appearing very tired, looked at my face close by, and said, "Don't you think we are leading a really corrupt life?"

I did not answer and just smiled faintly.

"When did you come to the United States? Have you been here a long time?"

"Oh, about two years. How about you?" I asked in turn.

"It'll be exactly five years come winter. It's been like a dream."

"Where do you go to school? Of course, right now, you must not be going anywhere because of the summer recess. . . ."

"That's right. At least for the first two years, I took schooling seriously. Besides, at that time my education was being paid for by the folks at home."

"So you are not exactly a penniless student working for a living."

"I may not look like it, but at home I am something of the young master." He smiled sadly.

Indeed, his whole appearance, from the smiling mouth to the intensely gazing eyes, does suggest something fragile and gentle, not like the other young men who used to be doormen, freeloaders, student servants, or in other such circumstances before coming to the United States. He seems physically quite strong, with stout, muscular arms underneath the rolled-up sleeves of his summer shirt, but even this may just indicate that his body, rather than having been strengthened by hard work, has been carefully nurtured through sports and gymnastics, which cost both money and time. He may have been a [rowing] champion once on the Sumida River.

"Where did you go to school in Japan?" I asked.

"I attended higher school once."

"'The First'?"

"No, I tried Tokyo [First Higher School] twice but didn't make it. So I had to go to Kanazawa [Fourth Higher School] the third year and barely got in. But then I was kicked out in no time."

"Why?"

"I got sick during my second year and had to repeat the same grade. The year after that, I again couldn't advance to the next grade because I flunked the math course. . . . The rules in those days said you couldn't stay in the same grade for more than two years, so I was expelled."

"That's why you came to America?"

"Not right away. After I got kicked out, I hung around the house for about two years, doing nothing. I learned every naughty trick then, like chasing a female *gidayū* [ballad narrator] or crashing in Yoshiwara [a pleasure quarter in Tokyo].

"My mother cried, my father was angry. But they couldn't just let me be, so they decided to send me to the United States to study."

"Did you come to New York right away?"

"No, I went to a school in Massachusetts. I worked really hard for two years or so. Don't think I am a total playboy. It's true that when I flunked the entrance exam for higher school or, later, got expelled, I thought I was finished, but once I set my mind to studying, I found out that I wasn't that inferior to the others."

"Of course."

"At the school in Massachusetts, there were three students from Japan, but I was the best, at least in language. . . ."

"Did you graduate?"

"No, I quit in the middle."

"That's too bad. Why?"

"That's how it is. I can't cry over spilled milk. And I am not about to.

"You may think I am hopeless. But I quit school because I came to a certain decision. I don't think I'll ever open another book for the rest of my life."

I stared at his face.

"It wasn't that I had any great idea, but it's simply more fun to hang around in a place like this rather than working for a degree or getting some sort of a titled position."

"You may be right in a way."

"You could say I was possessed by some evil spirit, if you believe in superstition. It was through a chance event that I became like this."

"Tell me about it!"

"It was during the second summer after I entered school. I took advantage of the summer vacation and came to New York to look around . . . so far so good, but when fall came and it was time to go back to school, for some reason the money I was supposed to receive for my education didn't arrive. I was really stuck. I waited day and night for it, and was soon short of money not only for the return trip to school but even for lodging, if I lingered much longer. I had never earned a living through my own work. I didn't know how to support myself. So no money was going to come from home . . . well, it would come sooner or later, but it felt as though it were never going to arrive. I couldn't even sleep at night. I felt terribly hungry. Kept dreaming that I had become a beggar."

"No wonder."

"I didn't have much choice but to pay my bills at the boarding house with the money I still had and moved to a cheaper inn run by a Japanese. Waited there for two weeks, but still no money came. I said to myself, this is it. I've got to think of alternatives. . . . But what could I do in America where I had no friend, nobody to consult, nothing like that? Finally, I made up my mind to become a live-in servant at a Westerner's home."

"To do housework?"

"Yeah. Folks staying at the inn were all people like that, so I gained some idea of the situation while talking to them every day. It didn't seem like as much hard work as I had imagined, so I thought things might work out somehow. . . . I was half desperate, but I managed to gather myself much more than previously. First, as you might know, I went to the *Herald* office, as people do in such circumstances, and placed an ad saying something like: Japanese student, very trust worthy [sic], wants position in familly [sic], as valet, butler, moderate wages.

"In two or three days, there were already two, three responses. But I had no idea which house to choose, so went to one of them for no particular reason and decided to work there for thirty dollars; that's the amount they mentioned. It amazed me that in America you could be paid as much as thirty dollars a month for doing domestic service like a maid."

"How could you take it? You told me your family used to send you money for schooling, so you must be one of those so-called greenhorns. . . ."

"Well, think of it as a reaction. Precisely because I was a greenhorn, I was able to take it. Not only that, I even came to enjoy it. You may not understand. It's a little hard to explain . . . but I am going to tell you why. But first of all, I'll have to tell you about my family."

"What does your father do?"

"He is a scholar, head of the — School. As my parent, as a gentleman, he is almost impeccable socially or personally, but things can be too perfect for their own good. Clear water is avoided by fish, as they say. . . . Because I grew up in too wholesome a family, corruption set in rather unexpectedly."

I wanted to ask him a question, but he stopped me by raising his hand and continued.

"It's almost silly to brag about my parent's reputation in a place like this, but in fact my father does seem to have been highly respected by others, just as people said, and our house was always like a private school, with seven, eight, or even more student-servants. You may have come across my father's name in some book. Anyway, from early on, I don't recall exactly when, I would be told by our student-servants or neighbors that my father was a great scholar, but I didn't know why it was so, or how great he was, so naturally I believed that I too would become a scholar when I grew up. But, I think it was from about the time that I was to enter higher primary school, I became very poor in math and almost had to repeat the same grade, and my teacher said to me: 'Your father, as the world knows, is a great scholar of law. Unless you study hard, not only you but your father's reputation will suffer.' A warning was sent from the school to my house, so upon returning home, I was scolded by my mother and then admonished by my father and told to stay up till ten o'clock every night to study my lessons diligently.

"In my innocent child's mind, I came to the realization that I was no good at studying and felt awfully distressed, and for a week or two afterward, I couldn't even bear to be seen by our student-servants. . . . I didn't go out much but remained in my room, staying up till late studying as Father had told me, but in no time I began to be terribly worried about the future; although I was still a child, I wondered if I would ever become a great man like my father, no matter how hard I studied. Such worries . . . apprehension about the future, you can say that was the worm that afflicted my spirit. As I advanced from primary to secondary school, academic work became more and more difficult. In contrast, my father's reputation and status continued to rise. . . . Former student-servants who used to be my father's doormen become university graduates and come back to pay their respects. I just feel so small and insignificant. But some of our student-servants and relatives still say that I shall inherit Father's household and also become a great legal scholar like him, making me feel that perhaps I have an obligation to become one, even that I would like to do so. . . . . The more I thought about these matters, the more

I worried about my ability, and even as my father's admonitions sunk deeply into me, I grew desperate . . . saying to myself, without any particular reason, that I was no good.

"Of course, this is a mere child's thinking without any understanding of the world, and as you grow older you are bound to become bolder. Still, what you sense as a child will stay with you for the rest of your life. It was the same with me; even now, in America, where I was sent after I was expelled from the higher school I had worked so hard to get into and became a little desperate . . . whenever I receive a letter from my father, I have a strange sensation that I am being supported so generously by him but that I really have no ability to succeed in scholarship. Even when I know I can accomplish something without difficulty, I always give up because of such 'imagination.'

"Can you believe it, it was exactly in the middle of such desperation that suddenly I felt greatly relieved, perhaps because I was receiving no money from home and so, in a sense, my connection with them was being severed—relieved because I no longer had an obligation to succeed by all means and return home loaded with honors. Now it was up to me whether to live or die. Even if I died, I began feeling, it didn't matter because I no longer had a parent to grieve over me."

Tired from talking, he fell silent for a while.

"That's why you put up with housework as a dishwasher?"

"That's right. I did receive money shortly, but it was too late. Two weeks' work washing dishes at the back of the dining room thoroughly corrupted me. I don't know if you've had the same experience, but it's a carefree life. Of course, in the beginning it was hard work since I wasn't accustomed to it, and I even felt sorry for myself and confused, but it's never a very complicated job. All you have to do is carry dishes around like a waiter while the family is eating in the dining room, there's nothing to it. After your employers have finished their meal, you wash the dishes and then go downstairs to the kitchen to eat at the wooden table with the old hag of a cook and the maid; but beware of circumstances. It's uncanny that washing dishes like that makes you behave like a dishwasher. Besides waiting on the table three times a day, morning, noon, and evening, I also had to clean the living room and the dining room, so I was physically exhausted, and when I had no work to do, I would just doze off. Gradually I stopped using my mind, like thinking or worrying about things. . . . Instead, it is amazing how your appetite for flesh and food increases. Nothing beats the taste of supper after a day's work. After you eat all you can, you begin to feel like just dozing off, and in no time you are fooling around with the maid sitting nearby. You want to hold her hand, even tickle her, and she pushes you away, which is all great fun. But even though the maid is angry at you, she also begins to feel something's wrong with her unless she is teased. It's not a matter of falling in love, or anything like that. The maid and the male servant . . . it's inevitable that they will come together."

The day was gradually breaking. As electric lights faded one after another, so, apparently, had the women from show places disappeared, and as the whole area grew steadily lighter, somehow everything was becoming even quieter. . . . All one heard was the sound of waves lapping against the beach.

"So, my destiny was all sealed. On one hand, I am more embarrassed than ever about facing my father and am really stricken with a bad conscience, but on the other, I am enjoying this sort of animal-like existence more and more. In other words, the more I agonize, the deeper I fall, and so in the winter I work as a waiter in this house or that, and in summertime, when families evacuate their city dwellings and travel to their resorts to avoid the heat, I knock about from one place to another like this every year."

"But what are you going to do eventually?"

"What am I . . . going to do, what will happen to me?" His face showed he was worried, but he shouted, "No, no. I'm doing these stupid things so I won't have to worry about such matters. I work, drink, eat, and buy women so I won't have any brain power left to think about my own future. I just try to use my body like a beast."

He walked away briskly, leaving me behind, apparently because he could no longer bear his agony.

A flash of morning sun began gleaming above the tall tower of a show house. . . . Oh, what a beautiful light. Unconsciously I knelt before the light, feeling as if I had been rescued from an evil den to which I had been confined all night.

(May 1907)

Two Days in Chicago

March 16—this is the day I have set aside to go to Chicago.

People are saying that it has been unseasonably warm; most of the snow that accumulated last year has melted away after a rain that has fallen for two or three days. The sky is still overcast, but the town, which has awakened from its long winter's sleep, has a completely different look. The low sleighs that used to glide over the snow have turned into large-wheeled carriages, and the drivers' forbidding fur coats have been transformed into lightweight raincoats. Young boys and girls who, in tasseled knitted caps, had been skating on ice now run up and down the rain-soaked cement sidewalks, clacking the heels of their new shoes. One need not be a child to leap with joy in anticipation of the soon-to-come spring, as one notices the appearance of dark and moist soil in people's gardens or orchards, as well as of the green grass after it had been buried under the snow for a winter.

To catch the 9:30 A.M. train, I hastily packed my small traveling bag, hopped onto a streetcar at an intersection at the outskirts of town, and headed for the Michigan Central [sic] station downtown.

I am told that it is exactly one hundred miles between Kalamazoo and Chicago, and that we shall arrive in exactly four hours. Immediately after the train leaves the town of Kalamazoo, it runs through rolling, undulating hills where trees are sparse, and along apple orchards blackened by winter's blight so that, passing scenery like the white-spotted patches created by the leftover snow in scattered pockets across the hills or the water from melted snow pushing down rotten fences of meadows and gushing out of the banks of tiny brooks, I am often reminded of the landscape described in Russian novels.

Once the train reaches Indiana, dirty little towns with numerous factories increase in number, and after a while we reach the edge of Lake Michigan. But a dense fog from the cloudy sky is covering the surface of the lake completely, and all one can see are huge chunks of ice floating near the shore and countless seagulls flying above; I wonder if the Arctic Ocean is like this, since I haven't seen it.

Running along the lake, the train soon entered the city of Chicago and arrived at the Illinois Central station. I left the platform and climbed up the stairs and, as it was about half past one in the afternoon, I proceeded to the waiting room and entered a restaurant at one of its corners.

Inside, the restaurant is divided into two sections, of which one is called a "lunch counter" and is somewhat like a Japanese tavern. It is for quick meals to be consumed while standing, whereas the other is a regular dining room with white linen-covered tables and chairs. The former was crowded, with virtually no empty space, since it was both speedy and economical; it was strange to see pretty, considerably well-dressed ladies among the unceremonious male customers.

After finishing my meal, I went down a broad flight of steps to the street, but, being a stranger to this city, I had no idea which way I should proceed to find the house of the friend I was to visit.

As there were carriages at the foot of the stone stairway, with drivers waiting for their customers, I waved at one of them and asked him as he came closer, "How much would it be to go near the University of Chicago?"

"Two dollars," he replied.

I knew it was fairly far away but still thought this was a bit outrageous, so, accustomed to doing shameless things while abroad, I returned to the station and asked one of the employees there, who told me kindly, "The best way is to exit the station and catch a train there that goes across town and then get off at Fifty-fifth Street." So I paid an additional ten cents for the ticket and waited on the platform for the train.

Soon a three-car train arrived; when it stopped the doors opened without any help from station employees, and as soon as it started moving, they again closed automatically. In the cars there were few female passengers but many men who looked like tradesmen. As I was planning to visit a friend of mine living in the vicinity of the University of Chicago, I turned to the young man sitting next to me and asked how I could get to a certain street where my friend was staying . . . whereupon he gave me detailed directions as if I were a child and even pulled out a map from his pocket notebook.

As I thanked him profusely, doffing my hat Japanese style, the man said, apparently taken aback at my excessive formality, "You don't have to thank me, we'd all have problems in a foreign country." Maybe in America men don't take off their hats when greeting each other. He continued, "Actually I am a foreigner too, a Dutchman. I've been in this country for some ten years. . . . How about you? Do you like America?"

"Do you?" I asked in return, to which he answered, smiling, "The best place in the world is really the land of your birth. . . . Don't you think?"

He told me he was a sales clerk at a certain store and was about to boast about his homeland when the train reached the station where I was to get off, so, thanking him again, I got out of the car and went out to the street.

The gaslight at the intersection reads FIFTY-FIFTH STREET. My destination is Fifty-eighth Street, so I just have to walk three blocks. It is so easy to find one's way, even in a new place, because one of the most convenient things about American streets is that they are numbered consecutively or named in alphabetical order. Building numbers too are arranged in such a way that, for instance, if odd numbers are on the right-hand side of the street, even numbers will be on the other side, so that the situation familiar to Tokyo residents who cannot find a street number even in their own city simply does not exist.

I walked leisurely, feeling at ease. The winter clouds that earlier had covered the sky for a long time were moving in layers, gradually revealing blue skies and an agreeable sunlight. Since the melting snow had turned the streets into marshes, I picked my way along the relatively dry sidewalks. The weather must have been rather abnormal, for it felt like a balmy day in May; sweat started pouring down my forehead, and my overcoat, which had felt comfortable till this morning, became terribly cumbersome.

Soon I found the address of my destination among a row of three-storied rooming houses all of the same stone. This area didn't look like part of the bustling city of Chicago, and only a few people were on the streets; on one side of the area there was a grassy open space (I later learned that it was called "Midway" and had been part of an international exposition some ten years earlier, after which it had been converted into a park) and beyond this space to the far right, the gray-colored University of Chicago could be sighted, while on the left two or three skyscrapers, quite probably hotel buildings, blended harmoniously with the clouds busily moving back and forth after the rainfall and strangely drew my attention. So I just gazed at the landscape for a while and stood at the door of the house that I was about to visit without ringing the doorbell.

I then heard a young woman's voice from the second-floor window, which I could not make out, but soon there was a clattering of someone coming down the stairway, and the front door opened.

"Aren't you Mr. N——?"

She was a slightly built young woman of perhaps seventeen or eighteen, her blond hair loosely swept back from her forehead, wearing a white waist jacket and a navy-blue skirt. She had a most lovely round face, with almost artificially charming dimples at the corners of her mouth, and she said in a bright, innocent, candid, and gentle voice characteristic of American maidens, "James hasn't come back from work yet, but he has been looking forward to your visit for some time. Do come in."

She took my hand and led me to the living room.

A sofa, an armchair, a desk, a framed lithograph, and a well-worn piano were about all the decoration there was in the room, as if that were enough to prevent it from looking forlorn. I was surprised by its lack of splendor, which I had expected to find in a Chicago home. The master of that house is a judge, and the person entertaining me is his only daughter, Stella, who is engaged to my friend James whom I came to know in Michigan.

Yes, indeed, how often has James told me about this young woman! And how many times has he shown me her beautiful picture, which he always carries with him, pasted to the back of his pocket watch. James's parents live in Michigan, and so we became good friends while he was back home some time ago. He is a graduate of an electrical engineering school in Boston and, since becoming an engineer at the Edison Company of Chicago, has been a boarder at the young woman's house. He was good at the piano since his student days, while Stella, the daughter, enjoys playing the violin, and so they have often played together after dinner, each evening drawing them closer together in mutual affection, and eventually they became engaged. I have already heard from James that it was when they played Schumann's "Träumerei" together that for the first time they swore their love from the bottom of their hearts, so I said to her, "I do hope you will play that piece tonight."

At this she looked quite startled and, lightly pressing her cheek with her supple hand, exclaimed, "The Dream!"; she already appeared overwhelmed by the remembrance of past events and, taking a deep breath, asked me, "Has James told you even such things?"

"Yes, everything. . . ."

"Oh, my," she laughed with a clear voice like a bell, that of a maiden who, like others in this country, did not keep her emotions under control, and I felt as though I could almost hear the palpitation of her heart filled with fragrant love.

She suddenly got up from the automatic [sic] chair* and went briskly to the adjoining room, then immediately returned with a photo album; drawing a chair close to me this time, she opened her album on her lap and said, "These are our pictures. We have taken them every Sunday."

Pictures they have taken of each other at various parks they have visited together on Sundays are pasted with dates written down. What a wonderful record of memories.

Stella explained where each picture was taken: the lakeside at Jackson Park, the embankment at Michigan Avenue, under some trees at Lincoln Park . . . even as she did so in a hurried manner, her deep green eyes shone with the self-assurance that she was one of the happiest girls in the entire world; certainly nobody would be unmoved by the sight of such honest emotions.

I felt from the bottom of my heart a sincere prayer for Stella's happiness, but at the same time I could not help envying her good luck at having been born in a free country. Let Japanese scholars steeped in Confucianism consider the situation. They would have labeled her an immodest woman or a nymphomaniac, but in a free country, no cumbersome creed exists that goes against natural human feelings, except for the gospel of love.

———————

*In later editions, the word "automatic chair" was changed to "easy chair."

That evening, I had a most memorable and pleasant dinner. Stella's sweetheart, James, came home, and her father, the elderly judge, returned. After they had dinner, joined by her mother, the young couple complied with my request and played that "Träumerei." Under the dim light from a colored electric lamp with a flower-shaped shade, he sat at the piano with his broad-shouldered back turned in our direction, while she stood right next to him, holding her violin and almost leaning against him. Near them were the gray-haired mother and the bespectacled elderly judge with a large, bald head, and outside the glass windows footsteps of someone hurriedly walking in the slightly humid March night.

Before long the young couple finished their playing, and as soon as the young woman put down her instrument, she threw herself into James's arms, as if she could no longer wait, and twice kissed him passionately. Her parents eagerly applauded and asked them to play again, but she kept her face firmly pressed against his chest, as if she were unable to restrain her deep emotions. But then she straightened herself suddenly, picked up her instrument, and this time played that merry tune, "Dixie," a great favorite of Americans, to which even the elderly judge responded by beating time with his feet as he sat on the sofa.

Oh, how I wish that such a pleasant family scene could be duplicated soon in our homeland.

Think, for instance, of the way I was brought up at my home, by a father whose warm human blood had been chilled by the Confucian classics, and a mother who had been restrained by treatises on womanly virtue and behavior. In such an environment, there is no room for music or laughter. My father would indulge in the pleasure of drinking with his friends till even past midnight and assail my mother, already exhausted from the day's chores, for the way the *sake* was warmed or the food cooked; alas, looking at my father's face on such an occasion, vicious and autocratic, and my mother's sad, lethargic face accustomed to blind obedience, I used to think, while still a child, that nothing in the world was as detestable as a father, and nothing as unhappy as a mother. But if progress is the law of the world, such a barbaric, Confucian age will soon become a thing of the past, and our new era will sound a triumphal tune.

Presently the clock chimed nine. James had told me that since there was, unfortunately, no extra room at Stella's, he would take me to a private boarding house three houses down the road; so I said good night to the whole family and went out with James.

I looked for words to tell James, "How blessed is your love!" but I was distracted by the irregular movement of the night clouds in the sky, so walked silently, while he whistled a popular tune, and in no time we reached the entrance to the boarding house.

Even though it was called a boarding house, there was nothing special about it. It seemed that the number of rooms and their layout were almost identical to those of Stella's house. I was taken by the mistress of the house to the best room available for rent, located at the front, and, after James left in five minutes or so, quickly changed and quietly lay down on the bed.

I had put out the gaslight in the room and so had a full view of the night sky from the windows with shades raised. Even though the sky was dark, it was faintly light outside, perhaps because the moon was hiding behind the coming and going of the clouds, enabling me to discern the trees by the roadside and the faraway buildings standing like so many shadows; fortunately, however, I was so tired after the train ride that before I could think of anything, I fell soundly asleep like a heavy stone sinking to the bottom of the sea.

March 17—When I woke up, it was eight o'clock and I saw the morning sun sparkling on the thoroughly wet windowpanes. Standing near a window as I dressed, I looked out at the windblown twigs scattered here and there over the wet pavement; there must have been a storm.

It was amazing that I had been able to sleep throughout the night without even a dream. It is the lot of us poor humans to be endlessly tormented by various dreams. But thanks to last night's dreamless sleep, for the first time I was able to achieve comfort and happiness away from daily toil, like those animals who lie down under shady trees in the meadows.

I went down to the dining room for breakfast, which, I had been told, was set for nine o'clock.

There are three small tables, each seating four people. By the table at the far end, two middle-aged men, apparently tradesmen, are reading the *Chicago Tribune*. At the center table is a woman who looks like a student. The mistress of the house brings me to this table, and the woman who has been wearily waiting for her breakfast immediately begins talking to me, seeing that I am a foreigner.

But her questions are typical of those asked by just about ten out of ten people— When did you come to this country? Do you like America, aren't you homesick? Don't you think Japanese tea tastes good? Aren't Japanese kimonos beautiful? I am crazy about things Japanese. . . .

I wanted to switch the conversation to anything but this, and as soon as possible, when, fortunately, a young girl of about fourteen or fifteen whose long hair was tied with a black ribbon brought over our breakfast; so, seizing the opportunity, I asked as I picked up my knife, "Are you a student at the university?"

"Yes, in the literature department," she answers. Feeling somewhat encouraged by this, I continue, "Literature . . . then you do read novels?"

"Yes, I love them," says the woman without hesitation. It seems that in America, unlike Japan, there are no unfair regulations explicitly prohibiting female students from reading novels.

She rattled off numerous titles of recently published novels and discussed them, but unfortunately, as I had not paid any attention to

American literature till then, I was not particularly able to appreciate her learned argument. Bret Harte, Mark Twain, and Henry James are about all the American writers I know. I think it was at the end of last year that a friend of mine in New York sent me some works by two or three famous authors, but I only managed to read about half of each book and didn't go beyond that. I still occasionally flip through a magazine, but for some reason I don't seem to be able to find, among the works of this new continent, gentle features like those in Daudet or Turgenev. It may be that lovely works like theirs, filled with imaginary visions, do not appeal to American taste.

Breakfast was over sooner than I expected. The female student said, "The spring convocation will be held tomorrow afternoon on campus at Mandel Hall, so you may be interested in coming," and, picking up a book that lay on the table, left the room, smoothing out her bangs with one hand.

Almost at that very moment the doorbell rang, and the girl who had served us told me, "You have a visitor."

I went out and saw that it was James. Wearing his derby slightly tilted back, he said, "Good morning," several times in his usual casual voice, adding that as he was going downtown to work, I might go with him and do some sightseeing. I readily agreed to his proposal, and we went out into the street to take the train to the city from the same station where I had gotten off yesterday afternoon.

As this is the time of the day when all sorts of Chicagoans go to work for various firms and stores downtown, the cars are filled with men and women, and practically no seat is empty. They are voraciously reading newspapers with the fierce look of those who want to take in the maximum amount of information within the minimum length of time. At stations where the trains stop every five or ten minutes, there is not a single person who is waiting for a train without a newspaper. What a newspaper-loving people they are. They will say, the people of a progressive nation must try to find out as much as possible what is happening in the world, and at the earliest moment. . . . Ah, but don't they realize that there is nothing unusual or strange about the world's affairs, the same old muddle repeating itself again and again? In diplomacy, it is the conflict of interests between A and B; in wars, it is the strong that win; banks going bankrupt, intrigues during elections, train derailments, thefts, murders, such daily occurrences of life are always the same and monotonous to the extreme. Hasn't the French writer, Maupassant, already suffered unbearable pain from this excruciatingly boring life and written in his diary, *On the Water* [Sur l'eau]:

> Blessed are those who are unaware that the same abominable things are endlessly repeated. Blessed are those who ride today and tomorrow the same carriages, drawn by the same animals, and have the energy, under the same sky, in front of the same horizon, to do the same work in the same way, surrounded by the same pieces of furniture. Blessed are those who do not realize with an unbearable hatred that nothing will change or happen in this weary and tired world. . . .

In that sense, Americans who yearn to know about the events of this monotonous life as ardently as the starving crave food should be considered the most blessed ones.

The train keeps running along the lake's shoreline. I hardly have the time to reflect that it feels somewhat like passing by the vicinities of Shinbashi and Shinagawa [in Tokyo, along Tokyo Bay] when the train reaches the terminal, and the passengers hurriedly stand up from their seats. James tells me that this is called Van Buren station, the entrance to the busiest commercial center of Chicago.

The innumerable men and women pouring out of the train go across the sturdy stone bridge that is connected to the platform, almost rubbing shoulders. Michigan Avenue, where many cars come and go as quickly as the wind, can be seen beyond the bridge, and tall buildings, all more than twenty stories high, are vying with each other on all the wide streets running westward from Michigan Avenue. The sky is overcast, which is typical of the month of March, and besides, these tall buildings obstruct the sunlight from both sides of the streets, with the result that one notices something black like darkness, neither dust nor smoke, swirling there. And the multitudes of men and women who have just crossed the stone bridge have fast disappeared, as if they were being swallowed up, into this darkness—this darkness that is Chicago.

I was struck with a great sense of terror. At the same time, I felt an irresistible urge to join the destroyers of civilization, even before I had time to consider its pros and cons. The honest Japanese farmer comes to Tokyo, the capital of Japan, as a tourist and is overwhelmed by its prosperity (if one can call it that) and goes back to his thatched-roofed cottage full of admiration and respect, but the young man who has been exposed to the ideas of the age even once is prone to engage in the wildest of fantasies, the more he sees and the more he hears. At the thought of all this folly, I stopped walking and lingered on the stone bridge, when James turned back and, smiling for some reason, called to me as if he were asking me a question, "Great city!"

"Yes. Big monster [sic]," I answered—how should I describe it, except to say, as people often do, that it is a monster?

James pointed to the tall buildings on Michigan Avenue ahead of us and explained: that is a hotel called Annequis, the next one is a theater called the Auditorium, the distant one is the tower of a company dealing in wholesale orders [Merchandise Exchange]. After having pointed to this and that building one after another, he suggested that, as there was still time, he would take me to a large store called Marshall Field's.

"The largest in Chicago. . . . Even New York doesn't have such a large store. So we can say it is the largest in the world. There are some seven hundred female employees alone."

169

James must not be wrong. A visit to this store is almost a duty for any traveler who passes through Chicago. It sells all kinds of daily goods such as clothes, furniture, notions, shoes, and cosmetics, and stands like a castle at one corner of State Street, which is the main street of this city. I slipped through the crowd and took the elevator to the top of the building, which is close to twenty stories high, and looked down, leaning against the well-polished brass railing.

The building is just like a huge tube with a hollow center, enabling the sunlight that enters through the glass ceiling at the top to reach all the way down, so that it is possible to enjoy the rare view of people walking in and out of the bottom, stone floor several hundred feet below! Men and women are hardly as big as our thumbs, and they worm their way through, moving their arms and legs; are there more comical playthings than these? But realizing that the same small and helpless-looking people had been able to build this tall, large building that reached the clouds, I could not help feeling proud of the glory of human development, even though I had but a short while earlier cursed civilization.

People will laugh at the frivolity of my undecided mind. But it simply means that the human mind changes and floats always and endlessly according to circumstances and surroundings. For instance, it is just like our hoping for the cold weather of winter on a summer day and longing for the warmth of summer on a winter day; there is no absolute truth, whether in Luther's Protestantism, Rousseau's liberty, or Tolstoy's peace. These are all voices called forth by circumstance.

James said he had to go to work, so we went down together by elevator and parted company at the store's entrance. As for myself, I intended to go to the Art Institute on Michigan Avenue.

(March 1905, Michigan)

The Sea in Summer

I am staying at the residence of my elder cousin Sosen, which is seven or eight miles away from the poor quarters of the East Side, where people sometimes die as a result of the scorching heat; though it is still within the city limits of New York its uptown location is very quiet, and from its fifth-floor windows you can see, in the west, the upper reaches of the Hudson River, and in the east, the deep woods of Columbia University. On the other hand, the heat searing into the paving stones and bricks turns all the rooms into hothouses even before people wake up, and as sweat oozes from all over our bodies like oil, we have no appetite at the breakfast table and don't even want to finish our bowls of oatmeal.

As it is a Sunday, Sosen proposes to show me around and take me to New Jersey's Asbury Park, a bathing beach that is something like Zushi or Ōiso [on the outskirts of Tokyo].

We left home at once, rode the subway for just thirty minutes or so, from the northern to the southern end of the city, climbed up the stone steps of the station, walked through the downtown streets of New York where the tallest buildings stand, that is, the quintessential New York, and reached the south pier. There were people everywhere, on the decks of the steamship moored alongside the pier, at the ticket booth, in the park in front of the pier; even Americans are said to marvel at the number of people everywhere in the city when they first come to New York, so for someone faint-hearted like me, it was discouraging, and "we won't be able to get on" was my natural response. But Sosen, who has long been accustomed to this sort of crazy scene and is what you call "smart," wasn't the least fazed and, taking my hand, forced himself into the crowd and somehow found a path for us to climb up to the deck of the steamship and even to sit down on folding chairs he found somewhere.

The ship unmoored in about five minutes, and by the time the dresses of women going back and forth on the pier began to look like flowers in a garden, a grand view of the Hudson's estuary was totally spread out before us. I believe there must be few scenes as grand as this. At the center are the tall buildings of New York rising high in the brilliant summer sky, at the right [sic] the cities of New Jersey with their smoke trailing out like clouds, and on the left [sic] the great Brooklyn Bridge, under which freely pass numerous steamships coming from the world's harbors, then the town of Brooklyn. A most amazing battleground of peace. And the Statue of Liberty gazes down on it in one sweep, raising a spear [sic] with one hand and soaring high above the sea far away from the harbor.

I have never seen a bronze statue of such dignity. Unconsciously, I felt an urge to kneel down at her feet and pray, and though at first I wondered if I had inherited some sort of idol-worshipping instinct from my ancestors, I came to the realization that this profound emotion was induced by the impeccable choice of the statue's location, which is the first principle of constructing statues. With any work of art, it is impossible to maximize its effect if the so-called accessories are neglected, and I think this is particularly true of statues and monuments. Nobody who, traveling on a tiny leaflike boat, comes within a distant view of the great city of the democratic nation and looks up at this enormous statue rising above the Atlantic Ocean will fail to be moved by a certain emotion. This statue is a representative of the new continent, an exponent of the new ideology, and at the same time, a protector of the American spirit that is far more formidable than a million fortresses. I have heard that this statue was a gift from France, but I think the power of the artist who created it is equal to God's.

Perhaps in Japan too some may be making plans for the construction of a huge monument, representing the Orient in the wake of the Russo-Japanese war. But if it is going to be carried out by the Japanese government, a government that equates artistic work with the building of roads, I must hope such a plan won't materialize. Japan's beauty is known and loved throughout the world not through the statues of Kusunoki Masashige [a fourteenth-century warrior] or Saigō Takamori [a nineteenth-century figure], not through the brick buildings in Hibiya [in Tokyo], but through cherry blossoms scattering like clouds or geisha dancing like butterflies. So our mission as Orientals is not to be drunk with the dreamlike illusion of harmonizing East and West, as someone suggests, but to turn the whole island nation into a pleasure center of the world, with all our men devoting themselves to growing flowers and all our women becoming dancing girls.

The steamship carrying me sailed away into the vast open sea, rendering the beach scenes unrecognizable, but then it shifted course and moved along the quiet coastline. The summer's bright sunlight permeates the clear blue sky and shines upon the pure white peaks of the clouds floating over the horizon, the smooth sea, and the trees along the waterfront with branches thick with leaves, adding indescribably pleasant luster to the white of the clouds, the deep blue of the water, and the green of the leaves. As we look around, the coastal area is a stretch of low-lying ground like a meadow, and the surface of the water is often interrupted by sandbanks with tall, overgrown reeds, behind which immaculately white sails of yachts glide past, while a flock of seagulls fly like scattering blossoms. What a joy it is to stumble upon such a small-scale landscape, just like a watercolor painting, in an unfamiliar place; it exceeds anything one encounters in world-renowned tourist spots or historical landmarks.

Last year, when I passed through the Rocky Mountains and Niagara Falls, I was not as moved by these world-famous sites as I had expected, while by contrast, I was unforgettably touched, poetically inspired by a Missouri village buried under fallen leaves or by a Michigan orchard's twilight—these celebrated mountains and majestic waters, gathering together nature's engineering, have long marveled and awed people, and may be likened to Milton's *Paradise Lost* or Dante's *Divine Comedy*, while the twilight scenes at those obscure villages are just like poems of unrequited love by an unknown poet. It is said that Tolstoy was more moved by the evening singing of *muẓhiks* [serfs] than by Beethoven's music, that George Eliot preferred a little Dutch painting to the famous masterpieces of antiquity; so it might not be totally because of my lack of learning that I find small pieces by Turgenev or Maupassant more interesting than the grand epics of the classical period that have become trifling objects of experts and scholars.

After making two or three stops at piers of smaller beaches, the steamship arrived at a similar summer resort called Pleasant Bay. The lowland in the whole beach area had been made into a park, in which there were small music halls, restaurants, and rolling-ball parlors amid trees. From here it takes a little over one hour by train to reach our destination, Asbury Park, and all along the way is an uninterrupted stretch of summer hotels, summer rentals, and meadows with cool-looking clumps of trees.

Young sisters stretch themselves out on a hammock hung from maple trees in their little garden and are reading novels; a young couple sits in armchairs placed side by side on a veranda overhung with vivid green leaves, chatting happily to each other while looking out on the street; young lovers are returning home along the iron-fenced road with flowers they have picked in the meadow; clusters of young girls are holding each other's hands, running around, singing songs; several groups of good-looking boys are visiting their friend at the front door across from the flower garden; and everywhere there are pleasant laughter, voices, whistling, and the sound of piano-playing.

Indeed, on such a clear, bright summer day, and with such an agreeable sea breeze, this village by the water is no hiding place for old folk disillusioned with life but a paradise for young men and women to indulge in the pleasures of youth, the idleness of youth, and the dreams of youth.

From the moving train, I saw countless beautiful women and handsome men. Nothing makes me feel more attached to this world and makes me enjoy my own existence more than seeing beautiful women and handsome men. Just as an innocent young girl does not know, not being a scientist, if the beautiful flowers blooming in the fields are poisonous or not, so do I feel, not being a moralist or a policeman and thus incapable of judging what may lie hidden underneath the human body, be it good or evil, that every place where handsome men and beautiful women tread, laugh, and enjoy themselves is like an ideal heaven. This is the more the case because this seaside in summer is less like a heated room in a wintry city, such as a theater or a dance hall where dresses and jewels are blooming, than a village where the fragrance of thinly clad snowy bodies are filling the air.

Men are wearing light jackets and straw hats, while women don't even wear hats underneath their white parasols and walk in the bright sun like so many birds flying in the sky, proudly showing off their curly blond or brunette hair, displaying, from the hems of their short skirts, wrinkle-free silk stockings and charming small shoes, rolling up the sleeves of their thin waists [shirtwaists], which are almost transparent, swinging their hips, and beating time with their shoulders.

I am the first to admit to admiring the physical beauty of Western women, the first to love everything from their most curvaceous waistlines, expressive eyes, statuelike smooth shoulders, and broad chests to their feet encased in small high-heeled shoes, and to pay the highest respects to their ingenuity in make-up and their swiftness in adapting to fashion. They skillfully choose the color and shape of their clothes to match the color of their hair, facial features, and build so that even an average-looking woman is enhanced to attract men's attention, while in Japan, men and women seem totally deficient of this ability. It may be that the Japanese are a people accustomed to censure and meddling so that women brought up in that society are too timid and intimidated to be capable of enhancing their natural appearances.

The train stopped at an intersection in a town overlooking the Asbury Park beach.

The verandas of four or five tall wooden hotels facing the vast expanse of the Atlantic Ocean, the drugstore at a corner of the intersection, the esplanade jutting out over the waves are all filled with men and women, their white clothes and parasols reflecting the blue color of the sky and the sea and producing in onlookers an indescribably pleasurable sensation.

Sosen and I go down the steps of the esplanade to the sand by the sea and look around for a place that might rent out a swimsuit so I may immerse my five-*shaku* [five-foot] body, which was raised under the Far Eastern sun, for the first time in the waters of the Atlantic Ocean,* but strangely enough, there is not one person swimming, though so many people are strolling along the sea, and no place is open for changing clothes.

――――――

*The part of the sentence from "so I may" to "Atlantic Ocean" was omitted in later editions. In reality, the author was a very tall person for a Japanese.

THE SEA IN SUMMER

"I don't understand it, the sea isn't that rough," I say, and Sosen too looks around inquiringly; but then he remembers and says, "It's because today is Sunday."

There are places in the United States that forbid any kind of amusement on a Sunday for religious reasons. Asbury Park is one of them.

A prohibition! Regulations! Nothing looks more foolish than formal rules promulgated by religion. Do they really think there is sufficient religious significance in going to church on Sunday, singing hymns, and praying? Are these enough to help solve life's riddles?[**]

Sosen told me that there are certain towns in this state with a ludicrous contradiction, which forbids all amusement on Sundays but allows the driving of carriages and automobiles.

The two of us sat on the sand and spent a little time gazing at the infinite ocean where only clouds floated, and after a while we returned to the esplanade; after quenching our thirst with a glass of lemonade, we decided to go back to Pleasant Bay Park where we had disembarked and take a nap till the return boat was due, and jumped onto the approaching train.

After getting off at the entrance to the park, we walked to a shady spot under the trees at the edge of the water and sat on the soft green grass. The scenery before our eyes reminded me of nothing as much as a peaceful Dutch painting, with roofs and windmills of farmhouses peeking out from among the low stretch of summer trees, across the calm inlet that reflects the shadows of white summer clouds.

I somehow felt inexplicably happy and, lounging on the grass, I took out a cigarette from my pocket and had a smoke; when I looked

---

[**]This paragraph was omitted in later editions.

toward the quiet surface of the water, there was a pure white boat in the middle of the lake-like inlet, which had made its appearance I knew not when. It looked like Lohengrin's white swan, which alighted unexpectedly from midair. But there seemed to be only two people aboard, a young woman and a young man, the latter rowing with all his might so that the boat swiftly moved away and in no time disappeared behind the sand bank where reeds protruded. Simultaneously, I too threw myself back flat on the grass as if I were lying down on my bed; my eyes were then at the same level as the surface of the water, and it felt as though the brimming sea were in no time going to soak me, while the summer sky glimpsed behind the green maple leaves seemed even higher and wider than usual, in sharp contrast to the floating white clouds, which appeared to be slowly descending to envelope me. With what joy did I wait for it to happen, with what should I compare the sensation of being surrounded by a haziness as if hidden in a mist, with only a breeze occasionally coming this way over the surface of the water, gently lapping my face, so that my entire body, all its bones and flesh, melted into vapor, leaving only the fragile skin that was like silk and sensitive to everything, enabling me to float between the full-bodied water and the languid clouds, more lightly than fish or birds . . . ah, what a daydream!

When I was back home, I used to think nothing was as refined as an afternoon nap on a summer day in a small room overlooking a small garden where safflowers blossomed, while listening to the sound of a wind bell outside the reed screen; or at a geisha house by the river where the sound of *samisen* could be heard far away; but away from home, I find that it is an even more charming and simply indescribable experience to lie down on the luxuriant wild grass under the immense sky of this foreign land.

When I was living in a remote rural community in Michigan, it was exactly at the end of May, in the middle of spring in this northern country, that fresh leaves of huge maple, elm, and oak trees thickly enveloped the village; apple, peach, and cherry blossoms bloomed in the orchards climbing up the hill, as did purple lilacs, white snowballs, and red roses in the tiny yards of people's houses. Robins and black-birds that leave the south and flock to this place in spring and summer keep singing carefree songs at the top of their lungs, in yards, ceme-teries, towns, villages, wherever trees and flowers are blooming. It continues to be sunny during the day, as is often the case on a conti-nent, and the strong sunlight reminds one of the July heat in Japan. I decide to take a break from my small room and walk along the train tracks amid the small hills rising from the edge of the village and grad-ually wander into the uninhabited oak woods. As I fling myself onto the wild grass resplendent with white daisies and golden buttercups, numerous squirrels, startled by the sound, scuttle in all directions on the grass and, promptly jumping from one oak treetop to another, begin to squeak.

As usual, I brought a collection of poems in my pocket, but before mysterious nature, any painting, any poem seems but a grotesque exaggeration, at times even a total falsehood, and I no longer desire to touch any such artificial object. Rather, I stretch myself out to my heart's content, and as I look at the sky beyond the tall treetops, smell the scent of moist soil and grass, and listen intently to the singing of birds or the squeaking of squirrels, I feel as if I had completely renounced the world, or been renounced by it. In Japan, where even in remote mountainous villages land is almost everywhere cultivated, one feels the din and bustle of the world, but, as can be expected, in the vast American continent, everywhere there is such an uninhabited area just two miles outside a town; in addition, my own subjective sentiment of solitude in a foreign land gives me an inexplicable sense of pathos and beauty as I watch the luxuriant foliage, the flowing water, and the clouds sailing across the sky, and wild fantasies well up in my mind, imagining, in view of the chilly pleasures of a wandering life, how it would be if I rode a camel in the desert side by side with an Arabian woman and slept with her under a tent, or, in contrast, if I fell ill on my journey and became bedridden in a back alley where the sun never shone. . . . At this I shudder in spite of myself and wonder if I should not go back to Japan tomorrow; I am driven from one extreme thought to another and eventually fall into a confused dream, emotionally exhausted.

Oh! Daydreaming in a foreign land! It was these dreams that gave my monotonous life an unlimited charm I had never experienced. Today, as usual, I lay down by Pleasant Bay, into which the tides of the Atlantic Ocean flow, and heard in my dream the sound of some exquisite music; I then awoke with a start and realized that at the restaurant at the end of the park, a band was beginning to play some quiet classical piece.

But I was still in a state of torpor after my nap and casually fixed my gaze upon the scenery in front of me, from the bay to the woods and the clouds, as if viewing a place I had visited more than ten years earlier; then, hearing footsteps behind me, I turned around and found Sosen. He told me that he too had just awakened and had been to the pier to check the schedule for our return trip.

The two of us left the shaded area and, after stopping at the park restaurant where music was playing to quench our thirst with chilled fruit and ginger ale, we boarded the ship past five o'clock in the evening.

The sun set in the west while we were on board, enabling us to enjoy thoroughly the view of the Atlantic Ocean aglow, and by the time we slowly approached New York harbor, we noticed a bright light starting to shine in the hand held high by the Statue of Liberty. This was followed by the glittering, all at once, far away beyond the high-heaving afternoon waves, of New York's buildings reaching the sky like a mountain range, the numerous ships moored by the

Brooklyn Bridge, and the row of piers; this scene was even more beautiful and seemed even more full of meaning than what we had seen in daytime.

It was exactly eight o'clock when the steamship reached the pier; Sosen and I went to Fourteenth Street, which is particularly alive at night, to eat our dinner and entered a certain French café.

(July 1905)

Midnight at a Bar

From New York's City Hall Plaza, go past the entrance to the Brooklyn Bridge, which is always crowded with people and horses, and walk on Third Avenue for four or five blocks alongside the elevated train tracks, and you will come upon Chatham Square, a large and dirty intersection; to the left is the Jewish section, to the right Chinatown and then Little Italy.

Called "Poor Alley" for short, this area is a slum inhabited by immigrants from various countries as well as laborers; it is still part of the city of New York, but in contrast to the West Side, which represents the New World and a haven for the successful, this East Side is a different world, a hiding place for those who have not yet succeeded or who have failed.

As a result, whereas on the West Side people show off their beautiful clothes while riding the subway, here women do not even wear hats but cover their heads with dirty shawls and walk with their mouths full of food. Men wear weather-beaten hats but no shirts with collars, exposing their hairy chests through their torn undershirts; thrust whisky bottles into their trouser pockets; and walk while spitting saliva yellow with chewing tobacco everywhere.

As a result, the surface of the sidewalks is slimy with the phlegm and saliva of these people and, besides, littered with strange, suspicious-looking waste paper, rags, and sometimes even torn women's stockings lying limply like decomposed dead snakes. The street is everywhere paved with stone thoroughly worn by the wheels of heavy wagons, while the constantly flowing urine of packhorses fills the nooks and cracks, stagnating there in dark, muddy green.

There are various shops on both sides of the street, and among them is a tattoo artist whose sign on the glass window—PAINLESS TATTOOING WITH ELECTRIC DEVICE—amazes you that such a thing should exist in the West. Elsewhere, here and there, and almost all in a row, one's attention is caught by dubious-looking jewelers and secondhand clothing stores, in one of which an elderly Jewish man bent with age is restlessly watching the world from behind the poorly lit counter, while at a roadside eatery an old Italian woman is dozing off among buzzing blowflies as if she had no mercenary desires.

It is everywhere like this; what strikes you, from the long rows of houses to the clothes people wear, is their uniformly gloomy coloration, while the air is always murky with the combined stench of meat cooked at roadside stands, sweat, and other indescribable filth, and weighs heavily on one's heart. So once you set foot in this neighborhood, any idea of life's glory and pleasure is completely obliterated, making you feel as if you were solely overcome by a gloomy nightmare.

One day—it was a winter night. I was walking in this area aimlessly after having seen a Yiddish play in the Jewish quarter. It seemed to be already past midnight, as the secondhand clothing stores and jewelers, as well as all the other shops, had turned off their lights, with only the saloons at various street corners proudly displaying their electric lights as if to say now was their time.

I pushed open a door and found, upon entering, a group of laborers leaning against the counter and chatting loudly, each holding a cup in one hand, but I also noticed the faint sound of a battered piano and voices of women merrymaking in the back. So I penetrated farther, and as I tried to push open the door at the end of the hall, I found my body sliding with the door into a pitch-dark corridor.

Sensing that the women's laughter was coming from behind a door five or six steps ahead, I moved on unhesitatingly and approached this second door, whereupon, perhaps hearing my footsteps, someone inside opened it. It was the guard who had been watching through the keyhole, and as soon as I entered, he shut the door again with a bang.

Who outside would have imagined that there would be such a huge hall in a place like this! All around the room, close by its walls, many tables and chairs were laid out, and at one corner there was an old, large piano. A huge man in a vest, his arms sticking out of a dirty shirt, is playing the piano, mopping his brow from time to time with one hand; sitting next to him, a skinny, hunchbacked man is playing the violin, exposing his pale profile, while men and women at the tables stand up in pairs and weave their way through the room dancing!

None of them is dressed in a particularly notable way. Mingled with sailors in wide trousers, some men are wearing clean collars and neckties, as if they had smartened themselves up for the occasion, but fingers that look even thicker than a child's arm and shoes with soles as thick as a horse's hooves give away the fact that during the day they are the type that repairs roads or carries bricks.

As for the women, they hardly look human, and it is difficult to tell if they are old or young. They have plastered their entire faces with white powder, with rouge on their cheeks, and there are even those who have lined their lower eyelids with eyeliner. Wearing worn-out crumpled skirts and shabby summer tops, they nevertheless must want to follow the city's fashion, for they have put on narrow shoes with high heels, as if they were going on stage, and an excessive amount of fake diamond pieces glitter among their hair filled with false tresses that make it look as though the women were wearing wigs, as well as around their necks and on their arms and fingers.

As the piano and violin played on, the sight of sailors and laborers embracing these women and dancing chaotically, as if in a frenzy, in a dim electric light that was yellow from the dust on the floor, the smoke from cigarettes, and the smell of alcohol, gave me an indescribable sensation of pathos, going beyond disgust or detestation— just like the time when, back home, I heard some singing and string music from a faraway pleasure quarter, somewhere near the dark village of Negishi.

The dance music has stopped, and as men and women return to their respective tables, waiters in white jackets circulate among them to take orders; some sailors, already drunk and hardly able to stay on their feet, are still gulping down whisky, while some women are quaffing equally potent punch, sometimes banging on their tables and loudly ranting, using some of the basest swear words in the English language.

I sat at a corner table, sipping beer alone, and cast my eyes around the strange scene that surrounded me, and then to the framed pictures hanging from dirty board-lined walls.

There is a picture of four or five women together, perhaps professional football [sic] players, holding hands and standing, exposing their robust muscles from their fleshings; then next to it is a portrait of a demonic-looking boxer with both hands held before him in fighting stance; and on the opposite wall two or three pictures of uniformed firemen are hung, suggesting perhaps that this neighborhood is their ground.

Suddenly a couple of women came and sat in empty chairs at my table, and when I, driven by curiosity, winked at them, which is a signal that is used only in this kind of society, they, apparently totally unconcerned about racial differences so long as they could make money, immediately pulled their chairs close to mine, and one of them asked, "Do you have a cigarette?" while putting her elbow on my shoulder.

I gave her a cigarette and called to a waiter just walking by; the woman ordered a cocktail, but I don't stand such drinks and so ordered another glass of beer, after which we carried on small talk while I paid

the closest attention to them in order to learn more about their background. But I was getting nowhere. . . .

"I don't have any name. Just Kitty . . . Kitty the brunette is how
they know me."

"Where do you live?"

"My home? . . . It's everywhere, every inn in New York or
Brooklyn. . . ."

"Have you got a beau?"

As I asked, she started laughing and, saying, "Any chap with
money is my beau," abruptly kissed me on the cheek and started
humming, rocking her head and shoulders right and left, ". . . will
you love me in December as you do in May. . . ."

Just then, another round of piano and violin playing drove people
back to their dancing.

The woman suddenly pulled my hand, which she was holding,
and asked, "Tonight. It's all right, isn't it?"

"What is it?" I responded, pretending not to understand what she
was talking about, but then she became very cross and said, "You
know, of course . . . I'm talking about a hotel."

I smiled but did not answer.

"You don't want to? I see," the woman said and, hitching her
shoulders a little, turned her face away and resumed her humming to
the tune of the dance music.

I was taken aback and watched her for a while, but soon she
noticed a bunch of sailors at a distant table who were winking at her
and hurried away without as much as saying a word to me, and was
again gulping down some whisky.

I was thinking that I must also be going when two musicians
entered the hall from the opposite doorway.

"It's George, Joe the Italian!" shouted one of the waiters, seeing
the mendicant musicians, while another man at a nearby table, looking
like a local tough, accosted them.

MIDNIGHT AT A BAR

"You haven't been here for a long time. Did you manage to get a fat job?"

"Oh no, nothing big, we've been doing the countryside for a while." So saying, one of them moved to the piano, sat down on an empty chair, took down a musical instrument called a banjo that he was carrying on a strap around his neck, and rested it against the wall, while the other, holding a small mandolin on his lap, greeted the pianist from a distance, without standing up. "How are things, boss?"

"Just as usual," answered the pianist, in rolled-up shirtsleeves and vest, in a husky voice. "Have a drink, anyway."

A waiter brought some beer over to a nearby table.

"Great! Thanks." The two Italians emptied their glasses, and the pianist said, very much with the air of a boss, "Don't mention it. Luckily, we've got many customers. . . . Let's hear that beautiful voice now."

The two Italians picked up their banjo and mandolin, stood erect by the piano, and began singing a Southern European popular song whose meaning escaped me.

But the tune was very slow as in an Oriental song, and the voices with vibrato suggested a certain slight sadness, so that all were entranced, drunken sailors, prostitutes, workmen, as if they were listening to *shinnai* [music originally played at puppet theaters] at a pleasure quarter, and for a time a hush fell over the place.

Here and there, five- and ten-cent silver coins were thrown on the floor as tips, so I too decided to be generous and took out a twenty-five-cent coin from my pocket. Actually, I would not have hesitated to give them fifty cents, even a dollar, if I had not wanted to keep from drawing attention.

The sound of Italian words that mostly end with a vowel is so marvelously appealing to my ear, but on top of that, the appearance of these mendicant musicians with their crooked hats, torn velvet clothes, and bright red printed handkerchiefs around their necks, as well as their dark hair hanging over their foreheads in abundant curls, black eyelashes, thin moustaches, and their dark complexion baked by the warm sun of Southern Europe—all these somehow brought out a deep poetic inspiration in me, who have always longed for the southern country.

The two finished singing, collected the silver coins, tips scattered all over the floor, and soon were approaching my table, so I seized the opportunity to ask, "Where in Italy are you from?"

One of them looked up at me and answered in broken English, not in the least perturbed by the face of a different race, "From the island, the island of Sicily."

"How long have you been here?"

"It's been only nine months. I came here thinking I would make some money, but I'm a rake by nature and love wine and gambling. But beyond that, what I like most is playing the banjo and singing. I'm not like those guys who come here from Northern Europe to earn money and work so hard, at the bottom of the earth or in the fire; a lazy bum is a lazy bum anywhere, you know, so I just go from place to place, singing like a bird. But I've been OK, thanks be to God; at least I don't go hungry."

The dance music resumes. Once again, men and women dance along here and there in the smoke-filled room, like people in a dream world. The two Italians, having gathered all their tips, retreat to a corner table and drink two, three more glasses of beer.

I had been confined to a roomful of impure air for so long that I decided to get up and cool off in the chilly air of the deep night. Farewell, strange people of midnight. . . . Good night. . . .

(July 1906)

Fallen Leaves

Nothing is as fragile as autumn leaves in America. In September, although it is unbearably hot in the afternoon and people complain about the lingering summer, dew-soaked leaves of oaks, elms, lindens, and especially the large leaves of maples, which are like *aogiri* [Chinese parasols], begin to fall heavily and languidly in the evening, even when there is no wind, without even changing their summer colors.

They touch me with a deeper sense of sadness than when fall is in the air everywhere and yellowed dead leaves fly about like a rainstorm in the chilly morning and evening wind. They somehow remind me of the premature death of a young genius.

I sat down one evening on a bench near the pond in Central Park. How quiet it was on a weekday in contrast to the Sunday bustle. This is just about the time when everybody in this punctual country must be having supper. Sounds of carriages, cars, even of footsteps of people taking a walk have stopped, and only the squeaking of squirrels who have collected their last morsels of food can be heard way up in the treetops. The gray sky that seems to presage rain in the evening is darkening murkily and heavily as if it were dreaming. The surface of the water, which is as vast as a lake, is shining darkly like lead, while yellow gaslights have started flickering through the gradually fading shrubs surrounding the pond.

From the tall elm treetops nearby, slender leaves are falling constantly in groups of three, four, five, or six. As I listen, it is as if I can hear the sound of leaves sliding down among other leaves. They must be whispering among themselves, luring each other toward their fall and destruction.

Some land on my hat, others on my shoulders and knees. Still others fall on the far-off waters, even though there is no wind to lead them, and are carried farther and farther away by the stream.

As I sat with my elbow on the back of the bench, thinking of this and that, I suddenly recalled the "Song of Autumn" by Verlaine.

> Les sanglots longs
> Des violons
>   De l'automne
> Blessent mon coeur
> D'une langueur
>   Monotone.
> Tout suffocant
> Et blême, quand
>   Sonne l'heure,
> Je me souviens
> Des jours anciens
>   Et je pleure.
> Et je m'en vais
> Au vent mauvais
>   Qui m'emporte
> Deçà, delà
> Pareil à la
>   Feuille morte.

"The melancholy sound of violins weeping in autumn tears my heart. When the bells toll, I turn pale, sigh heavily, remembering the bygone days, and cry. Like a fallen leaf I wander here and there, carried by the wind of my ill fate."* This is not the first time that life has been compared to fallen leaves, but because of it it always touches me deeply. Especially as I recall my own state as a traveler. . . . Ah, how often, and in how many different places, have I watched fallen leaves buried in this foreign land.

In the fall of the year when I arrived, it was on the Pacific Coast; the following year it was in the fields of Missouri, on the shores of Lake Michigan, and in the streets of Washington; and now this is already the second time with New York's fallen leaves.

Last year, when I saw falling leaves for the first time in this city, how arrogant, elated, and happy I was. I imagined that I had seen everything about the different social and natural conditions in all regions of the new continent and, unreasonably confident that I was about to observe life in this, the second largest city in the world, I would come near this pond every Sunday and watch the crowds of people walking.

Soon all the leaves had fallen, cold blasts had broken tree branches, and snow had covered the grass completely—the season for art and social life had arrived.

Seeing various kinds of plays, from Shakespeare and Racine to Ibsen and Sudermann, I felt as though I had taken in the classical and modern dramas of the whole world. I believed I appreciated and understood Wagner's visions and Verdi's craftsmanship. Not only that, I felt I was, had to be, one of the founders of the new musical drama that was bound to arise in Japanese society in the future. I heard symphonies played by orchestras and enjoyed the refinement and beauty of classical music and the unrestricted passion of modern romantic music; I admired the dissonance and formlessness of the unprecedented music of [Richard] Strauss. Furthermore, I often

---

*Literal translation of Kafū's own translation.

visited art museums and argued about Rodin's sculpture and Manet's paintings.

Programs, catalogues, and newspaper clippings piled up on my desk, but even as I was sorting them out, the season changed; the once desolate treetops were now adorned with young shoots and blossoms, while people cast off their heavy coats and switched to light spring clothing. I followed their example and bought new clothes, new shoes, and new homburgs. But American fashion is that of a commercial country and therefore in poor taste. Just to demonstrate that I would never be influenced by American utilitarianism, I worked hard at finding the right way to groom myself and concluded that I wanted to look like the portrait of young Daudet when he wrote "L'amoureuse," or even like Byron, so every morning I curled my hair and tied my wide cravat with a studied casualness.

People would laugh at my folly, but I myself do not think I am either foolish or out of my mind. I read in a Boston paper shortly after Ibsen died . . . that Ibsen had an unsuspected weakness; apparently he enjoyed looking at himself in the mirror wearing the medal the king had bestowed on him, rumpling his white hair intentionally to give the impression that he never combed it.

I won't question if this is true or false. Whatever Western poets have done moves me to tears, and I cannot help but imitate them. So I too tilt my hat slightly, again in an intentionally offhand manner, carry a cherry walking stick in one hand and a book of poetry or some such thing under my arm, and, after scrutinizing myself thus standing in front of the mirror for a while, finally go out and proceed toward the park where people gather on spring afternoons. After walking around the pond, as usual, I always go up to the tree-lined avenue where the bronze statues of Shakespeare, Scott, Burns, and others stand side by side, sit down on a bench facing them, and leisurely smoke a cigarette.

Then at some point, as soon as I slip into a reverie induced by the warm spring sun, I feel as though I had taken rank with these great poets of immortal fame. The muscles on both sides of my mouth loosen themselves to form deep dimples. Finally, I cannot help feeling embarrassed at myself and look around furtively, then notice the beautiful young leaves of the trees lining both sides of the avenue, the clear blue of the sky seen through the treetops, the deep, pleasant green of the grass spreading on both sides of the road like an ocean, and the soft, sweet fragrance of the flowers wafting from some unseen place. I must never have been so happy in my life.

In front of my eyes, women wearing light dresses pass me ceaselessly, driving in carriages or on horseback, and they all appear to be smiling in my direction as they go by.

Whenever I observe the smiling face of a very young, incredibly beautiful woman, I find myself daydreaming about a happy love affair. . . . I write something in elegant English, and a female reader wishing to meet the author visits me. We talk of life, of poetry, and finally of each other's secrets. In due course, I am married and settle down in the country within one or two hours' train ride from New York, perhaps Long Island or the New Jersey coast. It is a small painted cottage surrounded by cherry and apple orchards, and beyond the woods at the back of the house there is a pasture, and farther away we can see the ocean. On a spring or summer afternoon, at dusk in autumn or at noon in winter, I lie down on a couch by the window and doze off, exhausted from reading. Then I am awakened by the sound of piano music coming from the adjoining room, preferably something very gentle like a Liszt sonata, played by my wife. . . . At this point I awake with a start and find myself sitting on a bench, the cold evening wind blowing against my face.

The spring of such daydreaming, then the summer have gone by and ah, it is already autumn, when watching the leaves falling and scattering is like recalling the lost love of bygone days.

The leaves will soon be all gone. With the cold north winds, the theater and concert season will return. Street corners and train station walls will be adorned with theatrical posters and musicians' portraits. But will it be possible for me to remain the same bold, outrageous, happy observer of the arts as I was last year? And, come spring, will I again be able to indulge in such ephemeral daydreams?

Dreams, intoxication, illusions, these are our life. We perpetually crave love and dream of success but do not really wish their fulfillment. We merely pursue the illusions that appear as though they might be realized and want to intoxicate ourselves with this anticipation and expectation.

Baudelaire says—to be intoxicated, this is the only question. If you want to avoid feeling the horrible weight of Time that presses on your shoulders and bows you to the ground, you must not hesitate to get drunk. Whether with liquor, poetry, morality, or whatever, it does not matter. If at times you awaken from your intoxication on the steps of a palace, on the grass of a valley, or in a desolate room, ask the wind, the waves, the stars, the birds, or the clocks, anything that flies, moves, revolves, sings, talks, what time it is. The wind, the waves, the stars, the birds, the clocks will answer, it is the time to be intoxicated, it does not matter whether with liquor, poetry, morality, or anything; if you do not want to become miserable slaves of Time, you must be intoxicated all the time. . . .**

All around me, night had fallen. The woods were dark, the sky was dark, the water was dark. But I remained on the bench, watching the shadows of the leaves scatter against the electric lights shining among the trees.

(New York, October 1906)

———————

**Literal translation of Kafū's own translation. The original poem, "Enivrez-vous" [Get drunk], can be found in Baudelaire's collection of prose poems, *Le spleen de Paris* [The spleen of Paris, 1869].

Chronicle of Chinatown

There are times when I feel happy beyond reason, strange even to myself, just by looking at the clear blue sky; as a reaction, however, sometimes I find myself suddenly in deep despair without any reason or cause.

For instance, on a chilly, rainy evening, when I happen to hear the voices of people talking beyond the wall or the meowing of a cat, I feel like crying, gritting my teeth, or I am tormented by all kinds of sinister fantasies, as if I wanted all of a sudden to pierce my heart with an ice pick and kill myself or to throw myself into the depth of an indescribably frightful vice or degradation.

Once I am in this state of mind, everything becomes topsy-turvy so that what has seemed beautiful, to the world and to me, begins to look not only meaningless but also loathsome and hateful, while what has appeared ugly and evil impresses me as even more beautiful and mysterious than flowers or poems. All crimes and evil deeds now appear grander and more powerful than any moral good, and I feel like praising them from the bottom of my heart.

So just as people go to the theater or a concert, when evening comes I wish for a truly dark night without stars and without the moon, and throughout the night, driven by an irresistible passion, I wander in search of dead men, beggars, people dying in the street, or anything else that looks ugly, sad, and frightening.

Thus, I have been to just about every slum, every disreputable place in New York; however, alas, nothing seems to fulfill my dreadful desires better than the tenement houses of Chinatown, which are most detested and feared. Yes, Chinatown—its seamy tenement houses. This is the place that exhibits the ultimate in human depravity, an exhibition hall of vice, shame, disease, and death. . . .

I always take the subway and get off at the small station just before the Brooklyn Bridge; this area contains rows of wholesalers and warehouses, and after the hustle and bustle of the day is over, not a single person passes by; in the night sky, which is barely spared pitch darkness by the city lights at each street corner, boxlike buildings with neither windows nor gable roofs stand tall and alone. Those accustomed only to the lively evenings of central Broadway must be surprised that such a desolate place should exist in New York. Empty packing boxes are piled up mountain-high by the roadside, and many carts separated from their horses are cast loose; once you pick your way through them, you are already at the edge of the slums, beginning with Italian immigrants' quarters; to the left is a wide vacant lot with a row of benches, and to the right, a series of little houses with crooked roofs. As I continue on the bumpy paved road and climb up a gentle slope, I know at once that I have come to the main street of Chinatown by the unpleasant smell of the place.

Chinatown consists of a very small area, with the main street overlooking at a distance the tracks of the elevated trains; it divides into two winding roads lined with houses, but they converge once again into the main street. Those who come here for the first time must feel creepy about the way the bumpy paved road winds its way seemingly without end. The houses are all American-style brick buildings, but the various gilded signboards, hanging lanterns, and pasted notices on red Chinese paper put out on the doorways of numerous restaurants, general stores, and greengroceries, combined with the ugly row of houses of uneven heights and doorways, create a certain harmony for the whole scene that is unmistakably, gloomily Chinese.

At night, when the noisy sound of gongs from Chinese plays is heard from the end of an alley and the hanging lanterns of the restaurants are lit all at once, Chinese men who have been working far away during the day in various parts of the city steadily congregate, each with a long pipe in his mouth, and are engrossed in roadside conversations about lotteries and gambling; this scene must strike foreigners* as quite strange, for swindlers, always quick to see an opportunity, bring curious men and women from distant uptown in a sightseeing automobile with a huge sign saying CHINA TOWN [sic] BY NIGHT—and there are also those who come in fine carriages, accompanied by prostitutes from the Broadway area, to spend the evening at a Chinese restaurant out of curiosity.

This, however, is just the surface of Chinatown. Once you go behind its restaurants, stores, and other buildings, you will find four- or five-story buildings standing straight like walls, each crowding around a small yard paved with stone and with dirty laundry hanging from its windows.

It is to one of these buildings that I go late at night, stealthily . . . it is a tenement house subdivided like a beehive.

To get into this place, you have no choice but to pass through the small front yard, but its stone pavement is littered with waste paper and rags thrown down from all the windows, which cling to your feet like snakes, and the sewage flowing out of the public toilet at the corner, which is enclosed with boards, sometimes forms a pool too large to hop over. From a row of tin trash cans placed along the buildings'

---

*In later editions, the word "foreigners" was changed to "Westerners."

walls the stench from rapidly decaying objects unbearably pollutes the air, which cannot be ventilated out of this area. So once you set foot in this place, even before you take a look into the buildings in the back, you sink into a sensation as if you had been totally separated from your daily life, just as you do when you smell the burning incense inside a temple and are struck by the place's solemnity, although these are two sharply contrasting circumstances.

There are occasions when a momentary sight gives such a strong impression that it will almost stay with you for the rest of your life. . . . One clear winter night, if I remember correctly, as I sneaked into this place, as usual like a criminal in hiding, pulling down my hat over my eyes and turning up the collar of my overcoat, I noticed a large half moon in the narrow winter sky, visible between the buildings. Its dull red coloring could have been compared to that of a woman's eyes swollen from crying. Its dim light glided down the sides of the dirty buildings and cast an indescribably ghastly shadow on a corner of the far distant yard. There was light escaping from the doorways and windows with drawn curtains, but not a voice could be heard. Suddenly a big black cat, appearing from I knew not where, looked up above the boards of the public toilet and, raising its back high, turned its face toward the sadly falling moon, meowed once, twice, three times, and then vanished like a ghost. I had never felt so tormented by fathomless superstition. . . .

On another occasion, on a summer night, the walls on all sides had been in the sun all day long and not only did not cool off easily but shut out the breeze so that inside the yard it felt like a pot full of oil. The warm repulsive smell from the overflowing sewage stifled one's breathing like a visible fume, but the stuffiness inside the tiny rooms in the buildings must be even worse, for half-naked women were thrusting their bodies outside the completely open windows, almost turning themselves upside down. Bright light streamed out over their shoulders so that, entirely unlike in the winter, the color of the night that fell on the yard was bright and shiny. From the windows facing each other, ear-splitting voices of women resounded, cursing or chatting, but higher up, in the attic of a building, one heard the creaking of a *kokin* [harp], perhaps being played by a Chinese, which set one's teeth on edge . . . repeating a monotonous Oriental tune endlessly as if paying no attention to such cacophony. As I stood still for a moment, exhausted by the foul smell and heat around me, and listened half consciously, I felt, oh! what harmony, what unity! I had never heard a piece of music that sang of people's ruin and downfall in such a heart-rending way. . . .

At the very end of the yard is an entrance without a door. Right inside is a narrow staircase with remains of spittle here and there, and as you climb up fearfully, on each flight a dim, naked gaslight is on the old wall of the narrow hallway, and you are assailed powerfully by the smell of slow-cooking pork stew and green scallions as well as the scent of incense and opium; you can never smell such things anywhere else in the United States.

All over the painted doors red Chinese pieces of paper are pasted with various Chinese characters in thick brush strokes, names such as "Li" and "Lo" or invocations of auspicious omens, and inside people are talking in Chinese, sounding like the screeching of monkeys; at some other entrances, however, with ribbons tied in bows as their signs, American women with thickly painted faces open the doors halfway as soon as they hear some footsteps in the hall, calling out in the Chinese or Japanese they have picked up.

Poor women, they have come together in these tenement houses with only Chinese, the very people whom Americans in general consider not so much an inferior race as animals—the same way they consider a certain class of Japanese—as objects. In any human society, the distinction of winners and losers, upper and lower ranks, cannot be avoided. Even after women throw themselves away in the seas of lust, even in those seas there are some that are pure and others that are impure, and some of these women attain queenly glory and become objects of envy, while others exhibit such misery after having tried everything in vain.

These women have exhausted all their respective dreams befitting their situations and brought only their flesh marked "female" to this abyss, having lost any sense of sorrow or happiness, desire or virtue. A sure sign of this is the fact that when they stop a man lingering at the doorway, they merely want him to give the crucial answer right away instead of using tiresome devices such as a seductive expression or suggestive gestures, as an ordinary prostitute would, in order to lure him step by step into the deep. If the man doesn't say yes or no but tries to tease them, partly for fun, hell will break loose, and they will immediately begin howling like rabid dogs and spit out every abusive word available.

It really seems that they are just unbearably angry with no particular cause. It is not uncommon that, when they do not find an opponent to pick a fight with, they will burn their guts by gulping down glass after glass of strong whisky and writhe on the floor loudly damning their fate, or break cups and glasses and tear their hair. Not a few, on the other hand, have already gone beyond even such a stage of madness and calmly enjoy an empty peace, holding, whenever there is a chance, an opium pipe like a lover.

Ah, the paradise of poisonous smoke! A certain French poet called it PARADIS ARTIFICIELS [sic] (artificial paradises). To reach the stage of enjoying this dreamland, one has to endure the long journey of unusual despair, pain, and degradation, but then it is possible to escape completely the worldly ties of anguish or regret. Look at their bright eyes while they are asleep! Whenever I gaze timidly upon them, I feel an irrepressible anger at myself for lacking the courage and determination to degrade myself likewise, being held back by what is left of my conscience.

CHRONICLE OF CHINATOWN

Besides these queens of evil, empresses of sin, and princesses of corruption, there live in these tenement houses not a few who, being unable to inhabit bright, sunny places, at last find their repose under the awning of sin and evil.

There is the old Jewish man who comes to sell various stolen items and fakes to these women who are his best customers. There is the gray-haired peddler who spends his life wandering on one journey or another, holding his livelihood in the small box hanging from his shoulders. There is the black woman who makes a living by shoplifting and sells these goods from place to place at bargain prices. There is the orphaned, homeless delinquent boy who runs errands for the whores like the "errand boy" in the pleasure quarters of Japan. But among these people the most pitiful and frightful are the pack of homeless old women whose lives are uncertain even this evening, let alone tomorrow.

We prematurely conclude that the plight of those prostitutes is the ultimate depth of human degradation, but there are those lower than even the lowest. Alas, how often and how much do people have to endure ill fate in order to reach the ultimate ruin, the ultimate peace!

Their twisted bodies are barely covered with rags, their eyes resemble rotten oysters and discharge mucus, their disheveled white hair looks like shredded cotton yarn as if it has been preserved for the sake of lice; they take refuge from the elements in the corners of the tenements' hallways, under the floors, or behind the public toilets, and sometimes they officiously do the laundry and other chores for the whores in order barely to scrape a living. But they seem to believe that this is ultimately more comfortable and freer than society's constraints called charity or prisons called old people's homes; if they foresee that there is a chance of a policeman's footsteps being heard in this hole, they disappear with amazing alacrity, but otherwise they are wont to roam the world and, under cover of the night, make the rounds of the whores' rooms here and there to beg for money. Even the women are no match for them. If they beat or kick them in a fit of temper, they may die on the spot, but if they push them out of the door just a little, they may wail loudly all night or collapse nastily right there and start snoring. One time I heard these harassing words:

"OK, if you are so mean, I won't ask for your kindness anymore. But soon you too are going to learn your lesson when you've run out of luck. . . . You think you are still young and will be able to do your business as much as you want, but in no time you're going to be like me. Don't even bother to look in the mirror; the poison you've been taking in, who knows for how long, is going to gush out at one point. Don't pay attention to your wrinkles, it's your hair you should worry about. Your nose'll shrink, your hands'll get crooked and start shaking. And you'll get cramps in your legs, and you'll be bent in the back. Here's proof . . . just look at my hands. . . ."

The woman who was doing her face for the night in front of a mirror uttered a cry in spite of herself and, covering her face with both hands, lay prostrate on her bed. The old hag of a beggar laughed in a creepy way and, bidding her farewell, came out of the woman's room into the hall; I had been peeping in the doorway but became suddenly frightened and fled from the spot in a hurry.

All of this reminds me of the poem, LES PETITES VIEILLES [sic] [The little old women], which Baudelaire dedicated to Victor Hugo, in which he exclaims, "Ruines! ma famille! ô cerveaux congénères! (Devastation, my family! Congeneric brains!)**

Oh, I love Chinatown. Chinatown is a treasure house of poetic material for "the flowers of evil." I am constantly concerned lest so-called humanitarianism and charity should wipe away this world of its own from a corner of society.

** Literal translation of Kafū's translation.

Night Stroll

I am fond of nighttime in the city. I love its brightly lit quarters.

As you well know, I preferred twilight in Ginza or an evening at Yoshiwara to the moon of Hakone or the waves of Ōiso, and stayed alone at my house in Tokyo even during the summer, rather than going to a resort.

So it goes without saying that since my arrival in New York, the evenings of this great city on the new continent, where there is no place without bright lights, have given me so much pleasure. Oh, New York is an amazing nightless city. It is a bright, dazzling, and magical world of electric lights that must be very hard to imagine in Japan.

Once the sun sets and night comes, I leave home almost unconsciously. If I don't see the world lit by those glittering lights, be they in the streets, at street corners, in the theaters, restaurants, train stations, hotels, dance halls, or anywhere else, I am so lonesome and sad that I become despondent as if I had been separated from life. The colors of the lights have really become necessities of life for me.

Not just instinctively but also intellectually, I am fond of these colors. They are red like blood, pure like gold, and at times blue like crystal; how such colors, and such luster, arouse an exquisite sensation! Nothing, not even the charm of a beautiful woman's deep blue eyes or the brilliant luster of precious stones, comes close to them.

To my young romantic eyes, the lights appear as the symbol of humans' every desire, happiness, and pleasure. At the same time, they also seem to suggest that we have the power to go against God's will, to oppose the laws of nature. It is these lights that save us from the darkness of night and awaken us from the sleep of death. Are these lights not the manmade sun, flowers of sin that mock God and boast of knowledge?

Ah, that is why this world that has obtained and is shone upon by lights is a world of enchantment. Because of these lights, women of shameful trade appear more beautiful than chaste wives or virtuous virgins, a thief's face is as tragic as the Savior's, and a rake's mien is as noble as a king's. The poet of depravation incapable of singing of God's glory or the immortality of the soul has, for the first time and thanks to the lights, found beauty—in sin and darkness. Baudelaire's verse goes:

> Voici le soir charmant, ami du criminel
> Il vient comme un complice, à pas de loup, le ciel
> Se ferme lentement comme une grande alcôve,
> Et l'homme impatient se change en bête fauve.
> (The tender night, friend of sin, advances as
> stealthily as a wolf, like an accomplice in crime.
> As the sky is gradually closed like a most
> spacious bedroom, the tormented man also
> becomes like a foolish beast.)*

Last night, as usual, I left home as soon as lights came on in the city and, having had dinner at a place where many people congregate and the sound of music streams out, entered a certain theater. It was not in order to see a play but to become intoxicated with the light of the lamps

---

*Literal translation of Kafū's translation.

glistening in the high, gilded, vaulted ceiling, the spacious stage, and the box seats all around, so I chose an unsophisticated musical comedy where many dancing girls performed and noisily sang popular songs.

Having spent half the evening there, I went outside with the crowd, sent off by waltz music signaling the theater's closing, when the cold wind quickly hit my face. . . . I can never forget the charming sensation of this moment, which always happens when I leave a theater. The surrounding scenery of the city was in sharp contrast to the hustle and bustle of the early evening when I had entered the theater but was everywhere pregnant with the shadows of the deepening night; feeling as if I had come upon an unfamiliar street, I had an urge to walk aimlessly, driven by some vague sentiment of uncertainty coupled with a sense of curiosity.

Indeed, the charm of the city late at night is precisely this uncertainty, the mystery evoked by doubt and curiosity.

If someone is lingering behind a store whose lights have been turned off and doors closed, I am curious who he is and what he is doing, even if I don't suspect that he is a thief; and if I see a uniformed, formidable-looking policeman at the corner of an alley, without particular reason I think of a crime. All men walking with their hats pulled down over their eyes and their hands in their pockets look as if they have lost money at gambling and are contemplating suicide; a carriage emerging from darkness and driving past me into another darkness makes my heart pound, and I become incessantly ruffled as I imagine an adulterous love affair, an illicit relationship, concealed inside when I see, at a far distance, the bright lights of hotels and saloons triumphantly shining upon the deepening night. It is as if they are suggesting that all the pleasures of the world reside only there. The silhouettes of men and women swarming around, going in and coming out, are like butterflies that dance playfully in the flower garden of dissipation; and aren't their laughter and voices, which drift over from time to time, a seductive music of indescribable sweetness?

It is the moment of dreadful "destiny." The women who suddenly appear at this moment, at this very instant, in the flickering lights of the street, swishing their skirts like winds and emitting the scent of make-up into the evening air, are the spirits of the night. They are sin and baseness incarnate. They are the angels of the evil world summoned by Mephisto to appear at the doorway of the young Marguerite. They are goddesses who can see through the destiny and every thought of every young man who wanders in the night, from his past to his future.

So when the man hears their voices calling out to him and sees them coming close, he feels as if he is witnessing his past omens right in front of him and, accepting his fate, resigns himself to holding the cold hand of ignominy.

After I left the theater, I kept on walking along Broadway in the dead of the night, passing a tall building of twenty or more floors that soars like a stone pillar at Madison Square and conjures up a castle in dreamland, and soon came upon the clump of trees at Union Square in all probability and the lights coming through them. As I came closer, I heard water dripping from a fountain behind a tree, sounding, in the quiet night, as if someone were sobbing, so I sat down on a bench beside it and gazed at the reflection of the lights moving and breaking on the surface of the water, indulging in idle thought that kept welling up within me.

I heard the footsteps of someone approaching me and some whispering in my ear, but after a while I resumed my walk . . . but how could I have been trapped? I found myself walking with one of those evil women of the night, who led me by the hand to an unfamiliar back street.

I looked around and saw tenement houses on both sides of the road, red bricks darkened with grime, doors slanted, and lightless windows; as I climbed up the low stone steps and entered the front door, darkness was lurking, and from the basement some damp air streamed out and assailed my nostrils with an offensive odor. The woman stopped suddenly, studied my appearance a while under the nearby streetlight, and then smiled, revealing white teeth between her rouged lips.

I shivered in spite of myself. And yet I didn't have the willpower to shake off her hand and run away but rather was driven by an ardent desire to fall voluntarily into darkness.

It is strange how one develops a taste for evil. Why is it that the forbidden fruit tastes so delicious? Prohibition adds the sweetness, and transgression increases the fragrance. As the flow of a mountain stream does not become violent unless there are rocks, so too is man incapable of discovering the excitement of crime, the pleasure of evil, unless he has conscience and morality.

I let myself be led away through the dark entrance and up the dark stairway. As there was no covering on the stairs, the sound echoed throughout the deserted house like ice being crushed, and a cold dampness, gushing forth from heaven knows where, brushed against my neck like the hair of a dead person.

We mounted to the second, third, and finally what I thought was the fifth floor, where the woman opened the door, click-clacking her keys, and then pushed me inside.

Thick darkness was filling the room as well, but as the woman lit a gaslight the clouds of mystery dissipated, and all at once, like magic, a torn sofa, an old bed, a clouded mirror, a washbasin filled with water, and various other pieces of furniture scattered all over the room appeared before me. The room was apparently in the attic, and although the ceiling was low and the walls stained, it suggested a rather cozy dwelling, judging from the dirty nightdress, drawers, and old stockings strewn about here and there. However, this must be the same kind of coziness you feel when you peep into a dog's house with unkempt straw for its bed or a bird's nest covered with droppings.

While I was looking around, the woman took off her hat and then her dress, and, wearing only a short white chemise, she sat on a chair beside me and began smoking a cigarette.

I folded my arms firmly and gazed at her in silence, like an archaeologist looking up at the Sphinx in the Egyptian desert.

Look at her, at the way she exposes her stockinged legs even above her knees, crosses one leg over a knee, bends the upper part of her body backward, revealing her breasts from her low-cut undergarment, holds the back of her head with her raised, naked arms, and exhales smoke toward the ceiling with her face turned upward. Ah! What is this if not a cruel yet brave stone statue of defiance and ignominy that does not fear God, does not fear man, and has thoroughly cursed all worldly virtues? Does her face not betray the tragic beauty of the sun setting on a solitary castle, the face that has struggled against destructive "Time" by means of powder, rouge, hairpieces, and fake gems? The color of her eyes, which are neither asleep nor awake under their heavy lids, may be compared to the surface of a large swamp that emits poisonous chemical gas. Was Baudelaire, the father of the Decadents, not referring to the eyes of this type of woman when he wrote:

> Quand vers toi mes désirs partent en caravan,
> Ces yeux sont la citerne où boivent mes ennuis.
> (When my desires like a caravan head toward you,
> your eyes are the water of the cistern that soothes
> my troubled soul.)*

and again:

> Ces yeux, où rien ne se révèle
> De doux ni d'amer,
> Sont deux bijoux froids où se mêle
> L'or avec le fer.

———

*Literal translation of Kafū's translation.

(Your eyes, revealing not even joy or sorrow, are
like cold jewels where iron and gold are
blended.)*

I can no longer be satisfied with only the loveliness of a Koharu
[heroine in Chikamatsu's *Love Suicide of Amishima*] or the melancholy
of a Violetta or a Marguerite. They are too frail. They are flowers that
have scattered under the rain called custom and morality, and they lack
the unyielding spirit of noxious plants that do not wilt in the storm of
punishment and discipline but stretch their vile vines toward the sky of
death and destruction and spread their sinful leaves under it.

Ah, queen of evil! When I press my troubled forehead against
your bosom, where your cold blood resounds like the dripping of wine
onto the bottom of a dark wine cellar, I do not feel love of a lover but
a sisterly intimacy, the protection of an affectionate mother.

Debauchery and death are linked together. Please laugh at my
usual foolishness. I spent the entire night yesterday with this prostitute, sleeping like "a corpse lying next to a corpse."

(April 1907)

---

*Literal translation of Kafū's translation.

A June Night's Dream

The French steamer, *Bretagne*, has left the pier at the mouth of the Hudson River on schedule, carrying me, the wanderer, from North America to the shores of Europe.

High in the July sky, the buildings of New York soar like a strange ridge of clouds; the Brooklyn Bridge, which lies across the sky, is larger than a rainbow; and the Statue of Liberty stands erect in the middle of the water—the familiar scenery of the bay to which I have become accustomed during these years is steadily disappearing between the sky and the waves . . . and soon the ship glides along the deep green shores of Staten Island and is about to float out into the vast expanse of the Atlantic Ocean from the strait of Sandy Hook.

Ah! This moment may well mark the last time in my life that I see America's hills and waters. Once I leave this place, when, on what occasion, will I ever have an opportunity to come again?

I leaned over the railing of the deck and desperately tried to see for one last time the unforgettable Staten Island, its woods along the shores, the roofs in its villages—ah! It was on the very shore of this island that I spent over a month while the summer was at its prime, till last night when I boarded the ship—but, how unfortunate, the scorching heat of the July morning was covering sea and sky with a lead-colored vapor, blurring not only the woods and the houses but even the prominent hills like a cluster of trailing clouds.

The sorrow of parting, regret, attachment—ah! Is there a more cruel, more unbearable suffering than this? I might go out of my mind and even jump into the water if, tonight, the moon should gently shed a sad light upon my cabin's window . . . I am such a weakling, and besides, traveling all by myself. If I want to cry, I shall cry. When I am sad, I shall chronicle the sadness, that may be the only consolation. So, rocking along on the Atlantic Ocean, I pick up my pen. . . .

Looking back, it was four years ago that I left Japan. America has now become my second home. Among the many things I remember fondly, what is particularly hard to forget concerns, alas, the maiden from whom I parted last night, the well-being of the lovely Rosalyn.

It was early this summer, when the apple blossoms in the orchards had completely fallen. During the preceding four years, I had seen just about everything in American society that I wanted to see or examine, and so, as I had to wait perhaps till the end of the fall for travel funds for Europe to arrive from home, I moved to the shore of Staten Island, which lies at the mouth of the bay, in order to get away from New York City during the summer.

Staten Island must be known to anyone who has spent a summer in New York. It is an island dotted with show grounds, places to cool off, and swimming areas like South Beach and Midland Beach. But the place I chose for my respite was (although on the island) a remote, inconvenient, tiny village near the ocean little known except perhaps to fishing enthusiasts who come from the city on a Saturday or Sunday, if at all.

You reach the shore by crossing the waters on a large, flat, oval steamboat that looks like a *yakatabune* [roofed pleasure boat], and from there it is about a thirty-minute train ride. To go from New York City, where greenery is rare, to this island is to be suddenly struck by the fragrance of the air and the beauty of the fields; the sharp contrast makes one wonder if one is in a dream. As I had become completely bored by the rambling and monotonous scenery of the American countryside, which is of course continental in nature, I was particularly pleased with this island's scenery, which was the exact opposite, smaller scaled, lovely, and full of variety. On one side of the railway tracks, there are small woods and green fields with tiny streams beyond which one sees the expanse of the calm inland sea, and on the other, hills covered with various kinds of deep green trees roll high and low, somewhat reminding one of the scenery near Zushi or Kamakura. Not only that, there are also picturesque meadows covered with countless yellow and white asters as far as the eye can see, as well as swampy places where various water plants such as reeds, cattails, and candocks grow thick, making you feel squeamish.

After I pass through four or five small wooden stations, watching such scenery without becoming bored, the train reaches the village station where I must get off. As I come down from the wooden platform, I note that on opposite sides of the street there are two bars operated by Germans and, in front of them, stage coaches that are regularly sent out from the inns along the beach. This area is rather crowded, with little shops selling daily necessities such as a hardware store, a greengrocery, a butcher, and a shoe store, where the screaming of babies and children or the loud chattering of housewives can be heard; but once you leave this place and follow a road, either to your right or to your left, and go for two or three *chō* [200 to 300 yards] under a row of leafy maple trees, all you see are copses on both sides that look as if they have never been touched by a hatchet, as well as dirty roofs here and there in the shadow of hills where beautiful wildflowers and green grass grow luxuriantly. All through the area, small birds keep chirping, and from time to time the barking of dogs and clucking of hens echo farther and farther into the distance.

If you leave this main road, which is already very quiet, and take a small winding road that goes up the bumpy little hill and ultimately to the faraway beach, you will find by the roadside the house in which I lodged. It is a two-story house with a porch, and at the front of it tall weeds and miscellaneous trees form a dense thicket as if to deny any wind its passage, while the whole rear is enclosed with a thick oak woods. At the edge of the porch two old cherry trees are hanging over the roof, while on the grass a short distance away are two similarly tall apple trees with low-hanging branches.

The landlord is a small, redheaded man about fifty years of age and has been employed by the island's railroad company for about twenty years; he commutes to the main office by train every morning. For an American, he was a rather reticent, quiet man, but once, through an agent, I finalized my agreement to rent and moved in from the city for the first time, he treated me like a relative he had not seen for ten years; together with his plain wife with bad teeth, he showed me around the house, then from the vegetable garden in the backyard to the chicken coop, even introduced me to their dog named Sport, explained the geography of the entire Staten Island, and, finally, brought out a Webster's dictionary that must have been at least twenty years old and had been sitting in the living room, instructing me to consult it in case I didn't understand some English word.

I rented a room on the second floor, facing the oak woods at the back; in the morning I would sort out various catalogues, documents, and such that I had collected but had not gone through during those years in Chicago, Washington, St. Louis, and other places in the United States that I had visited, and in the afternoon I would read or take a nap by a cherry tree in front of the porch, enjoying the cool breeze that came from the sea over the hill while waiting for the sun to move on till the arrival of the evening, when I would set out for a walk.

It would be about half past seven when I would finish supper with the family, and I would take a walking stick and always walk down the path amid the various trees and weeds in front of the house toward the seaside. The whole shore is a damp meadow, but unlike the seaside in New York proper it has no rocks or stones against which surging waves break; when I first saw the pleasant and gently curving outlines of the bright green, long stretch of floating grass plot, which is like a swamp or marsh where reeds grow, sticking out onto the dark blue ocean, I somehow felt it was like a nude beauty lying ever so languidly, having tired of her dreams of pleasure.

Behind this floating grass plot, numerous fishing boats of the neighboring villages and small yachts and motorboats are moored, taking advantage of the fact that the inland sea is usually calm and its currents gentle, but as they are all painted white, they look like swans floating on a pond in a park. By twilight after the sun sets, their coloring presents an indescribably beautiful contrast to the red hue of the evening glow, the blue of the darkening water, and the verdure of the entire floating grass plot.

I no longer had the desire or the leisure to look for other scenic sights on the island. Every day, I would stand on the same spot and gaze at the same bay and floating grass plot without becoming bored; after a while, as it would steadily grow darker all around, and even the whiteness of the boats that had remained visible till the last moment would disappear from sight along with the darkening water, it would be the quiet, bright summer night of June. . . . In America, twilight comes and goes fast.

Ah, the summer nights of June! What a world of imagination, of fantasy! As the days have grown hotter, there are so many mosquitoes around, but at the same time innumerable fireflies flit about all across the fields and the forests like a rain shower. Evening tides sob at the roots of the thick growth of reeds, while the leaves of water willows and maples whisper in the night breeze. Amid the constant songs of crickets and frogs, the chirping of some unknown little bird can be heard. The air is filled with the scent of wild grass, which seems to be trying to grow as much as possible during the night. As a wanderer, I might someday encounter summertime in Switzerland or a winter evening in Italy, objects of every poet's dreams, but I thought I would never forget such a sight as the summer evenings in Staten Island. That is because right now, as I behold the sleeping ocean in front of me and the restful woods in the back, bury myself halfway in the tall wild grass, look up at innumerable stars in the infinite sky, eavesdrop on nature's every whisper, and especially watch fireflies' tremendous blue showers of fire, I feel, with a strong sense of mystery and ecstasy, as if I am no longer on the North American continent where winter is approaching but am wandering under the skies of the "Orient," the dreamland of the poets of the so-called Decadent School.

It was on the evening exactly a week after I moved to this island. As usual, I watched the floating grass plot in twilight to my heart's content and then walked aimlessly along the path in the grass, without realizing that I was heading home, and came to the foot of the hill.

It may have been because of the weather. The fireflies were glowing bluer than usual, the stars were shining equally brightly, and the scent of the wild grass was still more fragrant; and I felt more than ever, oh, this truly is a delightful summer night! It was as if there were on this earth neither a winter nor a storm when flowers wither, neither death nor despair, nothing, that all there was for my body and soul was to be intoxicated by the ecstatic sensation of summertime. . . . At the same time, feeling an urge to sleep comfortably in the wild grass covering the whole area as long as possible like a hare or a fox, I leaned on my cane and looked up at the distant, starfilled sky all over again. . . . At that very moment, suddenly, from the single house atop the hill, the sound of piano-playing and a young woman's singing could be heard. . . .

Anyone can imagine immediately how strongly this moved me. I was instantly all ears, but the sound of the piano vanished like dripping dew, and the song too halted and then stopped abruptly, suggesting that someone was softly singing just a short passage to kill time;

the bright and quiet summer evening returned. All I could hear now was the singing of insects and the croaking of frogs.

Oblivious to the mosquitoes swarming around me, I stood still on the grass for a long time and even sat down to gaze at the house on the hill. No matter how long I waited, there was little chance I could hear the song again. Suddenly, the light from the window seeping through the trees went out, followed by the barking of a dog a couple of times, and then I heard the sound of the small gate of the fence being opened with a quiet click.

Awakened from my dream now, somehow I felt extremely tired and, deciding to go home quickly and go to bed without doing anything, I walked hurriedly over the hill and followed the winding grass path; then suddenly I recognized a pure white form moving just four or five *ken* [twenty-four to thirty feet] ahead. . . . It was the retreating figure of a small woman. Despite the dusk, the light from the summer night's sky, the shining stars, and the glow of fireflies enabled me to discern her clearly, from her thin fingers occasionally waving a Japanese-made fan to chase away mosquitoes, to her white dress and even her white cloth shoes. There are times when minute details can be distinguished all the more clearly in darkness or haziness.

As the grass path turned, the woman disappeared once, becoming hidden in the wild grass, which was taller than she, but then I could hear her humming some tune, and to my great surprise, she stopped in front of the house where I was staying.

Startled, I stopped four or five *ken* away. The woman, not noticing it, called out "Ho! ho!" in a young, high-pitched voice as if in jest, to which the landlady inside shouted in a loud voice, "Come in," informality being the characteristic of American life. The woman did not enter but said she preferred to be outside in summertime despite the mosquitoes and sat down at the entrance of the porch, fragrant with climbing honeysuckle blossoms.

A JUNE NIGHT'S DREAM

This woman indeed was the person who had been singing, Rosalyn whom I can never forget, try as I might.

But when I was introduced to her by my landlady, I never suspected that things would develop this way—indeed, I did not even think we would be able to become good friends. That was because my experience those years had shown me how difficult it was to engage in a conversation with an American woman that appealed to my taste. They are too cheerful and their ideas too wholesome to engage in serious talk about the arts or the problems of life, so even when I was introduced from time to time to another woman at a new place, I made it a policy not to follow this up and expect a genuine conversation or a pleasant chat, except merely to practice my language and to observe human nature.

So with Rosalyn, whom I met for the first time that evening, I was prepared as usual, as a matter of a young man's courtesy toward a young woman, to talk about automobiles I detested, about churches, or about anything else. But from the very beginning, I was surprised to be asked if I liked the opera, and she went on asking more questions about Puccini's *Madame* [sic] *Butterfly*, about Madame Melba who had returned to the United States for the first time in four or five years and had once again enraptured American audiences, and about Strauss's "Simphonia Domestica," which had been performed for the first time that spring in the United States. Such questions were so unexpected that not only were my former resolutions forgotten, but I was almost driven to tears of joy as if I had met a friend I had known for a hundred years.

I have to admit that I do like Western women. Nothing gives me greater pleasure than to discuss Western art since ancient Greece under a Western sky, by Western waters, with a Western woman, and in a Western language, be it English, French, or any other. In other words, it was precisely because I had expected so much of American women that I had developed curious misconceptions about them.

Because the discussion was too sophisticated, and also because it is customary in this country for [an older person like] a mother or a teacher to leave young people alone to their conversations so as not to interfere with their interests, the landlady went out to the back of the house toward the chicken coop, ostensibly to check some noise.

Our conversation soon shifted to topics such as Japanese women's life, fashion, and marriage, and I asked Rosalyn casually if she believed in staying single, as typical of an American woman.

She seemed to take strong offense at being included among the unexceptional "typical" category and said, with a brief dramatic gesture of her hand, "I am not single as a matter of principle, but I think I shall probably end my life unmarried. But that won't be because of something negative, so I won't be like a despairing, pathetic, and depressed French widow or, for that matter, a narrow-minded, mean old maid of America. Though I was educated in America, I grew up in England till I was five, and both my parents are of ancient, pure English stock. English people smile as they fight till they fall. So even if I remain single for the rest of my life, I shall be like this till I die, a tomboy."

She finished, and her words contained a strong tone characteristic of the English language and at the same time sounded as if they were pregnant with an indomitable English determination. But as I looked at Rosalyn's frail, small frame, I deeply felt an indefinable sadness, all the more because her tone was intense. It may have been because the night, though it was still summertime, was so beautiful and quiet.

Soon it was my turn to respond to her questions about my beliefs. But what I have are not so much beliefs, assertions, or opinions as dreams, imaginings uttered in a delirium—in my heart, it was all dreams.

I answered that I greatly abhorred marriage. This is because I am disappointed in all reality. Reality is my greatest enemy. I long for love, but rather than hoping for its fulfillment, I instead pray that it fails. At its moment of fulfillment, love disappears like smoke, so I hope to spend my whole life just dreaming of true love by means of unattainable or lost love—this is my wish. "Miss Rosalyn," I asked, "do you know the story of Leonardo da Vinci and la Gioconda?"

The landlady returned to the porch with glasses of chilled water from the well in the rear, so Rosalyn and I shifted our topic as if conspiring, but soon, as the opportunity arose, Rosalyn stood up and asked what time it was. She was told it was already past eleven o'clock.

But the landlord, who had gone to a card game called poker held by the villagers early in the evening, had not yet returned. As I was the only man in the house, it would be my duty to take her home. I held a small lantern that the landlady had lit for me in one hand and lightly supported Rosalyn's arm as we followed the grass path that led to the beach. . . .

Ah, is there such a marvelous role in real life, not just on stage? After I came to America, I had often walked with a young woman, at night or during the day, but tonight for some reason I felt strangely agitated, as if this were my first experience.

Was it because the already quiet evening on this island was even quieter in the small hours? Was it because the sound of the leaves on trees and of grass rustling every now and then as if a shower were coming was strangely eerie? Was it because the chirping of insects and the croaking of frogs resounded with such indescribable clarity in the starry sky that I was forcefully driven by the consciousness that, in the entire universe now, just the two of us, Rosalyn and I, were awake? I can never explain the reason. I was simply desperate lest she should become aware of this indefinable agitation of my heart. Worried that the lantern I was carrying in one hand might expose my face as it shed light on the uneven path, I deliberately looked upward as we walked.

Rosalyn too kept silent and steadily went up the sloping road at a rather quick pace. The roof of her house became visible above the tall overgrown grass, but as soon as we reached the top of the hill, suddenly before us opened up the huge sky, expanding spectacularly; although the surface of the water was too dark to see, numerous lighthouse beacons could be observed here and there within the inland sea, while far away, near Sandy Hook, which empties out to the Atlantic Ocean, the reflection of the searchlight shining upon the dangerous strait all through the night could be seen. Behind us and just below us the summer village's clumps of trees lay, all dark.

I halted unconsciously and heard her say, as if talking in a dream, "Beautiful night, isn't it? I love to watch the lights on the sea [sic]." To me, these words sounded like nothing but a most agreeable, rhymed verse.

How should I respond? I simply nodded and hung my head down, but then she hurriedly pulled at my sleeve and said, "A bird is singing. What is it, could it be a robin?"

Indeed, a thin and high-pitched gentle tune, like the sound of a flute, broke off and started again.

This time I did not hesitate and gave a decisive answer—it must be the "nightingale" Romeo heard on the night of his secret rendezvous. I had heard that in America there was no Nightingale [sic] or Rossignole [sic] that sang at night, but now that we were actually listening to that gentle tune, it had to be the same bird that appeared in poems.

Actually, even though Rosalyn had grown up in this country, she did not know the name of the bird, but we decided without much argument that this must be "the bird Romeo heard" and wanted very much to hear another cry or two, but it seemed to have already flown away somewhere.

I accompanied her up to her house, which was just a couple of steps down from the top of the hill, on the right-hand side of the road, and shook her hand for parting and said "good night" across the fence that encircled a large lawn and flower garden. Thus I took leave of her and returned home.

When I awoke the next day, the events of the previous night seemed as if they could only have been a dream. For it was too poetic, too beautiful to have actually happened. At the same time, I felt strangely empty that such a thing would never happen again in my life.

At lunchtime, even before I asked, the landlady told me a great deal about Rosalyn. Her father was a businessman from Britain and, after coming to the United States with his family, left Rosalyn in a religious boarding school and went to South Africa, to the Cape Town area, where he accumulated a sizable fortune, and returned home seven or eight years ago. Then he built a country house in the present location and retired there. So Rosalyn had grown up practically out of the reach of her parents, and perhaps for that reason was of a strong yet solitary disposition; she had not made particularly close friends and always made up her own mind independently, instead of consulting her parents or anybody else, and never appeared lonely or sad.

After finishing my meal, I went as usual to the shade of the cherry tree to open Mallarmé's prose poems, which I had started reading two or three days earlier, and then, as my interest was drawn to them, gradually forgot all about the previous night's events, about world affairs, and about my own situation and, noticing only the shadows of the trees lying on the grass and the dazzling sunlight falling upon the road, all I felt was the beauty of the summer. Only toward evening, the time for me to take a walk, did I realize that in order to go to see the floating grass plot that night I would have to take the road that passed in front of Rosalyn's house.

I wanted to see her, yet I didn't want to see her; my mind was confused as I walked on the usual grass path, but before I reached the top of the hill, I heard Rosalyn singing like a lark—"Hallow! here I am! [sic]"—amid wild grass that was beginning to grow dark like smoke. She told me that she was going to visit my landlady again this evening (she didn't openly say she was coming to see me).

So we talked again that night till late, and like the previous night I escorted her back up to the fence of her house, walking on the night road with a lantern in one hand and once again listening to the singing of the unknown night bird; but then the following morning I ran into her unexpectedly on the village main street, where she said she was going to the post office, and we walked together in step under the parasol she held over us.

Given that it was such a small village with few roads, where the timing of my walks did not vary much, it soon developed that practically every day I would meet her at least once somewhere. As a result, when it happened that it continued to rain for about two days, making it impossible to go out and chance across Rosalyn anywhere, I felt so lonesome and couldn't stand being alone at night, listening to the sound of the rain beating on the roof of the farmhouse—although this may have been due to the fact that I had never heard anything resembling the sound of a quiet rain during the two years I lived in New York. Every night before going to bed I would look up at the stars in the sky from my window and secretly pray for good weather the following day so that people would be able to take a walk.

As I hoped, the dry summer weather brought fine days, except for some occasional passing showers during the day. Above all, the moon rose at night. I had never watched the new moon grow bigger and bigger every night as regularly as I did this year, this summer.

Ah! Looking back now, I loathe precisely this moonlight. If only there had been no moonlight, no matter how lovely the summer nights of June with the evening birds, the chirping of the insects, the fragrance of the grass, or the rustling of the leaves, I . . . Rosalyn . . . the two of us would never have so heedlessly come to kiss each other.

A JUNE NIGHT'S DREAM

I would probably have to leave America before the island's green leaves turned yellow and then red. I had already confided this to Rosalyn. On another occasion, I had told Rosalyn that I would like to have a blond friend as a long-term pen pal, as a memento of my four years living in America . . . to which she responded, laughing, that she would send me letters written in the difficult new Rooseveltian spelling. So it must be concluded that from the beginning the two of us were fully aware of our respective positions and circumstances and were merely enjoying each other's pleasant company during these lovely summer evenings.

Yet alas, the summer nights were too lovely for young people merely to enjoy each other's company. The moon, from the time it was like a thread, every night without fail cast its gentle light upon our shoulders as we talked and lured our souls, spontaneously and without our knowledge, into the faraway dreamland.

I really would not like to say that I did not have strong willpower. For I was conscious to the very end that I could never love Rosalyn, that, however I might have felt at the bottom of my heart, I should never confess it to the young woman.

We spent one evening watching the full moon till past midnight, discussing inconsequential topics, for instance, Rosalyn saying that in America they say the moon shows a human face, I responding that in Japan we see a hare standing there, and both of us trying to determine which view was more correct. On the following day, I received a communication from home sooner than expected, making it imperative that I depart for Europe within two weeks, without waiting for the fall to arrive. I mentioned this situation quite coolly and casually, almost without hesitation, as if I were just going away to New York City for fun.

Rosalyn, on her part, did not seem too surprised and asked me whether France or Italy was my destination and such things while engaging in the usual chitchat with the landlord and his wife.

However, past ten o'clock, as I went outside to take her home as I had done every evening, the light from the moon was even brighter than on the previous day, this being the sixteenth night of the lunar month. Although we were used to watching the moon every night to our hearts' content, it was so beautiful that we walked in complete silence on the grass path till we reached the hill, when suddenly I was overwhelmed by an indefinable sorrow permeating my whole body and realized I must pull myself together. Just at that very moment, Rosalyn seemed to have stumbled on a roadside stone and abruptly leaned toward me. . . . Alarmed, I held her hand; she let it rest in mine and pressed her face tightly against my chest.

For over half an hour we stood there, embracing each other in the moonlight, without uttering a word, till our clothes grew heavy with the evening dew. There really was no word to utter. For we knew, without saying so, that no matter how much we were in love, I was a traveler, and she a daughter with her own home and parents, circumstances that dictated that we would never be able to indulge in this dream of happiness for long. There were then only two alternatives to consider. Should I sever all my ties with my homeland and seek a livelihood in this country forever, through my own effort? Or should I have Rosalyn leave her parents' home and the land of America that had thus far raised her? Only these two. But no matter how desperate I felt, I simply could not suggest such things. Rosalyn too would never be able to ask anyone to give up everything in the world for the sake of love.

Alas, were we, after all, creatures of common sense? Did the force of circumstance called America compel us to act thus? Or had our love not yet developed to full maturity? No! No! I truly believe that our love was never less than that of Romeo or Paulo and Juliet or Francesca. We knew well that once we parted we might never see each other again—a beautiful dream of one instant brings lifelong sorrow; still from the following day on, we would go to the deserted woods at the edge of the village every afternoon and share deep kisses, in order to show we would live on and sing of love, forever lost. . . .

Alas, what a pity! The ship has already crossed the Atlantic altogether and is set to arrive at Le Havre, France, soon. People say that they saw Irish mountains in the morning.

I no longer have much time to continue writing. Within the span of just one week, how far have I been separated from her!

The farther I am separated, the more vivid her face appears in my mind. She had blond hair slightly tinged with dark brown. She always casually bundled her unusually long and dark blond hair for a Westerner, and the way she constantly pushed back some stray locks from her forehead with her fingertips was full of charm. When we were standing side by side, she barely reached my chin—for an American woman she was of quite small build, but since she was plump and always kept an extremely erect posture, she looked quite tall and big at times. Her deep blue eyes, which were like a lake, and her narrow and somewhat pointed features understandably betrayed an oversensitivity when she was engaged in an earnest conversation, but when she kept her poise she revealed an indefinable dignity and a strong and valiant melancholy. That is to say, she was just the opposite of a cheerful, bewitching beauty of Southern Europe with clear-cut outlines one is tempted to transfer to a canvas, and belonged to the type of women fairly common among the Anglo-Saxons of the North in whom a certain sharpness conceals a melancholy, and the melancholy contains a characteristically feminine gentleness. . . .

All of a sudden, clamorous voices can be heard on the upper deck. They are saying they can see the lights of Le Havre. In the corridor outside the cabin, some are saying, "Nous voilà en France [sic]," and running.

In the deck area, men and women were beginning to sing "La Marseillaise":

Allons enfents [sic] de la patrie
Le jour de gloire est arrivé.

I have finally arrived in France.

Ah, but what could I do about the unabated pain of my heart? Quite unconsciously, I was recalling the poem Musset had dedicated to Mozart's music—

Rappelle-toi, lorsque les destinées
M'auront de toi pour jamais séparé,
....

....
Songe à mon triste amour, songe à
        L'adieu suprême!
....
Tant que mon coeur battra,
Toujours il te dira:
        Rappelle-toi.
(Remember. If destiny forever separates me from
you, remember my sad love. Remember the
time we parted. As long as my heart resonates,
it shall tell you, "Remember.")*

Reciting it in my mind, I walked step by step toward the deck in order to pay tribute to the mountains of France, which I was going to see for the first time.

---

*Literal translation of Kafū's translation from the original.

A JUNE NIGHT'S DREAM

Rappelle-toi, quand sous la froide terre
Mon coeur brisé pour toujours dormira;
Rappelle-toi, quand la fleur solitaire
Sur mon tombeau doucement s'ouvrira.
Tu ne me verra plus; mais mon âme immortelle
Reviendra près de toi comme une soeur fidèle.

      Ecoute dans la nuit,
      Une voix qui gémit:
        Rappelle-toi.

(Remember, when my broken heart will forever
sleep under the cold earth; Remember, when the
solitary flower on my grave gently will open.
You will see me no more. But my immortal soul
shall come back near you like an intimate sister.
Listen attentively in the night. There is a voice
that whispers, "Remember.")*

      Alas, alas.

        Rappelle-toi___Rappelle-toi___

                (July 1907)

---

*Literal translation of Kafū's translation.

A Night at Seattle Harbor

One Saturday night, I wanted to see the Japanese quarter in Seattle and furtively walked in that direction.

I say furtively not without reason. I had been told when I landed, by a member of the crew with whom I had become well acquainted during the voyage, that in Seattle I should refrain from going to the downtown area where there were many Japanese. He warned me that this was not a place to be visited by anyone with the least sense of honor. But as so often happens, such advice only feeds one's curiosity, so I walked down the crowded, sloping road, without being noticed, from Second to First Avenue.

This is the most thriving part of Seattle, and although it is generally considered a newly developed city, the Ginza is no match for the way tall shops of stone and signboards are electrically illuminated in beautiful colors here. Besides, this is the early evening on a Saturday when many people come to take a walk, and innumerable men and women pass one another, rubbing shoulders and laughing under brilliant lights. At the intersections, a large number of streetcars full of passengers crisscross each other, while carriages thread their way through them. It is enough to dazzle you.

Bumping into people frequently, I managed to go down First Avenue and, turning left, reached a street called Jackson, where I found a totally changed atmosphere. The street was still wide, but there were fewer and fewer shops, and on the pavement covered with boards horse dung was piled high here and there, while an acute stench coming from sooty smoke somewhere was filling the air, naturally making it quite difficult to breathe. Those impressed with the bustle of First and Second Avenues must be even more startled at the drastic contrast of this gloomy, dark street. I let my feet lead me for several more blocks and came upon a strangely shaped building on one side of the road reminding me of the Panorama building in Asakusa, soaring in midair like a castle. Not only did the unpleasant stench grow worse, but the area was gradually turning pitch dark, with the overpass for elevated trains running along the left-hand side of the street almost blocking the light of the gray sky.

This was no place to linger for even five minutes. But when I noticed that this strange-shaped building was a gas tank, I realized the Japanese quarter must lie just ahead. For I had been told that the gas tank on Jackson Street marked the border of the Japanese quarter. I covered my mouth with a handkerchief and held my breath as I barely passed under the gas tank with its disagreeable smell; then dim lights came into view, flickering at a distance.

Coming closer, I found that the buildings on both sides were far different from those on prosperous First Avenue; they were all low, wood-frame ones, as is usually the case in poorer quarters. I happened to look up at the window of one of the two-story houses and noticed hanging there a lamp with some Japanese words, so I ran toward it and read the words, RESTAURANT, JAPAN HOUSE. I had heard about this place, but actually encountering it aroused a queer sensation in me, and I just stood there for a while, gazing at the sign for no particular reason. Soon I began hearing the sound of *samisen* coming from the second-floor window.

As it was a Western-style building with windows shut, I could barely make out the dim noise that was seeping through, but surely it was a woman singing a tune. It was a kind I had never heard in Tokyo, so I stood there, struck with a sense of amusing incongruity as if I were traveling in the countryside and listening to some comic songs in a distant post town in Japan, when all of a sudden I was startled by the sound of voices behind me and turned around.

"Oh, hell! They're having fun again tonight."

"It must be Oharu playing the *samisen*. Too pretty to stick around in America."

Three Japanese were talking and looking up at the second floor. They all wore homburgs and dark suits, but their long torsos and short and, moreover, bowed legs must look quite funny to white people, I thought. They were saying in voices with a trace of some provincial accent,

"I haven't seen her yet; is she that pretty?"

"When did she come? Looks like it was quite recent."

"Came on the *Shinano* (the name of the ship) the other day. I've heard she is also from Hiroshima."

I was eagerly trying to listen to this conversation, but one of them glared at me with a menacing look, and I realized all of a sudden that they must be those hooligans who are said to prowl around the Japanese quarter. So reluctantly, I left the area.

By now, all the signs that I noticed were in Japanese characters. It was exactly as I had heard on the ship; everything, from tofu makers and *shiruko* restaurants to sushi bars and noodle shops, was as one would find in a town in Japan, so that for a while I could only look around restlessly, in a state of shock. In the meantime, more people were crowding into the area, but most of them were my bow-legged and long-torsoed compatriots, and the only whites around appeared to be laborers with large pipes sticking out of their mouths.

Thinking that anything would make a good story, I first went near a hanging lantern that read SOBA NOODLES. The store was in the basement of a large house, so you had to go underground by going down the steps at the edge of the street. As you entered the sooty, open doorway, there was a huge room with a wooden floor partitioned into small sections with painted boards, each with a musty linen curtain drawn at the entrance as a screen.

Inside, four or five chairs were placed around a table, and a gloomy gaslight was lit. As soon as I sat down, a deep voice said, "Come in," and a man close to forty appeared. He was a big man with a dark complexion and a narrow moustache pointing down at the ends and was wearing an apron over his trousers without a jacket.

As I ask, "What can you make me?" he lists, twisting his finely trimmed moustache, tempura, *okame* [noodle soup with fish cake], *namban* [noodle soup with duck or chicken], and other dishes, and asks, "Would you care for *sake*?"

I order one of the dishes and smoke a cigarette, leaning against the chair; before long, footsteps are heard, perhaps of three or four people, who noisily enter the next room separated from mine by a board. As the moustached proprietor goes out to them, one of them says [in English], "Hello, good evening."

"Tempura as usual. Also Masamune, we want Masamune [a brand of *sake*]," another orders in a loud voice.

For a while, the knocking on the floorboards of chairs being adjusted, the sound of a match striking against the sole of a shoe, and such can be heard. And then one of them says, "After our drinks, why don't we go have a look?"

"That place? Forget it. Whatever you do, don't go whoring in America," another objects, while still another asks, "You don't want to? Why?"

"I'll tell you why: because it's not worth it. It's so cut and dried. It's all business, an 'all right' affair in return for cash. Couldn't be more ridiculous."

I smiled to myself, but then the proprietor brought over my order. He then must have gone next door with *sake* bottles and cups, for someone was saying in a reinvigorated voice, "Let's have a drink; it's hard to forget the taste of Japanese wine."

"How about the taste of women?"

"I'd better watch out, or else I could forget that. I should be practicing now."

"Ha, ha, ha, ha," they all began to laugh noisily.

"By the way, how is it at your place? Are you still busy?"

"It's terrible. Day in and day out, I am pushed around by the red-haired [Westerner] woman to help out in the kitchen. It's no easy matter, being a schoolboy."

"Well, we're all doing it, so don't complain. Just hope for a successful future."

"I don't know if I can. Has your language gotten any better?"

"Not at all. I don't understand. A grown man goes to primary school every day, with ten- or eleven-year-olds. It's been already half a year, and still no progress."

"At first I thought that if I worked as a schoolboy and listened to white guys speaking for three months or so, I would be able to understand an ordinary conversation, but anticipation and reality are totally different things."

"However, let's not despair. Despair is followed by self-destruction and then by degradation. We've got to be on our guard. There are so many examples of this, you know. There are those who come to America with definite intentions of working through school but who eventually become corrupt and continue to work at white people's houses when they are already thirty or even forty; such failures should serve as a warning. Haste makes waste, so let's just take our time studying."

"Yes, I agree," one answered but added immediately, "Let's not be too serious, it'll spoil the taste of *sake*. Today's a Saturday, so let's just have fun."

"Of course, of course! We've got to refuel ourselves."

A NIGHT AT SEATTLE HARBOR

The conversation ended up right where it had started. Even the one who had objected earlier didn't seem to protest when the company noisily went outdoors; perhaps he was too drunk for that.

Thinking I might be able to obtain some unusual material for my stories if I followed them, I quickly paid ten cents for my drink and hastily went out after them. Turning right at the straight main street, just as they were doing, I found that the road narrowed but was filled with more and more people, and saw on one side of it stalls grilling pork or beef with smelly oil. It seems that such a scene, with stalls in the poorer streets or bad quarters, is not limited just to Asakusa in Tokyo.

As for those three, they are hastily climbing up the dark and narrow staircase that leads from the front of a certain small tobacco shop—owned by a Japanese—to the back.

(Bungei kurabu, May 1, 1904)

Night Fog

It was one night toward the end of October. I came back to the city of Tacoma on an electric train from Seattle. The city clock must have already struck eleven. When I got off the train, there were very few people on Pacific Avenue.

As I look up, the windless sky is covered by its nightly darkness, and, turning around, I see a dense mist about to suffuse the earth. Such weather is not unusual around this time of the year. After the cool autumn is over, I am told, the Pacific Coast area will enter the gloomy winter season when it rains every day.

Even the nearest city buildings, five or six stories high, are totally covered by the thin fog, and I cannot discern their tops; lights beautifully flickering in windows or colored electric lights shining upon signboards are like blurry lanterns if they are only a block away, and the illumination of the tower of the city hall, which on a normal night will decorate a section of the sky in many colors, is also pitifully darker than the light of a magic lantern. I notice that from a fog-covered distance, a one- or two-car train is rushing this way. But there is no one inside the well-lit cars, and they have gone up the slope empty and vanished in the direction of the neighboring town, the sound of the wheels echoing like a storm.

Intending to go home, I walked on the cement-paved sidewalk of this large street with a bleak view. The shops lining the street had already locked their doors, but the electric lights inside were shining like daylight upon various kinds of merchandise displayed in the glass windows. In front of them, I noticed a number of passersby halting and lingering. A woman who appeared to be a poor housewife was lost in admiration in front of a jewelry store even as she shivered in the cold air, while a man wearing a tattered jacket without an overcoat was staring with sunken eyes at the breads beautifully displayed at a bakery. It was easy to know what was on their minds. But they did not seem to be embarrassed about it at all.

As I approached a corner, I heard some noisy music. Then the voices of many people became audible. It was a store selling liquor, and the colored glass door at the entrance was kept open, but as something like a screen was placed inside, I was prevented from looking into the far end. However, from an opening where the warm air polluted with the smell of liquor and tobacco smoke was oozing out, I was able to discern several kinds of nude paintings hung high up on the walls, brightly lit by electric lights. Laborers, wandering around town in large crowds at night with huge pipes in their mouths and their hands thrust into the pockets of their trousers, were pushing one another in quick succession at this entrance. The inside was apparently quite spacious, for the sound of shoes, chairs, wine glasses, every noise in the room reverberated against the high ceiling, while the monotonous music sounded at times like a storm charging into a cave.

For a while I stood still, feeling intrigued, but then fear welled up in my heart as I watched the appearances and faces of those coming in and going out. Not only were they all glaring suspiciously and shaking their drooping heads from time to time, but when they walked away they dragged their feet in thick-soled shoes as if their bull-like bodies were too heavy, and their retreating figures became obscure at once, like so many shadows, and vanished in the thin fog. Aren't their demeanors those of wounded wild animals who have lost even their willpower to run? I could not help being reminded of the terrible lives of laborers so often depicted by Western writers . . . especially in Zola's *L'assomoir*.

Just at that moment, a man stopped in front of me. Without a doubt, he had just come out of the saloon's door. Thinking that a drunken laborer of this country wanted to tease me, I was about to go away, startled.

Since it is the Japanese and Chinese who sell their labor for the cheapest wages and steadily encroach upon their territory, Japs must be among the laborers' most hated enemies. I knew that people in this area universally detested Japanese and so I tried to get away in great fear.

"You! Wait," the person called out from behind in accented Japanese, to my great surprise.

Astounded, I turned around.

"Aren't you my countryman? I've got to hold your hand for a little while."

So saying, he approached me falteringly.

"What is it?" I asked quietly.

He did not answer but stared at me with his sharp eyes. He must be over thirty years of age. While he is not particularly short, his legs are bowed in typically Japanese fashion, and the skin of his face with its protruding cheekbones is coarse and of a reddish-brown color; even to his fellow countryman, he simply cannot be considered nice-looking. He is wearing an old fedora stained with rain and dust, and underneath his torn, completely wrinkled suit he is not wearing a white shirt but a grubby flannel undershirt with a crooked tie. He must be either a laborer hired for railway construction work or else a servant employed as a kitchen hand by some white family, but certainly not of higher status.

"What do you want to ask me?"

When I questioned him once more, he looked at my face with even sharper eyes but then opened his thick lips and started shouting violently.

NIGHT FOG

"What makes you think I would have stopped you if I didn't have something to ask? Aren't you from the same country as I? Aren't you a compatriot? Then don't! Don't talk so coldly to your countryman. Don't."

"What's the matter? You misunderstood me. You must be terribly upset about something," I tried to speak with a calm voice, though I was astonished.

"Of course. I am hopping mad. I want to tear my heart apart, I am that mad at myself. I just gulped down several glasses of whisky to try to forget what's been bothering me for so long. I wanted to stop you to tell you something because you are my compatriot."

He grabbed my coat sleeve. I could not help but be extremely disconcerted, but there was no longer any way of escaping. Helplessly, I leaned against the wall of a store and lingered on.

"You know. I'm an uneducated migrant worker. I don't know the language of America. No, I don't even know many Japanese characters. But I have strong arms. I used these arms to make as much money as possible. Actually, I have already earned a few dollars. But, but . . ." He opened his eyes frightfully wide and once again grabbed my sleeve.

"What happened? But don't talk so loud. The passersby will become suspicious of us."

"Let them, if they want. I don't know their language, and they don't know mine. So who cares?"

He was about to howl once again, but behind him there were already two or three people lingering with the disdainful look that they show whenever they see Japanese; feeling totally embarrassed, I fell silent, red-faced.

"Who cares? Are you afraid of the Yankees? Have you forgotten the Japanese spirit that's within us?"

He stuck out his yellow teeth and looked around, smiling in a revolting way, but soon his bloodshot eyes fell sharply upon somebody; among the people standing behind him was a young woman leaning on a man's arm. Perhaps fearful of the night air, she was wearing her hood over her eyes, from which her disheveled blond hair was falling upon her pink cheeks; as he saw this seductive woman place her head against the man's chest and whisper something, looking at his face as if utterly disgusted, he screamed, "You whore!" as if he could no longer contain the anger that welled up in him, and spat in her direction.

His spit stuck on the woman's shoes, the woman screamed, and her companion came forward, clenching his fists.

I do not know to what sort of class such a woman belongs, being in the street so late at night. But the people witnessing this scene were all in an uproar to avenge her humiliation. Violent words were uttered, and I was completely at a loss, not knowing where to escape.

All of a sudden, a huge arm like that of a *Niō* [Buddhist guardian god] appeared. Stretching over the heads of the crowd, it caught the shoulder of this rude Japanese laborer like an eagle grasping its prey. Startled, I looked up; it was a towering giant of a policeman of this country.

Without uttering an unnecessary word and with the slow pace of an elephant, he easily dragged away the undersized Japanese laborer who struggled with all his might. People gradually drifted away, laughing among themselves as if this scene were funnier than a farce in town.

The night fog enveloping the city had grown even denser, and now it was virtually impossible to see a few inches ahead. The numerous jeerers, their victim who was my countryman, and the frightening policeman all were lost in the absence of light. I realized only after some time had passed that I was still leaning against the store's cold wall in a daze, yet I didn't know how to escape from this totally dreadful trance. I have no idea which dark street I managed to take to return home.

Several days later, I heard the following story from a Japanese of long residence in this area.

A certain immigrant who had worked on railroads for close to ten years and accumulated five hundred dollars deposited the money at a savings agency organized by a group of Japanese. However, some time ago, due to a certain event this savings agency went bankrupt. Distressed at having lost the fruit of ten years' hard work, the immigrant almost killed himself, but then half of his savings, two hundred and fifty dollars, came back to him as a result of the post-bankruptcy investigation and settlement. Alas, the great joy that suddenly overwhelmed him after despair had almost driven him to death made this simple-minded laborer go berserk. He probably ended up climbing the stairs to a gambling den. The very next day after he had received the leftover savings, he became a penniless beggar and began wandering about the streets.

He has now been thrown within the iron fence of an insane asylum on the outskirts of the city. You may not know this, but in this country, once you are committed to an insane asylum, in nine out of ten cases, chances are that you will never come out alive. So he too will suffer from improper treatment and soon die, after shouting all day long at the cold walls that he is going to tear his heart apart.

You ask where this asylum is? It is not very far away if you take the train. On a Sunday, perhaps, you can go and see. They say that besides him two or three other Japanese laborers are incarcerated there; despair has driven them to insanity. . . .

I merely nodded in silence, because I felt suddenly so moved.

(Written at a hotel in North America, November 1903
[published in Bungeikai, July 1, 1904])

Other Works in the Columbia Asian Studies Series

MODERN ASIAN LITERATURE SERIES

TRANSLATIONS FROM THE ASIAN CLASSICS

COMPANIONS TO ASIAN STUDIES

The text of this book was set in 11.25/14.25 Fournier, licensed from Monotype/Adobe, a facsimile of a typeface designed by Pierre Simon Fournier le Jeune (1712–1768) in the 1740s. The face was originally called St. Augustin Ordinaire in the *Manuel typographique*, in which it first appeared. The structure of its letterforms is inspired by the Romain du Roi of 1702 by Philippe Grandjean (1666–1714), a transitional face between the historical periods of neoclassicism and rococo. The present-day version of Fournier was first introduced by the Monotype Corporation in 1924 as Monotype Fournier. Rational and yet exquisitely florid, it is a typeface of clean look and even color.

This book was designed by Chang Jae Lee.
Composed at Columbia University Press by William Meyers.
Printed and bound at Maple Vail.